T...
BOOK 4...

Including . . .

Poul Anderson
DERELICTION

A giant anti-matter weapon—with a duplicated human mind—questions its own mission of destruction.

Larry Niven and David Drake
MOM AND THE KIDS

Khalian raiders capture a piece of Alliance machinery, and—unlucky for them—learn to make it work!

Diane Duane and Peter Morwood
PEST CONTROL

A seemingly lifeless, damaged ship drifts into Khalian territory . . . like the Trojan Horse.

Anne McCaffrey
A SLEEPING HUMPTY DUMPTY BEAUTY

A lady surgeon, smitten by a handsome but comatose soldier, learns that fairy tales really do come true.

David Drake
THE END

The warriors of the Fleet blast their way to a sudden, *suspicious* Khalian surrender . . .

AND MANY OTHERS!

Ace Books edited by
David Drake and Bill Fawcett

THE FLEET
THE FLEET: COUNTERATTACK
THE FLEET: BREAKTHROUGH
THE FLEET: SWORN ALLIES

SWORN ALLIES

THE FLEET

BOOK 4

_____ *Edited by* _____
David Drake *and* Bill Fawcett

ACE BOOKS, NEW YORK

This book is an Ace original edition,
and has never been previously published.

THE FLEET
BOOK 4: SWORN ALLIES

An Ace Book/published by arrangement with
Bill Fawcett & Associates

PRINTING HISTORY
Ace edition/March 1990

ISBN: 0-441-24090-9

Ace Books are published by The Berkley Publishing Group,
200 Madison Avenue, New York, New York 10016.
The name "ACE" and "A" logo are trademarks
belonging to Charter Communications, Inc.

PRINTED IN THE UNITED STATES OF AMERICA

10 9 8 7 6 5 4 3 2 1

To Joanne and Jody,
for understanding and patience far beyond the call
of duty.

With special thanks to those whose names don't go
on the cover: David S., George, Norman, Richard,
Gene, John S., Beth, Susan, John, and the rest of
the good people at Ace.

Contents

DERELICTION
by Poul Anderson

WE HAVE ALWAYS had our broken men, and I suppose we always shall. Nobody pays them any special heed. They are harmless, almost invisible, bits of wreckage that drift about until they sink from sight or the waves cast them ashore to lie among empty shells and strewn bones. Most never get far from the places of their ruin. A few somehow scrape together passage money or find berths on ships whose owners begrudge the cost of proper robotics. Thus they escape, once, twice, even a dozen times, telling themselves that beyond these next light-years there surely waits the opportunity, the luck, the fresh dream that is all they need to build their lives over again. At last they too strand and go no farther.

I met this one in Wang Fang's, on the Fever Coast of Selvas on San Valerio. Nothing much had changed in the years since my last visit. The west side of the building still stood open to catch any breeze off the bay, which glimmered oily black under the clotted red stars of Horn's Cluster. Nonetheless the tin roof trapped smoke and stenches, while you seemed less to breathe than to drink the air. Sweat plastered shirt to skin. At the far end Madame Sylphide's bulk still overflowed her throne. Half featherless, her parrot danced madly on the

1

tables in exchange for gulps from the customers' cups. The tunes out of the multi were as raucous as ever. They were local men, Chambois sailors and Maraisard swamprunners, who sat crowded, talked, laughed, growled, shook dice or slapped cards. A few girls circulated, cadging drinks. Now and then one of them got somebody, usually a very young fellow, to go into the back room with her. When he returned, his friends were apt to make game of him, and custom required that he merely reply in kind, not invite any of them outside for a slash session.

Often you'll see three or four foreigners as well, no tourists—the guides don't want to risk that—but old acquaintances like me, who drop in whenever they happen by. We have enough of the patois and we know how to behave, the ritual bow to Wang Fang's skull, the respects paid to Madame, the cognac bought for her and her bird, the offside table taken. Those men who care to talk with us will stroll over and do so; or we'll swap stories with each other, till the bayshore treetops turn orange with dawn and we walk back to our aircars through a field of knee-deep fog. It's a place for stories. That's mainly why we come.

On this night I was the only such. It didn't matter. Ancre-Jacques left his neighbors and joined me. We had much to tell from the time that had passed. I was third mate in the *Freuchen* when she took Sarauw's team to Grayworld on the expedition that found a ten-million-year-old machine still at work—

Jacques was describing his brush with a pirate submarine in the Amazonian Sea when abruptly he broke off and squinted past me, through the smoke, toward the entrance. "Why, there's La Balafre Triangulaire," he said. "I thought he was out on Cap Trahison." He raised a mighty arm and bellowed, "Eh-ah, rogue, over here!" In those parts, "*coquin*" comes near being an endearment. To me: "Poor devil, he's always pitifully glad to meet spacefarers. A decent sort, makes himself useful in small ways, and he saved two children when the Fou Rieur tidal bore caught them." They have small respect for the laws of God and man on the Fever Coast, but a great deal for physical courage, and in their fashion they are not unkindly.

Turning my head, I saw the newcomer approach. Though tall, he was so thin that I wondered how he had carried out the rescue. His build, sunburned fair skin, and sandy hair marked him out startlingly. In clothes faded and patched but clean, he made his way among the tables with a stiff carefulness that told me he was already half drunk. When he reached us, I saw the jagged scar from his right temple to the corner of his mouth that gave him his nickname.

Jacques invited him to sit down but didn't introduce us. That isn't done there, because some men have reason not to want it. My Firestar Line emblem identified me well enough. La Balafre Triangulaire nodded gravely and took a chair. Jacques shouted for more *eau de mort* all around. "My friend is newly in from Eisenheim, and was doing exploratory work before that," he explained.

Washed-out blue eyes seemed to kindle just a bit. "Eisenheim?" said Balafre. His voice was very low. I guessed that drink was what had hoarsened it and, from the accent, that the mother tongue was English. "Second planet of Schelling's"—he stumbled through a catalogue designation I didn't know but recognized as naval—"if I remember rightly?" I nodded. "Then did you earlier, by any chance, call at Belisarius?" His fingers gripped the tabletop. "It's a planet of Third Grigorian's. In the Canopus sector. Have you heard of it?"

"No and yes, in that order," I answered. "We had no reason to stop there. It's strictly a Fleet Base."

His words wavered. "But did you at least hear something of it, at some port along your way? Any news or— It's so bloody far from us. We're so isolated on this damned continent." He swallowed, drew the rags of his dignity about himself, and finished, "I beg your pardon. You wonder what cause a beachcomber has to inquire."

"Well, you've been a spaceman yourself," I ventured. He didn't seem dangerously touchy.

"Not quite," he sighed. "Not of your kind. Although once—but that was long ago." He looked vaguely beyond me. "How long? Let me see, I've been on San Valerio seven years, is it? That would be about five standard. And before then— No, never mind. I verge on self-pity, the most contemptible of emotions. Worse, I bore you.''

"No, no," I said, for I scented a story in him, and Jacques's expression confirmed it. The liquor arrived and I paid. Balafre regained graciousness as he thanked me. He sipped with care, obviously trying to maintain a precise, desired level of tipsiness.

I heard a few anecdotes from this vicinity. He had a shack under the bluffs, made his living by odd jobs and picking over the ebb tides for rock pearls, got his scar when he stumbled across a ripfish. They could have repaired the damage at the clinic in Senville, an hour away by a bus that landed weekly, but he preferred to spend the money on booze. Porto Blanco, across the ocean, might as well have been on a moon. Not that he was a mindless derelict. He spent most of his abundant free time at the little terminal in his hut, screening books, drama, music from the global database.

After a while we realized we'd slipped into English, and offered Jacques our apologies. He laughed. "It's practice for me to listen," he said. "I deal with outsiders more than you may think, me. But when you speak of . . . Aristotle, the name? . . . and of what is justice, that is water over this head and I bid you good drinking, my friends.''

He got up and sought back to his own kind. Balafre and I talked till morning. It took nearly that long to get the real tale out of him—not that he had never told anybody else, but I was a stranger and he clung to his remnant of pride. Yet I too had read philosophers and seen a fair amount of worlds. In the end he decided that my opinion was as worth hearing as some priest's or sea captain's or wise old fisher wife's. Had he received justice or was he the victim of a cruel wrong?

Assuredly they had not accorded him mercy.

"Lieutenant Arthur Laing, to report to Vice Admiral Derabina."

The ensign behind the desk nodded, touched a button, and said, "A few minutes, I think. Have a seat." He went back to whatever he was doing on a computer. Idle hours were scarce on Belisarius, and would be till Christina had been freed of the Khalia.

Restless, Laing ignored furniture and paced across the bleak little anteroom. Brought to this planet today, he felt light under two fifths of standard gravity. He wished the heaviness inside him could be abolished as easily.

Well, but wasn't he supposed to play a part in the liberation? An important part, maybe crucial—whatever it was.

At the wall he stopped and stared out. Before him was not a viewscreen, only a window. The Fleet had cut every possible corner in its haste. A year ago there had been nothing on this world but rock, sand, dust, ice, and the sole official name it had had was a catalogue number, unless you wanted to say, "Third Grigorian's IV."

When it shone in the skies of Christina, we used to call it Ruby, Laing thought. But that was just to ourselves, Tess and me.

Dwarfed, the sun hung low in a ruddy heaven. Away from it, a few stars were visible through the tenuous air. The light fell pale across wasteland and the spacefield. He saw a shuttlecraft, newly down from orbit, and several ground crewmen, their suits and helmets calling to mind robots or trolls. Along the edge of ferro-concrete stretched bare metal walls. The skeleton of a monitor tower loomed behind them.

Here in the office, recycling was less than perfect; a chemical harshness tainted the breaths he drew. He remembered odors of growth and blossoming on Christina. How rare life was in the universe, how infinitely wonderful and precious. It seemed wrong to destroy even Khalia.

But that had to be done, of course.

"Lieutenant Laing?"

The voice at his back brought him around to confront a man who bore commander's insignia. He saluted. The man responded, then smiled half shyly and said, "Never mind about ceremony. I'm Ian Maclaurin." His English had a slight burr. He was surprisingly young for his rank, slim, blond, boyish-faced. Promotion in the Fleet could be fast, though, when a war was under way and a person had special capabilities.

"Oh, the, uh, psychophysicist? I've heard your name mentioned, but I'm afraid I'm in the dark about what you actually do."

They shook hands. "I'm pretty ignorant about you, so that puts us on the same footing," Maclaurin said. "And we're also fellow Scots, aren't we?"

"Only by rather distant ancestry in my case," Laing replied. "I was born on Caesar. You?"

"Well, Dunbar, but they've kept the ethnos—recreated it, actually. People from the old country on Earth come to marvel at our picturesque ways." They sat down opposite and close to each other. "I hoped I'd find you waiting. The admiral's predictably behind schedule, as overworked as she is. Here's our chance to get a little acquainted. We ought to spend days on it, but we won't be granted them."

In spite of the immediate liking he felt, unease tingled in Laing. "How necessary is it?" he asked. "Not that I'm being standoffish, but— What do they want me for, anyway?"

Maclaurin watched him closely from behind the geniality. "Haven't you tried to guess?"

"No." Laing constructed a smile. "I'm a scientist by trade. It's bad form to make hypotheses in the absence of data. Nobody has told me anything except that this is secret and urgent. Obviously it involves my knowledge of Christina."

"Of what?"

Laing realized that Maclaurin must be new here himself. Besides, the name was unofficial, casually decided on at mess one evening in honor of an actress famous at the time. She too was beautiful. "The third planet, that the Khalia are on."

"Och, aye. Should have deduced that on the instant," Maclaurin said. "Yes, you're right, we require a person familiar, very familiar with it, and specifically with the territory where the Khalia are. Your name popped out of the data scan."

"Why me? Hundreds of people must have been on Christina from time to time since Grigorian reached this system. Yes, I know most of them didn't do work that involved them especially, or at all, with Mozart, as we came to call that area. But I could name you a dozen at least other than me, starting with my wife, who spent years there, and— It depends on what aspect of it you have in mind, but whatever that is, I'll bet I can tell you who's the real expert." Insofar as we have any, Laing's mind added. Christina's a whole world, as big and varied and mysterious as ever Earth was.

"I didn't make the choice, but I know the reason," Maclaurin told him. "They're civilians, who scattered from end to end of Alliance space after we evacuated them. Any whom we might locate and who might be willing to serve would lack naval training and not be subject to naval discipline. You're the one member of the Fleet who appeared to have the necessary information."

"Reservist. A glorified civilian, really."

Maclaurin shrugged. "Well, the Fleet could recall you to active duty and bring you here." He cocked his head. "Surprising that you're not a regular officer, grown up in the Fleet, if you were born on Caesar."

"Civilians are in the majority there too, regardless of any popular impression. My wife, now, she's a Fleet brat."

"But I gather that she never enlisted, while you did."

Laing bridled. What the hell right had this dipnose to probe him?

It was as if Tess stood beside him again, blade-straight, red hair ruffled by the wind that sent banners snapping and streaming, afire with pride as the graduating cadets paraded by, her brother in the first rank of them. Again she racked back a drunk in a bar, some kind of pacifist, who had sneered at the Fleet, till the wretch stumbled away from her, half terrified. Again she lay in his, her bridegroom's, arms and murmured, "Yes, I know I have something of a father fixation, but Dad *is* magnificent and, and it doesn't stop me from loving you, darling." Again she jubilated when he told her he had decided to join, and again when he received his commission, though she knew his reasons and respected them and laughed that she'd have made a dreadful wife for any officer bent on a real Fleet career.

"I'm sorry," Maclaurin said. "I do apologize. No wish to intrude on your privacy, I swear. Nor to insult your intelligence. I have studied your dossier and already know the general course of your life to date, plus your psychoprofile, medical history, et cetera, et cetera. But that tells me little about the inner you. The mission has a better chance of succeeding if I get a sense of you as a whole human being, not a disembodied file of data. My job is as much art as science, and I suspect more black magic than either. So, yes, I am leading you in conversation about yourself."

"I see." Mollified, Laing felt a perhaps irrational eagerness to explain, to justify. "My wife did dream of serving. Throughout her girlhood, she meant to. But gradually she found that what absorbed her more, and what she was best qualified for, was ethology. Loosely speaking, natural history. Really mastering that and doing it demanded full time." Again they stood on the university campus under a midnight moon and she wept, "I'm not disappointing my father too much, am I, am I?"

Maclaurin nodded. "More valuable to civilization too, I daresay."

"Well, somebody has to mount guard." Against the murderous likes of the Khalia.

"So you decided to enlist?"

"Not out of altruism," Laing admitted. "For one thing, the Weasels hadn't attacked anybody yet that we knew of."

Now I, the detached and broad-minded scholar, am talking of them, yes, thinking of them like the lowest-browed slogfoot Marine. Well, I am not ashamed of myself. What they have done, what they do, is a horror, a menace, an abomination. It must be ended. That they swept into this system and disrupted our work among the amadei—the Fleet got us out barely in time—is small indeed, set beside what they wreak elsewhere. But it is what has hurt Tess and me in our own lives. Not just the cutting off of the research. The amadei were like children to us, the children we have not had ourselves.

He pulled out of his thoughts and continued: "Ironic, eh, that I should be the one of us who did? But quite logical. You doubtless know how the Fleet helps underwrite scientific and exploratory projects that have potential value to it. Manhabitable planets like Christina aren't exactly common. Whether or not eventual colonization is contemplated—and in this case, our recommendation against it is as strong as we could find words for—they will likely sometime become involved in operations, as places to establish bases or resupply or simply give crews on long missions a bit of R&R in a pleasant setting. So they need to be studied beforehand. But the Fleet naturally wants personnel of its own on the teams. Well, I'm a generalized biologist. My work doesn't require the continuity that my wife's does. It doesn't suffer if I take occasional time off it. We found out that the Fleet would subsidize research on Christina, which we'd decided was our ideal lifetime project, if at least one of its officers was permanently engaged there. Her father pulled a few wires and, well, that's how it came about." He paused. "I'm rehashing what you know."

"Not entirely," Maclaurin said. "Or to the extent you do, I repeat, it's valuable to me to hear and see you giving me your perspective on matters."

"Don't get me wrong," Laing requested. "I didn't join grudgingly." It made Tess so radiantly glad—"I like the Fleet, its people, its traditions. My tours of duty have been short, agreeable diversions, a taste of the outside universe after many months in wilderness. But I am basically a scientist, not a warrior."

"Nothing wrong with that," Maclaurin assured him. "As long as you're prepared to do your duty—"

"Admiral Derabina will see you now, gentlemen," the ensign called.

They entered the inner office together. It was as cramped and gauntly functional as everything else on Belisarius, but not devoid of character. On the walls hung framed copies of citations for excellent service or outright heroism, together with pictures taken at the storming of Mount Satan and the defense of Kamehameha. On the desk, besides a terminal and communicator, stood a model of an attack ranger that Laing supposed had been Derabina's first command. He and Maclaurin snapped to attention and saluted.

The admiral returned the gesture crisply. "At ease," she said. "Be seated." It sounded more like an order than an invitation. Yelena B. Derabina was a stocky woman whose face, beneath the short gray hair, made Laing think of ancient

Tartars. En route he had occasionally heard her called a martinet and always heard her called humorless, but those who served under her and survived it developed a special esprit de corps. "Borisovna's Bastards" got things done, and done right.

The men sat without relaxing. "Are you prepared to go straight to business, Lieutenant?" Borisovna snapped.

"Yes, ma'am." Laing hesitated. "Except, well, I haven't been briefed, just rushed directly through."

"And you wonder why a flag officer takes you in charge. This is an extraordinary mission, Lieutenant. Nothing quite like it has ever been done before. The investment in it is enormous, the cost of failure larger yet. Although the danger of information leaking to the Khalia is small, still, the fewer individuals who know, the better. I want to be on top of the operation from start to finish. Giving you a few minutes gives me a chance to estimate your fitness. Your record suggests certain ambiguities."

Laing flushed. "Ma'am, nobody has ever questioned my loyalty."

"There has been no cause to. Your tours of duty were routine and non-combat. Most of your time you spent on Planet Three studying its wildlife." The clipped voice softened slightly. "I know that that has had its dangers and that you acquitted yourself well in emergencies. No slur on your character is intended. In fact, your psychoprofile shows a sense of duty well above average. It is only that we have to know the limits of your ability. This undertaking *must* succeed. We won't get a second try."

"If I may speak, ma'am," Maclaurin offered. At her nod: "Your ability is what we need, Laing, your capacity for quick perception, comprehension, decision, and action. In one sense, this is a suicide mission. Yet you'll be perfectly safe . . . yourself. So dismiss any worries and concentrate on the technical problems."

Insight sent a chill up Laing's spine and out to his fingertips. "You're planning a mind transfer?"

Maclaurin raised a hand. "That's sensationalism. Actually—"

"In due course," Derabina interrupted. "We'll take things

in order. What do you know of the military situation here, Lieutenant?''

Laing forced his consciousness to it. ''Well, ma'am, we—you—have the Khalia bottled up on Christina—on Planet Three.''

''Is that all you have heard?'' she asked with scorn. ''I should think you would be more interested in the scene of your dedication.''

Laing swallowed his anger. ''Ma'am,'' he said, ''the Khalian invasion came without warning, out of nowhere. The evacuation of Three was helter-skelter. My wife and I were swept onto different ships and taken to different systems. In the confusion, we had trouble finding each other's locations, let alone getting back together. Then we had to make frantic arrangements, housing, jobs, necessities. Meanwhile the campaign around Target completely dominated the news. We couldn't get anything but rumors from Third Grigorian's. When I was contacted and put on active status and immediately shipped here, the crew were under strict orders regarding secrecy. They didn't know why, so they didn't want to risk violation, and clamped shut whenever talk turned to operations.''

He felt surprise that Derabina heard him out and responded quite patiently: ''I see. Not your negligence.

''The basic facts are simple. The Khalia arrived well prepared, with more supplies and equipment for construction than for combat. What warships they did bring sufficed to stand off our initial counterattacks, for we did not appreciate the threat at once. We assumed they only meant to carry out nuisance raids for a while. The Alliance has consistently underestimated the Khalia, thought of them as mere pirates. We're gradually having our noses rubbed in the fact that they are far more.

''Barely in time, a scoutcraft managed to get sightings on Planet Three—and escape. Thus the Fleet learned that the Khalians had brought into being a complete, fully dug-in, fully outfitted stronghold. With such a base, plus ample ships, they could interdict this entire stellar vicinity, a catastrophe for the Alliance.

''An armada was on its way. Now alerted, the Fleet detected it. A task force of ours intercepted it and turned it back. The force went on to regain Planet Three. However, that attempt failed, with heavy losses. The Khalian defenses were, and are, too strong. The best we could do was erect our own base here on Four. From it, we do control ambient space. Thus far, the Khalia have not taken their remaining vessels out of shelter. We have them under siege. But we can't starve them out or wear them down. Given the resources of a terrestroid world, they can supply themselves indefinitely, now that they have the robots and other gear to exploit those resources.

"We cannot go away and leave them. Simply using the small craft they have on hand, they could make hit-and-run assaults for parsecs around. And, of course, their headquarters would be quick to send in much more force, as was originally planned.

"Maintaining the blockade is costly. It takes more ships than you, with your background, might think, Lieutenant. We must keep constant watch, in sufficient strength to repel any sortie. Additionally, we must patrol all space around the sun, out to more than a light-year, lest the enemy send reinforcements streaking in. Let those get past us and onto Three, or into low Three orbit, and they'll be invulnerable, remember; and so the Khalia could build up their reserves piecemeal until they were ready to come out and challenge us. Supporting this effort of ours takes more personnel and equipment, by an order of magnitude, than the effort itself.

"At the same time, the war is intensifying overall. For example, we would make a large difference in the Target campaign. Third Grigorian's has become an intolerable drain on Fleet and Alliance resources." Did the admiral barely, grimly, smile? "You might well say that the Khalia have *us* bottled up."

She leaned forward. "Do you understand, Lieutenant?"

"Well, uh, well, ma'am," Laing floundered. He mustered resolution. "No, ma'am, not really. Why can't you bombard from space? Saturate those defenses and blast a hole where the base was."

"That wouldn't be so good for the planet," Maclaurin observed.

Laing tautened. "No. Firestorms, fallout." The Mozart country become slag and ash. "But I knew from the first that it was likely."

"And Three doesn't have intelligent life."

"Well—" The amadei. But they aren't sapient. Smart, but still just animals. And their species has spread over more than half the world. It will survive. Life will come back to Mozart. The Khalia—probably the Khalia hunt the amadei for sport. "No. Anyway, I was thinking of rays and plasma as well as missiles. Energy weapons are . . . comparatively clean."

"What academy did you attend, Lieutenant?" Derabina demanded.

"Why, uh, Xiang on Celestia, ma'am. Where I happened to be when—"

"Their school of weapons must be deplorable. Even though you were not slated to become a line officer, you should have been better taught. Or have you forgotten your instruction?"

"No, ma'am, I—"

Derabina touched computer controls. She was doubtless putting in a reminder to herself to urge that the High Command order an investigation of Xiang, with possible courts-martial to follow. "You may try to explain, Commander," she said.

Laing was glad to turn his eyes on Maclaurin. The other man cleared his throat and began: "It's a quantitative matter. These Khalians possess an extraordinary concentration of defensive weapons. They've demolished every missile we've launched at them—and we've sent some barrages, huge by any standard—in the stratosphere or higher. You're aware total destruction isn't necessary. A strong energy beam that touches an incoming warhead, however briefly, or a nuclear burst some distance off, either of those will scramble the electronics and make the missile a dud. No shielding, backup system, or evasive action has worked against the kind of firepower the Khalia have. Remember, they've got robotic mines and factories producing arms underground.

"We've tried kinetic kill, large meteoroids sent in at high velocities. Radiation doesn't affect them. Unfortunately, it takes a lot of energy to move one capable of doing significant damage onto the right trajectory, and course corrections are slow. Khalian detectors pick the rocks up in plenty of time for small nukes to intercept and blast them into chunks of harmless size. Yes, we tried mounting automatic energy weapons in them, but between the defense missiles and the decoys, those proved inadequate.''

''What would 'harmless size' be?'' Laing wondered.

''We've seen up to twenty tons of fragment strike in the area at velocities up to fifty KPS. They've made craters, they may have taken out an emplacement or two, but the Khalia are dug into bedrock deeper than that, obviously with perfect-crystal reinforcing materials. By the same token, toxins or radioactive dust would harm nothing but the surroundings, not bother them in their dens in the least.

''As for burning them out with rays and plasma beams, surely you can see for yourself what an intensity and what a time that would take. As close in as our force would have to keep station, it'd be a sitting duck for the Khalia; their ground-based energy generators are more powerful than anything ships can carry. No, the attempt would be a disaster for us.''

''Targeting,'' Derabina said.

''Och, aye. Yes, ma'am. That's another problem we face. The Khalians chose their site on Three very well. They must have sent scouts and collected intelligence about the planet for years beforehand. You know how ruggedly mountainous that particular region is, how changeable and often cloudy the weather. Nobody foresaw a military need. It turns out that accurate maps never were put in the Fleet databases. Whatever such information existed was on Three itself, and left behind at the evacuation. Yes, incompetence, lack of fore-sight, and heads have already rolled—but my God, Laing, the Fleet's composed of mortal beings. Mistakes and oversights are bound to occur.

''The upshot is that without a precise grid tied to proper benchmarks, we can't pinpoint our fire except optically, at those short times when seeing through the atmosphere is close to perfect. Radar lacks adequate bandwidth, and the enemy jams it anyway. We can't do a real mapping job ourselves, because no surveyor could fly low enough long enough before the Khalians shot it down. Oh, we can always aim within a probable few kilometers. But that error is one reason why kinetic kill has been such a fiasco for us.

"If we had better maps, we'd still be handicapped by not knowing exactly where the enemy base is. We spy the above-ground stuff, but it's spotted across half the continent. Of the central installation, the heart and brain, we know only that it's below one of several deep valleys sheltered by surrounding mountains. The Khalia did a clever job of camouflage—forced regrowth of vegetation—and as for emitted radiation, it's diffused and most of it must be from dummies. None of us are familiar with that country. We can't tell what is natural and what artificial.

"Now you, Laing, you've spent years in it. You've tramped over it, flown over it, pored over the maps again and again. You must know it like the palm of your hand."

Laing dared a smile. "To tell the truth, I never studied the palm of my hand especially."

"You know what I mean. You don't have a geodetic survey in your head, no. But you could recognize landmarks instantly, I'm sure, though you glimpsed them through cloud or rain; and then you'd instantly know where any other given place was; and you could see which had been heavily tampered with. Correct?"

Laing remembered Vesper Peak soaring out of a thunderstorm beneath which lay the River Argent and the camp where Tess waited for him. "Well, yes. Within limits. Yes, I did get pretty good at finding my way around, also from the air."

"That is what we require," Derabina said. He looked back at the admiral. The fierceness of her gaze was like a whip-slash. "One way or another, we must end this stalemate, and soon. The Fleet cannot afford it much longer. We had resigned ourselves to ground assault. Under cover of as heavy a bombardment as we could possibly manage, we'd land an expeditionary force on a different continent. From that beach-head we'd expand and move. Surface-to-surface missiles should soften the Khalia somewhat, but air, armor, and infantry would have to finish the job. The cost is appalling. A million casualties, with corresponding losses in matériel, is a low estimate. Nevertheless, it seemed we must bear it.

"Then this new proposal was made. Commander Maclaurin was in the group that devised it. If it succeeds, he can share credit for saving a million Allied dead and wounded, plus the added casualties that their absence elsewhere would cause."

Maclaurin's eyes brightened, his cheeks reddened, and Laing suddenly understood the full meaning of that old word "accolade."

"You can bring the same honor on yourself, Lieutenant," Derabina said, and Laing understood why, in spite of everything, her people went bravely into battle.

"What . . . shall I do . . . ma'am?" he whispered.

Derabina's words were again dry, but her voice rang. "You, or rather your duplicated mind, will pilot the weapon that all by itself can end this standoff.

"It exists, ready except for the programming. In outward appearance it is an ordinary chondritic meteoroid adrift in space, a lump of fragile rock, its largest dimension about four meters, which indicates a mass of perhaps ten tons. Actually the mass is lower. We will maneuver it into such an orbit that it will strike the atmosphere of Three not far from the zenith above the enemy base. The Khalia should take that for a natural occurrence, especially since it will fragment high in the air as chondrites usually do.

"Suddenly one of the pieces, about three meters thick, will shoot straight toward the base. Probably the Khalian computers will deduce, or detect, that this piece has an engine inside. It will be too late for missile interception, but they will fire an energy beam to disable any electronics. That will be useless. The meteoroid will strike on top of them."

Derabina stopped. After a silence, Laing said, "Pardon me, ma'am, but I don't follow you. Evidently the object won't have a warhead, since you expect the Khalian defense would take any out. All you've got is a large boulder and ordinary cosmic speed; the motor can't have added much velocity. From what I've been told about the enemy fortress, I don't see how that would do so much as rattle their teacups."

The admiral had clearly invited his bemusement. She wanted to savor his reaction when she explained; she was that human. "Ah, but apart from the disguise, the engine, and auxiliary apparatus, what you will be piloting is five tons of antimatter."

Laing was allowed twelve hours to eat, sleep, adjust to Belisarian conditions, before he reported at Maclaurin's laboratory. Yet when he arrived the psychophysicist first took him into an adjacent domicile room, made coffee, and struck up a leisured conversation. It would be best if his subject was—not relaxed, which was scarcely possible without drugs, but not extremely nervous. Moreover, he reiterated, a degree of personal acquaintance would enable him to perform his task better.

"It isn't a simple business of gadgets scanning your nervous system, mapping it into an equivalent pattern, and putting that into a program," he said. "Nor can we just copy off your relevant memories. Intelligence is too subtle and complex. It has a certain unity. We need your whole mind, or we get nothing. An improperly run scan could give us the semblance of a mind, but it would be . . . untrustworthy. Insane, in any of a dozen tricky ways. If I'm watching you while you're in the circuits, knowledgeably observing your body language as well as your spoken responses to cues, that will be an important supplement to the instrumentation."

Laing leaned back in an uncomfortable chair and strove to make his muscles ease off. Maclaurin's living quarters were a help, neat but with homely touches, pictures of his wife and children and sailboat, a guitar, a few well-worn codex books, a chessboard for play against a computer. "I know hardly anything about mind transfer," Laing admitted. "It isn't done often, is it?"

Maclaurin frowned. "Please, I hate that phrase 'mind transfer.' May its inventor spend eternity in hell listening to every journalistic cliché of recorded history. Your mind is not a *thing* that we can lift out and stuff into a machine. It's an ongoing process, a function of your entire organism. What we do is—our devices observe it, derive a set of equations describing it, too many and too complicated for any organic brain to handle, and under the guidance of those equations write a program by which a special kind of computer operates correspondingly.'' He paused before adding, ''You are right, it's seldom done. Originally it was for scientific research purposes, and these days, almost always, we do best giving instructions to a robot.''

Laing sipped his coffee. The warmth and flavor soothed him a little. ''Matter of ethics too, I imagine,'' he said slowly. ''Shouldn't we pity that shadow self of mine? Bad enough being trapped in a machine body, but with a kamikaze dive ahead of him—''

''No, don't worry about that,'' Maclaurin replied. ''There are compensations. Subjects have described the wonders of direct sensory input from instruments you and I can only read, and sharing the intellectual power of a computer. Just the same, true, we don't do this sort of thing lightly. And, true, your alter ego is to be a sacrifice. But men and women have laid down their lives countless times that others might survive, and this is for a million or more.'' He drew breath. ''Besides, the ego won't mind self-immolation. Remember, it won't be you, nor an identical twin of you. Same memories, same ways of thinking, but no flesh, no glands— essentially, no instinct of self-preservation. To the extent that 'emotion' means anything in this case, it will be glad to serve so good a cause. We know that from earlier experience. If it were not true, our project would be out of the question. We have no way of laying compulsion on a consciousness without suppressing the capability of independent thought that is the very thing we need. The mind has to do what it does of its own will. That's another reason you were tapped. Your psychoprofile shows a high sense of duty.''

Laing grimaced. ''This won't be a pleasant duty. Understatement of the century.''

Maclaurin gave him a close but gentle regard. ''Yes, you do have to wreck the country where you lived and worked so long,'' he agreed. ''That entire continent will be in bad shape, and the background count will rise everywhere on the planet. However, we aren't going to sterilize it. Not even this weapon can do that. Life is tough, tenacious.''

Laing nodded jerkily. "I know. I didn't sleep much last night. Lay there thinking the matter out, as best I could."

"I'm fairly confident you and your associates can go back in a few years and pick up your research. The Fleet is mindful of those who have served it well."

"Not the same," Laing muttered. "The locale, Mozart Land, and the amadei we know—those won't exist. We'll have to begin all over again, among strangers, in a strange country."

"Uh, amadei?"

"Our team's informal name." Laing found himself curiously anxious to talk about them, regardless of how it hurt. "Officially, chrysodonts. The most interesting animal by far on Christina. They became Tess's, my wife's, specialty. I observed them as often as I could manage, and made friends among them."

Maclaurin raised his brows. "Friends? There are no sapients on Three." His voice roughened. "Are there?"

The Fleet did not condone genocide.

"No, no," Laing answered quickly. "Likening the geological histories of separate planets is ridiculous, but as a crude catchphrase you might say Christina is at a stage similar to the late Cretaceous of Earth. Except on mountains, climates range from warm to hot. No polar caps. No dinosaurs, of course, but creatures with many analogies to reptiles dominate animal life and have evolved a marvelous variety of forms. The chrysodonts are bipedal, comparatively large-brained. The species we call the amadeus is the brightest of them. About like Terrestrial monkeys, if that means anything to you."

"I saw a documentary about Earth nature once. How do they get that name?"

"Amadeus? They sing beautifully. It's a nickname we field workers hit on, like Mozart and, oh, damn near everything else." Laing tossed off his coffee and bashed the cup down on the table. "God, I want to weep for our amadei."

"Chances are the Khalians have killed those you knew."

"Yeah." Laing looked elsewhere. "Maybe my mind-copy will enjoy his task, in a way." Abruptly he wanted to think about that. "But must you really bring such a weapon to bear? Seems like overkill in spades."

"We have to make sure," Maclaurin explained. "Nobody's ever done anything like this before, and as the admiral said, we won't get a second try. Exercising emergency authority, by writ of the High Command, our agents collected practically the entire supply of anti-lithium anti-hydride in the Alliance. It's normally used in minute quantities as an industrial explosive where ultra-precision is necessary, you may know. The stockpiling was to free up the plants to produce heavier nuclei. Now it'll take them ten years to replace those five tons."

"Lithium?"

"The hydride. Solid, fairly dense, chemically stable, much easier to handle than anti-hydrogen or anti-helium, and more effective for our purposes. We've got it suspended by a tension field in a vacuum chamber inside our meteoroid. Impact will switch off the field generator and drive the stuff out, a ways down into the ground. Conversion of mass to energy will be total, of course. But we can't predict how fast it will happen, or how efficiently from the viewpoint of what we want to do. Gobs of material will be flung far and wide by the initial reaction, blazing through the air. We've got to be absolutely sure that enough force hits the Khalian base to destroy it utterly. Therefore we're throwing as big a lump as we could get together, and need a conscious pilot to make certain it strikes very near the target."

Maclaurin laughed. "What a fireworks display!" Maybe that was his defense against the expectation.

The hours of scanning were not a nightmare. Physical discomfort was minor, mainly due to prolonged immobility while connected to a labyrinth of tubes, wires, monitors, meters. Maclaurin and his assistants were *simpático*. The experience was eldritch, though. Forgotten moments of youth, childhood, infancy rose from the deeps to claim the whole of the universe and recede before others. Thought rambled dimly and without coherence, as it does on the verge of sleep. Emotions burst forth, objectless: love, anger, dread, lust, grief, mirth, primordial passions for which the waking mind had no name. They flowed into a oneness that exploded in a million whirling colors. Space-time dwindled to zero and stretched to infinity. Laing perceived the meaning of existence, but lost it again. He could not afterward remember any of those hours, except that he had dreamed such things. Finally a technician gave him an injection and he spun into oblivion.

He awoke in sick bay. Drowsily he saw that the various punctures in his skin were bandaged. They should soon heal, faster than his hair would grow back. He closed his eyes and slept onward.

At some later date he was more fully awake. Maclaurin came in, vibrant, and exclaimed, "It's worked, it's worked! Everything went top chop. The program's in place now, and our weapon's on the way."

We will never know what the pseudobrain thought, bound for its destiny. We have nothing but that last stark message, and the fact of what happened next. Still less can we know what it felt, as sundered from ours as its existence was. Yet I heard much, that night in Wang Fang's. Later, curious, I retrieved what I could from various databases whenever I was on worlds they occupy. And I already knew something about such machines. I had even talked with one. As said, I collect stories.

So let me reconstruct this, believing I am not far wrong.

Think of that rock, slowly a-tumble with hell in its belly on a long fall around the sun. The Laing mind does not see space as you and I do. It perceives through instruments attuned to the entire spectrum, to ghostly winds of atoms and ions, to force-fields and pulses and the rhythms of gravity as the planets dance about their mother. It sees the solar fire ahead in full incandescence, while at the same time it sees the maelstroms that are spots, flame-tongues of flares and prominences, lacy nacre of corona, and the zodiacal light outspread in great vague wings. Undazzled, it sees the stars in their manifold hues, crowding Heaven wherever it looks, for to these senses myriads stand clear that are too dim for our eyes. Space is not dark, it is radiant. Nor is it silent. The atoms between the stars sing in radio voices through which throbs that deep chant that remembers the birth of the universe. Here and there nebulae glow with new suns or the death-gasps of old. Clouds cleave the Milky Way, but they cannot hide the furious heartbeat of the galaxy from this machine. Sister galaxies gleam afar, outward and outward to that edge of observability where we descry the beginning and foresee the end of all things.

The Laing mind takes hours, days, to master its awarenesses. By itself it is merely human. It would be forever lost in bewilderment were it not conjoined to the computer that controls the whole. Given such a capability, the speed and volume of data handling, the immense library out of which it can draw whatever it needs in nanoseconds—given this, gradually it assimilates the flood of input. It understands and governs. Thus it can think afresh. No longer like a drunken god, but taking its godlike powers for granted, it recalls what it formerly was.

No, it realizes, that isn't accurate. It never was Arthur Laing. He is back on yonder ruddy spark in the sky. The mind makes an optical enlargement until Belisarius rolls big in vision, a desolation of rock and dust storms. Neutrinos from the powerplants stream through detectors, but maximum magnification cannot give sight of the Fleet Base. Life is so small in the cosmos, so transitory, intelligent life so rare.

Meanwhile the asteroid has orbited ever closer to Christina. Knowing that the Laing mind would need to settle down into its condition, the planners gave it plenty of time. Furthermore, by starting their missile off on this trajectory at such a remove, they denied the Khalia any possibility of noticing anything suspicious about it.

Christina waxes, at first a white star, then a tiny crescent, then a disc over whose dark part plays a faint phosphorescence. The dayside begins to show a shadow-limned intricacy of cloud-play. Streaks come and go, blue, sight of the oceans, greenish brown when the skies clear above land, but they are soon gone again. The planet has known ice ages, humans have seen the traces, but this is its great summer, in which it has dreamed for fifty million years. Two moons, of less size than Luna, shine scarred upon the cloud deck.

The Laing mind remembers.

Tess gripped his hand. From their seats they saw the world swell before them. "Our home," she breathed. "Oh, I know we'll be happy here."

He smiled. "I wish I could carry you over the threshold," he said, and felt how much he meant that. He wanted her in his arms, the dear weight and warmth of her. Well, they'd shortly be on the ground, in camp. There ought to be private quarters for them, if only a tent. There'd better!

The spacecraft growled, braking. Mist blinded the viewscreens. Suddenly they broke through and beneath them reached forest, mountains, a river like a silvery snake.

The Laing mind strains its instruments forward. Emanations from the Khalian base are discernible. They strengthen hour by hour, presently minute by minute, radio, infrared, neutrinos, out of a spot like an inflamed wound. A few little ticklings come from elsewhere, aircraft on errands—or on safaris? The Khalia seem to love killing in the way humans love sex. No matter. After the base is destroyed, hunting down any survivors will be a trivial chore.

The Laing mind has no fear of obliteration. It does not envy its other, original, self. It lacks a body to savor the sweetnesses of life and long for them. Here is a duty to perform, a deed more useful than most in history, service to Tess and humankind and decency. It is able to take pride in that.

Nevertheless, while existence remains and it is free of immediate demands, it wants to remember everything it can.

The overcast was seldom gloomy, but pearl gray. After you had learned how to see when shadows were dim or absent, you felt that somehow the whole air had gone softly luminous. Mountains reared into it wherever you looked, blue majesties, their highest peaks lost in the clouds, bared to the stars. The valley floor was half glades, half woods. Laing stood in tall, tawny, rustling growth that was not actually grass, near the trees. Those towered coppery-barked, spreading out in violet-veined leaf canopies where drops of water glinted. Rainbow wings fluttered among them. A breeze took the curse off the heat, though he was long since used to that anyway. It bore odors evoking childhood whiffs of jasmine and ginger.

The amadeus family was taking its ease at the forest edge. "Family" might be a purely human idea, but Tess had come to think it fitted. Amadei lived in groups, about half a dozen adult males and as many females plus their young. The couples appeared to be more or less monogamous. Extended family, you could perhaps say. From time to time several bands met, frolicking and singing for days, while newly mature members found mates. Afterward the families went back to their territories.

Laing was pleased to recognize individuals here. Often away studying different creatures, he hadn't developed Tess's intimacy with the amadei. (That was the reason for settling in Mozart; deep dales concentrated them, prevented wide wandering, and so you could observe them, win their trust, follow their lives year after year.) However, he'd gotten friendly with some.

They were a handsome sight, the adults of a size with him, body slanted forward, counterbalanced by a gracefully waving tail. The head was large, round, blunt-muzzled, on top of a rather long neck; the eyes glowed liquidly dark; the golden-gleaming teeth had seemed alarmingly large at first, and indeed the amadei did sometimes hunt lesser animals, but in their own company they were generally sweet-tempered. Their skin was delicately scaled, its blue-black shimmer suggestive of chain mail. Laing was fascinated by their forepaws. Those digits seemed well on the way to becoming true fingers, with opposable thumbs.

Gimpy hobbled about in search of berries. Tumtum, already sated, drowsed against a bole. Bella put food in the mouth of a hatchling, which she cradled in her left arm. Fussy made vain efforts to call two half-grown of hers down from reckless games in a tree. Another youngster poked a stick, sharpened with its teeth, into a myrmecoid nest and speared tasty bugs. Another adult watched—supervising?

Joe was quick to notice Laing. He uttered a warble of delight and bounded toward the man. He always was brash. The rest hung back for a couple of minutes. Thereby they let

Joe get the most and choicest of the treats, crackers prepared from local plants, that Laing had in his pockets. When they saw that, everybody crowded around.

They started to sing. An amadeus had its personal songs, and Laing had never heard exactly the same twice. Their vocal range was a full seven octaves, and the variety of sounds they could make was incredible: trills, whistles, roars, thuds, clangs, ripplings, rushings. Each was melodious, and the whole became a composition, music that sparkled and rejoiced.

Laing had also heard ominous cantos warning of danger; he had listened to males trying vocally for dominance, and courtship songs, and lullabies, and what he felt sure were laments for the dead. Tess believed the amadei communicated by music more than by signals and attitudes.

"Hey"—Laing laughed—"don't embarrass me. I'm out of goodies, and by now you should know I can't carry a tune in a basket."

The planet stands huge. Auroras flicker over the poles. Instruments go to full amplification. It would be most unwise to feel ahead with radar, but passive devices reveal much. Magnetic field variations, mascons, beds of radioactive minerals, and similar clues sketch the country below the clouds.

They are inexact. The radiation of the enemy base is more helpful, but fails to pinpoint it by too many kilometers. Deeply buried as it is, most of what comes out is weak and scattered. Also, the Khalia follow standard military practice in using baffler fields and planting dummy emitters far around. To everything but optics, the target is a broad, ill-defined smear. Light, including infrared, loses itself in the clouds, is absorbed and reradiated, comes forth essentially imageless. You must get below the vapors and look; and then you are within seconds of a missile strike, within less than a millisecond of an energy beam's reach.

Nevertheless the Laing mind has wondered what its purpose is. Couldn't a bomb like this burst half a continent away, and succeed? However, analysis of information from the databank confirmed what Maclaurin had said. The destructive power is known; $e = mc^2$, five tons of antimatter annihilating with five tons of our kind. But the dispersion will be enormous, the effectiveness unpredictable. Not only are the Khalia dug cavernously deep into hard, geologically stable rock, and shielded and reinforced and shockproofed, but they are beneath a deep, small valley, surrounded by guardian mountains. Just which valley is unknown. To be certain of a kill, even this doomsday blow must strike the right one.

The Laing mind will have a fractional second to identify the target, possibly through rain or haze, then calculate the thrust vector necessary to redirect its fall, and awaken the engine. Given its electronic senses and computer power, that should suffice—because *it*, the Laing mind, will see which of the green vales of Mozart has been so changed that the enemy must lair below. The Khalia have done a good enough job of restoration to fool outsiders, but Laing walked this land and flew above it for long, gladsome years.

Happy indeed. Junie let Tess hold her new hatchling. It fluted and cuddled close; amadei liked mammalian warmth and smoothness. She gave it a cracker. It took the tidbit in tiny paws and nibbled daintily. Having finished, it wriggled half free of her clasp. Holding fast by its tail, it nuzzled into her shirt pocket.

"Oh, it knows where crackers come from," Tess said. "Right away it knows. Don't you, kiddums? Smart little devil you've got, Junie."

The amadeus caroled. Tess handed the baby back to her.

"Eerily smart," Laing said; and suddenly the forest around them was heavy with awe. "I do believe we've met the ancestors of an intelligent race."

"Why, I don't doubt that at all," his wife replied. "Give them, hmm, ten million years at most." And they will make tools and poems, build, sow and reap, yearn, question, climb the high peaks and behold the stars, perhaps finally seek out yonder. And what of the music they will have made? If our spirits live on, will Bach and Beethoven and Mozart hear, and try to understand, and never quite do so, because that was not the peculiar genius of humankind?

Christina has laid hold of the meteoroid. It hurtles inward. Ahead are the Khalia. Left to itself, the part of the meteoroid that is the weapon will break free of the rest and crash somewhere on that land mass, or perhaps in the ocean. Devastation will follow, wherever the fall occurs. But it must be the intended devastation. Mathematics marches through the computer. The Laing mind prepares itself. It is full of purpose, inhumanly steady.

In the instant of vision, it shall decide on its target. The faster it does, the surer is victory. It reviews every aspect of the task.

Hitherto the Laing mind has not thought in astronomical terms. Nobody has, really. This is an instrumentality of war. But now, in passing, it sees that the impact, the energy release, will equal that of a fair-sized asteroid crashing into the planet.

Laing was neither a geologist nor a paleontologist. He had never been on Earth. His scientific education naturally involved some study of man's ancient home, but mostly, afterward, he forgot.

Today his duplicate mind has total recall.

Christina is a rolling white brilliance before it. Perhaps half a minute remains till atmospheric penetration. That is ample for a computer. In thirty seconds the Laing mind can think the thoughts and feel the anguish of thirty human years.

It breaks radio silence. The maser beam spears back toward Belisarius. "I cannot murder an entire future."

Its engine comes to life. The meteoroid veers, shudders. Pieces break off under the acceleration. Those drop harmless into the air, shooting stars. The death machine leaps from orbit. Outward it speeds, faster and faster, until by the time its fuel is spent no ship of the Fleet has any hope of overtaking it.

Thus far my reconstruction. I do not care to guess what the Laing mind thought while it flew straight into the sun.

The dawn mists were faintly red, as if the oncoming light washed them with blood. They hid the bay, but jungle on the shores hulked sullen above them. We were the last in Wang Fang's. Madame herself had gone to bed, and her parrot hunched asleep on its perch. She'd sold us the rest of the bottle we'd been working on before she locked up the bar. The boy hadn't come in yet to clean spilth, ash, stubs, and tobacco juice off the floor. Enough smoke hung around to

gray the air and make it bitter. Already through its coolness
I felt the day's heat inbound.

"The same thing happened on Earth," La Balafre Triangulaire said. His voice was dull with weariness. Stubble covered sunken cheeks and darknesses rimmed bloodshot eyes.
"At the end of the Cretaceous period, when the dinosaurs
were in their glory, an asteroid hit. It threw up such dust and
steam that for decades Earth was shrouded, most sunlight
reflected off and twilight laid on the days. A winter that went
on and on. Plants died, ashore and in the seas, plankton, the
animals that fed on them and the predators that fed on those.
Three fourths or more of living species became extinct. They
included the ammonites, that had been around since long
before the dinosaurs—and the dinosaurs themselves, except
for a few reptiles and the birds."

"I know," I said. "That gave the mammals their chance.
Many of them survived. They'd been insignificant, but now
they blossomed, and so we came to be."

Balafre nodded. "True. That wasn't inevitable by any means,
though. Humans weren't foreordained. Any of a million accidents could have stunted the development of the hominids, and
Earth would have borne only plants and beasts."

He raised a bony forefinger. "Do you know also, my friend,
that there in the late Cretaceous, the dinosaurs were working on
intelligence? They weren't sluggish lizards. Many of them had
well-developed nervous systems. Some were warm-blooded.
Among the advanced types were the dromeosaurs, bipeds, about
man-size, with large brains and the beginnings of hands."

"You're telling me that the antimatter bomb would have
had the same effect on Christina," I said.

He nodded again, and again, and again. "Right. That has
got to be what the electronic mind meant. I computed it for
myself, given the hint. Same energy release as for an asteroid
impact. Same pulverized rock turned into dust, water turned
into steam, and fireball air currents to carry them into the
stratosphere. If anything, the result would have been worse,
because the explosions would have been scattered more
widely. And radioactivity as well. Fimbul Winter. Mass ex-
tinction. Oh, the calculations indicated that smaller, more

primitive life-forms would persist. But the amadei, everywhere they are on the planet, they couldn't have.

"Don't mistake me," he added jaggedly. "The Fleet commanders aren't monsters. Not like the Khalia, not at all. They didn't think about the meteorology, because as far as they were concerned they'd simply kill off a lot of animals along with the enemy—regrettable, but better than the losses they'd otherwise have to suffer."

"That they did suffer," I said.

He slumped and stared down at his hands, which encircled his almost empty glass. "Yeah. They did." Lifting his head for a moment, voice cracking: "But that ghost of me, it saved a whole future!"

The Fleet had not appreciated the act.

I picked my words with as much care as the liquor in me allowed. "Ghost of you, you say. Not you. Why did they blame you, then? What were *you* guilty of?"

"Nothing," he said into the air. "I was as shocked as anybody. My superiors filed no charges. But—it had been my other mind. How could they trust me? How could they keep me safe from fellow personnel, once our men began to die by the tens of thousands?

"Have you ever been among people, your own people, who won't speak to you? By the time they handed me my 'undesirable' discharge, I didn't care. I was glad, in a burnt-out fashion, to get away. I went home. My wife had left me. So here I am."

"And you ask whether you got justice," I murmured.

"Yes. I don't know, myself. I didn't do the thing. But would I have? I don't know, I tell you. I never will."

We fell mute for a while. I couldn't think what to say, until at last: "Some people believe in a God who can judge us. Now, sorry, I'm worn out and have got to sleep. Busy time ahead of me." I lied. "Good-bye. Good luck."

I rose and went into the sunrise. Fog eddied about my shins. Beyond the bay, ocean shone steely under a sky turning hard blue. Everywhere around me lay silence.

INTERLUDE

Auro stared at the cube. Inside was recorded, so Buchanon had promised, all that any Fleet officer needed to know. It contained only two records, Allison's Rules of Command and the Standing Orders. All, at least, he would need to know to pass the lieutenants exam and make his brevet commission permanent.

Depressing keys on the side of the cube, the young officer began to study the text that hovered a foot in front of him. It was a page from the five-hundred-year-old classic guide to command that had been the final legacy of Admiral Allison, hero of the Cluster Wars and father of the modern Fleet.

To the recent cadet's relief, he saw that he had finally gotten through Allison's mathematical analysis of combat that had revolutionized war centuries earlier. Instead, Allison was now dealing with the softer issues of morale and medical support.

Admiral Dav Su Allison, retired
Rules of Command
14.246M3
Morale/Medical/Final Determinations

   For Fleet personnel to function effectively in a combat situation, one where they have virtually no control over their own lives, it is necessary to give them as much control as possible of those factors that they can affect.

Perhaps the most significant factor that is within the control of combat personnel is their treatment in the case of severe or debilitating injuries. The wide variety of religions and life styles found with the Alliance further demonstrate the necessity of leaving life and death medical decisions in the hands of the personnel affected.

While, like many of the rules of war, to allow trained personnel to perish when they might be saved may seem wasteful, this is not the case. Analysis (see appendix 54) demonstrates that the improvement in functional ability of such self-determined troops far exceeds the additional losses likely to be incurred in any but the most desperate battles.

A SLEEPING HUMPTY
DUMPTY BEAUTY
by Anne McCaffrey

"I DON'T KNOW if we can do anything with what's left of
sleeping beauty here," Jessup said pityingly.

"What?" Bardie Makem looked up from the Jefferson militiaman who had bled to death. She wondered why the corps-
mech couldn't read its own monitors. Except that it was
supposed to return any remains. Families always preferred to
know their relatives had been duly buried—somewhere. Even
space was more acceptable than MIA. With a sigh for him,
she consigned the militiaman into the organ-removal slot of
the triage area.

Then she craned her head over to Jessup's gurney and
caught her breath. The face inside the helmet was of a very
handsome man: tri-d handsome, though the strength of mouth
and chin suggested character as well as looks. She rubbed
muck and char off the helmet plate. Pilot, *Bonnie Parker*?
Headhunter troop carrier?

"You know, Bard," Nellie Jessup went on as she continued
her evaluation, "I think those new pressure suits actually
work. This one's managed to control his bleeding, even if the
limbs are mangled. The medikit is drained dry but I'll bet

that's why he's still alive. Whaddaya know! Science triumphs over slaughter!''

Moving swiftly as she noted his vital signs, Bardie Makem fed his ID into the hospital ship's main banks. They must have fixed the glitch that last Khalian missile had done to the internal system, because the terminal printed up large and clear.

"O'Hara, Roger Elliott Christopher." An O'Hara? She ignored the service garbage and scrolled down to the medical data she'd need, blood type and factors, latest jabs, previous injuries—and he had a fair number—good recovery from all repair jobs.

"Another thing, the Genital Cap worked, too, dented but the AI's all there." AI being Nellie's alphabet for "all important" when dealing with male patients. "Jeez! It's his own face," Jessup remarked, amazed, as she noted the medical log on Roger O'Hara. "Only the one scar: gives his face a roguish look. But, Stitches, I don't think you can reassemble all the parts of him.''

"What're the cerebral functions like?" Bardie reviewed the medical data.

"Not bad," Jessup said, scanning the gurney monitor. "Must be a tough mother. Left arm is hanging on by a skin flap just below the elbow, but whatever it was missed the joint. Most of the bicep is gone and the shoulder joint, left knee crushed, thigh broken in nine places, yeah, and his left foot's off. Left side of the rib cage is smashed, sternum cracked, lung puncture. Right fingers gone, right arm . . .''

"Damn," and Bardie, aka Stitches for her exquisite skill with the micro-suturer and flesh glue-gel, grimaced with disgust at O'Hara's records. "Clearly stated that he's not a brain donor, though he did sign a permit for organ use.''

"Hell," Nellie said with vehemence, "there's more of him still working outside than inside. Spleen's ruptured, pancreas sliced, punctured lung, one kidney, most of his liver's minced, guts are scrambled but they're easy. Eyes are okay!" Jessup liked to be positive.

"We can replace those," Bardie said, sighing heavily. "But he wants out . . .''

"Shame to lose a guy looks like that. How come you can't just transfer the head?"

Bardie appreciated team support but Nellie had a ridiculous notion that her superior could do anything. She glowered at Jessup.

"You know the rules about that as well as I do, and even if we could, there hasn't been a whole body in here all day. His head is legally out of bounds." She had been watching the vital signs monitor for the pressure suit had been hooked into it, thus saving any unnecessary manipulation of the injured man. Once again Bardie shook her head in amazement. "He's one tough fella. He should be dead from the trauma of such massive injuries."

"The suit did it. That'll look good in the report." Jessup smiled kindly down at the unconscious man; Bardie was surprised to see the tenderness on the woman's face. Nellie Jessup had developed the necessary tough outer callous objectivity essential in triage.

"He's just not giving up without a fight." His BP was low but steady, the heartbeat was weak but working.

"He deserves a chance, doesn't he?" Jessup was eager, her brown eyes imploring Bardie.

"I know I shouldn't listen to you, Nellie . . ."

"But you're going to!" Nellie Jessup's face radiated approval.

"Let's get to work."

There were twenty teams of highly skilled surgeons and surgical nurses on this theater deck, one of five on the hospital ship *Elizabeth Blackwell*, though all the teams constantly bitched about being understaffed when the flood of wounded arrived from the latest assault on the Khalian position. At the team's disposal were the most advanced, and sometimes experimental, implements and procedures available to martial medicine.

Bardie Makem was serving her compulsory two-year term as a combat surgeon and was going to be very glad indeed when her stint was up in two weeks' time. She'd had enough of battlegore for the rest of her lifetime. Nellie Jessup was on a ten-year contract—if she survived. She had already been wounded twice riding up the MASH courier shuttles.

Now Bardie and Jessup walked their patient to the stripper, a machine programmed to remove anything not flesh, bone, or sinew attached to a body. Its anti-grav cushion managed mangled flesh as delicately as a spider weaves a web. Its sensors also examined hard and soft tissue, sending the results to the theater hood; weighed and measured the patient; retested blood, bone, and tissue type, and could color dye the circulatory system to pinpoint punctures or embolisms. The speed with which the injured were prepared for surgery often made the difference between life, half-life, and death. They walked him through the sterilization beams that sanitized surgeon and nurse as well. And on into the surgical unit where Bardie began hooking up the heart-lung machines, the auxiliary anesthetizer, while Nellie slipped a shunt into the relatively undamaged right arm to start the flow of supplements into his bloodstream and to service his bodily fluids. She kept up a flow of vital-sign information until the wrap screens in the theater hood took over. By then the pertinent damage was also visible.

"Not quite as bad as it looked," Bardie remarked, assimilating information and making decisions as to what delicate repair to undertake first. It was her speed in assessment that made her the valuable surgeon she was. She seemed to have an uncanny instinct that had saved many almost irreparable bodies. She slipped her hands into the glove dispenser for much of her work would involve the highly adhesive glue-gel, or gg. The joke was "Adhere to proper procedures. Stick with the patient, not to him, her, or it."

"Organ replacements?" She raised her voice to activate the theater wrap system.

"Ready," said a disembodied voice. And it was, for the intelligence that managed the organ bank had once been a senior surgeon.

"Red? Got a bad one here. Give me the whole nine yards. O'Hara, R.E.C., spleen, left lung, left kidney, liver, new left shoulder joint, left elbow, wrist, knee, ankle . . ."

"He belongs down here, not up there," Red answered, but

already the chill-shute signaled arrivals, sacks bathed in the
fluids that maintained the organs. Jessup began the anti-
rejection procedures that would assure that each replacement
adapted to the new environment. The catch-as-catch-can procedures of the late twentieth century were considered bar-
baric, cruel, and inhumane. But it had taken the science of
several species and several horrific space wars to perfect such
repair for the humans who fought them.

"He didn't want his head on a plate!" Bardie said.

"What's so special about his head?"

"You're no longer in a position to appreciate it, Red," and
Bardie shot a glance at O'Hara's classic profile.

Jessup had glued the thin face laceration shut while Bardie
replaced the lung—but his own heart would manage after the
rest they'd give it—so the lung lay flaccid in the chest cavity.
Well, this sleeping beauty was also humpty dumpty so they'd
better put the rest of him back together again. They both
worked on the shoulder joint, the arm, and the battered sa-
crum and remolded the crushed ribs with bone-set gel. Liver
and kidney, spleen, pancreas. He didn't need the gall bladder.
Now they both began reassembling the intestines, repaired
the rip in the stomach wall, glued the skin back in place
across the lacerated abdomen.

"Nicely hung," Jessup remarked all too casually. "Unusual in a tall man."

Bardie merely grunted. It did not do to encourage Jessup's
earthiness. She could go on quite irrepressibly, with endless
variations on the theme.

"Me, I've always preferred short men." Today Jessup was
incorrigible. "BP picking up. Hey, he might make it yet. If
one of those et germs don't get him."

"He might at that," Bardie said, then began work on his
left leg.

There were many servo-mechs, robotics, and other
computer-assisted surgical machines but, as every human being was slightly different from any other, even the most sophisticated machine could not duplicate the instinct of a
human surgeon. Even the most gifted of the non-humans
didn't quite have the same knack with this species. Machines

did what Jessup called the grunt work, but nothing replaced a human on the work at hand.

By the time they had finished putting Roger Elliott Christopher O'Hara back in one glued, stapled, renovated piece, they were both exhausted. The monitor told them in its implacable voice that they were to log off immediately. Their efficiency levels were dropping below permissible levels for surgical procedures. It had taken four intensive hours of flat-out surgical skill and decisions to effect the resurrection, and O'Hara had not been the first patient of the shift for Bardie and Nellie.

An orderly came forward to move O'Hara's gurney from the theater, but Bardie and Jessup followed, one on either side, through the sanitize green light bath and out into the broad corridor.

"Officer?" asked the orderly.

"Yup!" Bardie said, the adrenaline leaving her slightly light-headed. She was clinging to the body cart.

"I can do it. Don't you gels trust me?"

Bardie grinned. "No, Naffie, I don't. Not with this one."

Naffie looked peevish because he had taken a very long look at the unconscious O'Hara.

"Oh, have it your own way. You always do. Not that he's any use to anyone for a while! Bay 22, Bed 4." The two weary women turned to starboard. "Monitor says he's unattached. How can you be sure it's you who can attach him?"

"Naffie, you've had more than your share lately," Bardie said firmly, and she and Nellie turned into ICU Bay 22. Naffie was deft with the anti-grav unit, slipping the unconscious patient onto the bed that folded its sensitive wings around its new occupant with tender intensive care.

When Bardie reached her cubicle, the first thing she did was program her screen for a ten-minute printout on O'Hara, Lt. R.E.C. She took a fan-bath: even a cup of water could make you feel cleaner. She dialed for hot hi-protein meal, inserted herself into her bednet, and ate. The buzzer woke her and she had to blink hard to clear her eyes enough to see the screen. O'Hara was holding his own. She stayed awake until the next report but with great difficulty. She reprogrammed the screen to rouse her only if there was a significant relapse and was asleep almost before she lay back in the net.

To her surprise, she got a whole ten hours sleep, waking up, feeling guilty when she saw the time. The screen was flashing a no-change and she had to think hard to remember why she would be monitoring a patient here. Then Humpty O'Hara's case came to mind and she tapped for a review.

He, too, had slept ten hours. His vital signs were strong, satisfactory all along the line, with no hint of rejection from any of the new organs. But no signs of awareness, no return to consciousness. Which, Bardie thought, was kind. No one had discovered the universal pain-suppressor. She didn't like to think of the pain, inevitable as it was in her profession.

She dressed, drinking the hi-protein glop that was supposed to be all she'd need for the day's efforts, and left her cubicle. The corridors were amazingly vacant and the sounds of personalized snores furthered the thought that there had been no new assaults. A lull in massacre was definitely welcome. She had only thirteen more days of this to endure before she was out of it. She alternated between wanting to be so occupied the interminable thirteen days would be over and done with or have time to adjust her thinking to a civilian standard.

She stopped in the duty room and discovered she and Nellie were in the next shift—if there was one. She had an hour's leeway. The information screen was scrolling through data on the last assault, but she had long since ceased to assimilate either victory or defeat—it all meant bodies to mend. She chided herself for letting that thought intrude. 'S'truth, but whatever victories were won against whatever enemy, she found no glory in it, no matter how necessary the action, how urgent the winning, or what odds and against what, whom, or why. She couldn't remember now what had prompted her to opt for a MASH assignment: apart from a momentary mental aberration. She had learned a great deal—maybe that's why she had come—but there was a large pit of nothingness that one day she would be required to look into, process, and put aside.

Bardie was somewhat surprised to find herself entering Bay 22 of the ICU, and stopping by Bed 4. The vital signs were as strong as could be expected: the new organs still functioning normally. There was even a healthy tinge to O'Hara's skin.

"Can't raise so much as a groan from him," Naffie said, slipping in to stand beside her, his bright eyes flicking from screen to her face.

"Have you tried, Naffie?" Somehow Bardie Makem resented that.

"In the line of duty, of course." Naffie grimaced. "He really ought to come to long enough to know that he's still alive! Gratitude, if nothing else."

Bardie grinned at Naffie's disapproval. "So you could hold his hand and reassure him?"

"I don't really think he's my type," and Naffie flounced off.

Bardie pulled back the sheet for a visual check. All the incisions and repairs looked good under their skinplas dressings. Of course, he hadn't been thrashing around with either delirium or pain. She laid her hand on his chest; the skin was warm on hers. She felt his forehead, smoothing back the crisp hair; it was unusually soft to the touch, not wiry as the curling suggested. He really had the most handsome face. Idly, she brought one finger lightly down his cheek, to the thin pink scar, and was surprised to see a faint smile appear on the sleeping face.

"O'Hara? O'Hara?" she spoke softly. "Roger?" She spoke a little louder for the smile was still there. "Roger!" He took a deeper breath and then seemed to settle further into sleep, his head turning ever so slightly to the left on the pillow, toward her, the smile still there. "Roger, lad. Wakey-wakey." His brows pulled fractionally together in annoyance. "Roger, I know you're in there. Open up!"

"You're having more success than anyone else," said the ICU duty nurse at her elbow, startling her. "And we've tried."

"Since when is a grimace an indication of alertness?"

"If it's the only reaction anyone's got out of sleeping beauty."

"It's not a coma," Bardie said, reviewing the signs.

"No, it's not. Normal sleep pattern. Doesn't even vary when the medication begins to wear off."

"More should have that facility," Bardie remarked as the patient in the next bed began to moan piteously. She walked as quickly as she could out of the facility.

Both she and Nellie stopped by Bed 4 at the end of their shift, which had been relatively light. Mopping up operations were rarely as hazardous to life and limb, though they'd had some minor repair work from pong-stick land mines and some of the nasty heat-seeking darts the Khalia deployed at such times.

At the top of the next shift, Bardie paused for another visit at Bay 22, Bed 4 where several colleagues had gathered, including the Head Psych.

"Ah, Surgeon Makem," Brandeis said, his wide smile resembling nothing more than a trap for the unwary, "I understand you did miracle surgery on this patient. Can you enlighten us in any way as to his current somnabulant state?"

"He hasn't regained consciousness yet?" Bardie was surprised and saw concern and disbelief in the other medics at the bedside. "Well, he did experience major bodily insults. Sufficient trauma there to keep him from wanting to know."

"Ah, then," Brandeis said, leaping upon her suggestion, "this could be psychosomatically induced?"

Bardie shrugged: she patched bodies, not minds. "His pressure suit kept him alive, maybe even conscious, but he had to have known that he was badly injured. The suit doesn't record how long its inmate is conscious, merely his vital signs."

"Good point!" Brandeis and the others turned back to regard the calm sleeping countenance. "Could be! And his records do indicate 'mercy' in preference to disembodiment."

From his tone, Bardie thought Brandeis was annoyed that another "subject" had slipped away from him. Brandeis did a lot of counseling to "brains."

"Dr. Makem did get a response from Lt. O'Hara," the duty nurse spoke up. She'd been standing to one side and Bardie hadn't seen her. She could cheerfully have beheaded her.

"Ah, when? And what?" Brandeis wanted to know, his expression almost avid.

"Oh, I just felt his forehead." Bardie felt silly: the hands-on was such an anachronism with so many sophisticated sensors to take accurate temperature readings.

"And?" Brandeis encouraged her.

"Faint smile. Might have been reflex." She could feel herself blushing.

"No doubt," someone murmured in a droll voice.

"One would have thought that such a handsome man wouldn't have objected to brain-duty."

"Who'd see him?" The words were out of Bardie's mouth before she could think and she blushed even more furiously.

"A perfectly natural vanity," Brandeis remarked with an equanimity not echoed in his hard eyes. Brandeis was a tolerably attractive fellow, in excellent trim, and according to wardroom gossip, plenty of activity in hetero relationships that were not at all professional, so Bardie wondered at the subtle envy. "Well, Dr. Makem, if you would be so kind as to repeat your gesture . . ." He stepped aside and indicated that Bardie move to the patient. Bardie did not like his expression, his manner, or the suggestion.

Reluctantly she stepped forward, and feeling more ridiculous than she had since a lowly intern, she put her hand on O'Hara's broad forehead.

"Is that all you did?" Brandeis asked superciliously, with a tolerant smile to the others when there was no patient reaction.

Bardie fought a desire to turn and run. Grimly she replaced her hand and honestly duplicated the incident. "Roger O'Hara! Roger!" She let her fingers drift backward from his forehead to his crisp, curly hair, then down the side of his face. When the faint smile again touched his lips, she didn't know if she was pleased or if she'd prefer the deck to open up and swallow her. But an experiment was an experiment.

"Roger, wakey-wakey, lad." And once again the brows moved into the most imperceptible of frowns as his head inched away from her. "I know you're in there. Open up!" Bardie paused, cleared her throat. "At least, that's about what I said."

There was a long and embarrassing pause as her colleagues absorbed action and reaction.

"And that's all you did?" Brandeis asked, frowning.

Bardie contented herself with a noncommittal nod, recovering her professional poise.

"That's more response than anyone else has had," the duty nurse said approvingly.

"If you will, nurse," and Brandeis motioned for her to repeat Bardie's hands-on. There was notably no reaction. "Interesting. Very interesting."

Bardie's collar alarm burred quietly. "My shift, Doctors. Excuse me." She was out of the bay as fast as was dignified.

Most of the casualties she and Jessup had that shift were fairly routine: amputations, the savage lacerations of the latest Khalian mankind-mangler. There was satisfaction in saving all the lives but Bardie suffered from a most insistent hallucination: O'Hara's smile on nearly every patient.

At the end of her shift, she went back to Bay 22, Bed 4 and read the latest chart entries. Technically Roger O'Hara had not regained consciousness. There was no one else in the bay. Feeling decidedly self-conscious, Bardie stroked his forehead, entangling his curls in her fingers, then let her finger ride down the side of his face. The faint smile appeared.

"Roger," she said softly, caressingly, "you're in there. I know it. Please don't keep hiding. It's all right to wake up. You're in your own body. We're not allowed to disembody you, you know. That's why you have the option. But you're all right. Really, you are! You're still in one piece and recovering far better than could be expected."

She repeated the caress and he stirred, a deep "mmm" starting in his throat, and he licked his lips. "Thataboy, Roger." She dipped her finger in the water glass and passed it across his lips which surprisingly were not as dry as they ought to be. "C'mon, Roger. Wake up." Again the frown.

"Don't want to wake up, do you? Well, it's okay to. You'll be just fine. Only wake up. I think Brandeis has some ideas about you, flyboy, that you wouldn't like at all. So I really do advise you to wake up." The frown was deeper, Roger's head turned as if resisting the request. "Do it for me, will you, Roger? Wake up for Bardie, will you?" She smoothed his hair back, fondling it, again surprised at its softness and the springiness of the curls that wrapped about her fingers. "You're some mother's son, Roger. C'mon, sweetheart, open your eyes!" She made her tone wheedlingly loving. The eye-lids trembled and the muscles in his cheeks and temples moved. "It's really okay to wake up, Roger."

She chuckled. "You sure don't like that word, do you?" The frown obediently appeared but it was deeper now. "I wonder why. The call to duty, or merely back to life again. A guy who looks like you wouldn't have much trouble with life. And you'll be out of this war—that is if you decide to . . . rouse!" She grinned as she substituted a synonym. Then, out of pure mischief, remembering what Jessup had originally called him, she bent forward, "Roger, sleeping beauty," and kissed him on the lips.

Simultaneously she heard movement just beyond her and saw his eyelids flutter open, blinking wildly to focus. She slipped from the bed and out of the bay before she could be hailed. Safely back in her cubicle, she dialed up Bay 22, Bed 4 and saw the alert readings of the Alpha waves. Sleeping Beauty had awakened.

She got her wish to be so busy in the final days of her contract that she had no time to think. She woke that last morning on the *Elizabeth Blackwell* with a feeling of such intense relief that she had survived her two years that she was almost in tears. To restore her composure, she used her entire day's water ration in the shower and shampooed her hair, blowing it dry and attempting to style it as a going-home preparation. She dressed in the smart unitunic, tight-fitting pants and boots, clothes she hadn't worn during her entire tour of duty. She even put on a touch of the scent that had lain unused on the shelf of her locker. Then she stuffed a clean shipsuit and briefs into her bag and the few personal things she'd been allowed to bring, and that was that.

"Hey, dressblues match your eyes. Nice!" Nellie said, widening her eyes appreciatively when she walked into the wardroom. Two of the other off-duty surgeons accorded her a long whistle before they served her the traditional farewell jigger of fleetjuice.

There were some letters consigned to her to bring home. Then Bardie left a good-bye message on the wardroom screen for the rest of her MASH friends before it was time to take the shuttle that would bring her on the first leg of her homeward journey. Nellie insisted on going with her to the airlock.

"Oh, Stitches, I'll never have another as good as you, I'm sure I won't," Nellie said, unexpectedly sobbing in their farewell embrace.

Bardie held her off, rather chuffed that the case-hardened nurse had such a sentimental streak. "How many surgeons have you survived so far, Nellie?"

"It doesn't matter," Nellie said, gulping. "It's you I'll miss."

"Not if the next one is handsome!"

"Speaking of," Nellie said, her sobs miraculously stanched as she looked down the ramp, "here's sleeping beauty himself!"

Bardie cast a glance over her shoulder and saw, in the stream of wounded being evacuated on this shuttle, Lt. Roger Elliott Christopher O'Hara on an anti-grav seat being guided by Naffie who was chatting affably to his charge. The pilot wore a pleasant enough expression but the slight furrow to his brows indicated more tolerance than interest. So he hadn't been one for Naffie after all. Awake, though still semi-recumbent, but responding, Roger O'Hara was really too good-looking for anyone's peace of mind. And his hair curled outrageously over a still-pale face.

"Amazing recovery," Nellie went on. "Brandeis had hoped to make him a special study case. I heard he woke up the moment he found out."

Bardie hurried the good-byes as much as she could, wanting somehow to get aboard the shuttle before Roger arrived at the airlock. She succeeded, wondering during the take-off procedures why she had run like a startled virgin at the sight of him.

Her reaction puzzled her all through the long boring run to the relief vessel. Then, just as the shuttle locked onto the mother hospital ship, she realized what had startled her: of all the men and women she had operated on, Lt. Roger O'Hara was the only one whose face she had recognized. And it hadn't that much to do with the sleeping beauty aspect of their patient-doctor relationship. She did ward rounds frequently enough but the patients were bay and bed numbers, wound descriptions, severity categories that she forgot as soon as she moved on to the next wounded body. And it couldn't have anything to do with kissing the man, or his startling return to consciousness as a result of that resuscitation. It certainly couldn't have anything to do with him being a sleeping beauty, a frog prince, or a humpty dumpty.

Fortunately the usual well-organized confusion as the wounded were disembarked first broke that remarkable revelation. Bardie caught a brief glimpse of O'Hara being air-cushioned out, his eyes closed. She wondered briefly if he'd made the trip all right: two weeks was not long enough to mend his desperate wounds.

She had received her cabin assignment and was settling into quarters considerably larger than those she had enjoyed in the *Elizabeth Blackwell*: she had space to stand in and a pull-down desk surface and stool as well as her own sanitary cabinet. She had just turned on the screen to familiarize herself with the ship's diagram when the buzzer went off and the screen cleared to a duty station.

"Major Surgeon Makem, please report to Deck C, Ward Station G."

"What's the problem?" The corpsman glanced down to his right. "You're surgeon of record to a Lt. R.E.C. O'Hara?"

"That's right. What's wrong?" Maybe he'd been evacuated too soon.

"He won't wake up."

"What?"

"If you'd please come, Major?" Long-service corpsmen could develop a tone that was tantamount to an order.

Besides being worried about O'Hara, Bardie was curious. She had seen O'Hara leave the shuttle with his eyes closed, but for him to have slept? With the normal bucketing, creaking, and groaning on even the newest shuttle, that was unlikely.

She keyed in the ship's deck plan and first located the anti-grav shaft nearest her quarters on H-Deck, then Ward G on C-Deck. When she got there, the officious corpsman was waiting for her with ill-concealed impatience. His expression said "you took your time" but he merely gave her a curt nod of his head, gestured for her to follow him.

"If you'll check him over, Major, since you're familiar with his case . . ." the corpsman said, stepping aside for her to enter the cabin. He shut the door immediately behind her and Bardie wondered if she should report his most unusual behavior to the Deck Physician.

But there was Roger Elliott Christopher O'Hara, neatly cocooned in his sensor sheet, and the printout over his bunk gave her no cause for immediate alarm. Except that he looked rather more pale than he ought. She approached the bunk, noting the light sheen of sweat on his brow. The sensor did not indicate any unusual amount of pain-reaction, and according to his chart, he'd been given medication two hours before.

Without realizing her intention, she laid her hand against his forehead, moist and cool. Her fingers, of their own accord, strayed to the crisp, but soft, curls.

"Okay, mate, what's this all about? You were in good shape when Naffie wheeled you in." Did she detect the faintest wrinkle of a frown? She stroked his forehead again. "If you're not careful, you'll still end up in Brandeis's files, pulling this sleeping beauty act."

"There's only one way to wake a sleeping beauty, you know," he said, his eyes still closed. "I liked it the first time. But I wasn't sure if you were real or not until I saw you ahead of me on the gangplank. Brandeis had me believing you didn't exist at all except as a wish-fulfillment dream." Suddenly he opened his eyes and they were a startling shade of clear green. He turned his head slowly to look at her. "But you did kiss me then, didn't you? And I had to wake up because that's how the charm works, isn't it?"

She couldn't believe his ingenuousness: He couldn't have lived through three years service and still believe in fairy tales, could he?

"You're no sleeping beauty, O'Hara. More humpty dumpty!"

"That's why I had to see you, Bardie Makem," he said so earnestly that his rather rich baritone struck answering chords all down her spine. "I knew how bad I was hurt before I finally passed out and I was terrified that . . ." His voice broke and he swallowed convulsively. No, Roger O'Hara hadn't believed in any fairy tales but he had feared to end up in a personal horror story. "I needed to know that you were real, Bardie Makem. And not a fairy tale."

"Alice in Wonderland . . ."

His smile had an almost breathtaking charisma to it. "Naffie told me it was wonders you did for me all right enough and no mistaking it, and not a king's horse in sight."

"So, you played sleeping beauty again to entice me into your clutches?"

"I sure as hell can't come to you awhile yet," and he twisted his shoulders restlessly, then his smile became mischievous. "Would you take as a given that I'm sweeping you off your feet, to plonk you on my white charger and carry you off into the sunset to live happily ever after together . . ." His face was merry with his smile but the intense look in his vivid green eyes affected Bardie far more than she had the right to anticipate. "At least for the duration of this voyage . . . that'd give me a good reason to wake up again." He closed his eyes, schooled his handsome face into repose, but a hopeful smile pulled at the corners of his mouth.

Laughing at his whimsy and more than willing to enjoy some happily ever after as anodyne to the past two years, Bardie bent to bestow on O'Hara the favor he had requested. The kiss became considerably more magical than Bardie Makem could ever have expected!

INTERLUDE

The test was in less than a week. Little enough time with
Meier off on an inspection tour leaving him responsible for
the fifteen merchants still orbiting Bull's-Eye. Without conscious thought, Auro drew up Allison's writings on the main-
tenance and inspection of depots.

Rules of Command
16.456.7L.1
Logistics/Forward Depots/Maintenance

A ship that is lacking supplies is crippled in combat.
Our hundreds of years of experience has shown that the
lack of even the most innocuous or seemingly useless
item can mean disaster during a confrontation. It is
therefore of vital concern that all units of the Fleet have
a readily accessible source of supply available within as
close of a proximity to any potential war zones as is
practicable.

The stores of these bases should be maintained in as
great a variety as possible. It is impossible and dangerous for those who are not actually on the scene to determine which items might be needed. The vital part played
by cotton cloth in the negotiations with the Ferelunxi or
the need to cover Marines in fish oils before combat on
Tessar both demonstrate the immense variety of needs

that can prove vital when days or weeks away from a trade center. This unpredictability also precludes any success by those not in the relevant combat situation from determining which stores may be considered vital.

The only conclusion that can be drawn from the impossibility of determining in advance which stores are going to be necessary is that each depot must contain the widest range of material possible.

While at first this may seem wasteful and not cost effective, it is in fact both. Stores, properly cared for and packaged, can be retained for long periods of time. Further, these materials then remain available for redeployment, it being easier and less costly to transport as opposed to create and transport supplies to a new theater of operations. Finally, when the cost of the replacement of warships and their highly trained personnel is included, the loss of even a few of these vessels far outweighs the expense of maintaining field depots.

14.456.7In
Logistics/Forward Depots/Inspection

For reasons similar to those stated above, it serves no purpose to have the readiness of any depot facility judged by other than an officer who has seen recent combat . . .

WAR PAINT
by Bill Fawcett

HE WAS THE best.

But now that meant nothing. Captain Abe Meier knew he was indisputably the best quartermaster in the Fleet. No one else among the Alliance's hundreds of planets could expedite needed supplies as efficiently. A tenth-generation Fleet officer, few men understood better the myriad of operations that let the star-spanning defense force operate. When at his console on Port, controlling the flow of material to thousands of ships and bases, Abe knew he was an effective and vital part of the service.

Unfortunately, at the moment Abe was crouching under a Mannerhein Transceiver module. It was serial number C-124673J8, the quartermaster remembered, though the information wasn't of any use. It certainly wasn't going to deter the three heavily armed Khalians who were tracking him through the stacks and rows of the supply depot.

The sound of explosions and torn metal reverberated for the third time inside the kilometer-long, ferro-concrete structure. The floor shook as a bin of com modules (ordnance number C-4624523U4 to be exact) near the entrance noisily collapsed as its supports were cut away by the actinic glare of a Khalian laser rifle. Even cowering a hundred yards away, the portly captain recognized the sound. Nothing made quite the same noise as amberson coils imploding. Abe gritted his teeth. The Perdidan-made coils had been in short supply for months, requiring special solicitations and emergency manufacture. With an effort Captain Meier stopped himself from mentally categorizing the loss and concentrated on staying alive.

Less than an hour earlier Captain Abraham Meier, newly appointed Field Inspector, Fleet Quartermaster Corps, and the sole cargo of the corvette *Johnny Greene*, had landed on Arcole. Abe's computer briefing had warned him that the planet's air was barely breathable, a sulfurous mixture of acids and smoke. As the corvette had descended toward the forward supply depot he could see the numerous belching volcanoes that dotted the rugged surface of this barely habitable Fleet outpost. After his short leave among the gentle breezes and verdant valleys of Bethesda, Abe found Arcole's acrid atmosphere an unpleasant contrast.

Abe had been tired when he landed, not quite recovered from the strain of Bull's-Eye. On this inspection tour he'd already visited over a dozen frontier depots in less than a week. He suspected that his grandfather viewed this as a vacation after the strain of trying to stretch the available supplies during the invasion of Bull's-Eye.

Not that the inspections were unnecessary, or the trip some sort of bizarre vacation. With twenty-three more stops scheduled in the next thirty days, it had promised to be an exhausting grind. Not that Abe felt tired anymore. Scared, panicky maybe—no, definitely—but hardly tired.

Fifteen minutes earlier Captain Agberea and Abe had been halfway through the inspection, Agberea looking bored and insulted as usual. The commander, a youthful quartermaster named Spellmen, was just stuttering out some excuse for an oversight Abe hadn't even noticed when the Khalian raider screamed over the horizon, her plasma cannons and lasers ripping deep gouges into the roof of the depot behind them. After their defeat at Bull's-Eye, there were hundreds of now baseless Khalian ships in desperate need of supplies and ammunition. These Khalians must have seen this new and still unprotected facility as an easy source of the supplies they needed to continue terrorizing Alliance planets.

The *Johnny Greene* had raised under emergency power, with three message torpedoes flashing out of her sides past her as she rose. Agberea had screamed, either from anger or frustration. The small ship was hit at least once as she dragged herself up from the planet, trying to gain fighting room. Since the Khalians later risked landing, Abe guessed that the *Johnny Greene* had either escaped into FTL space or had been destroyed.

That had been less than ten minutes ago. The Khalian ship had next landed on the ferro-concrete roof of the ammunition bunker a few hundred meters from where they stood at the entrance to the stores center. The alien pirates had swarmed off their ship and immediately begun blasting holes in the ammo bunker's roof. At this point Spellmen and Agberea had begun organizing a defense using the enlisted men who had rushed out of the warehouse's open blast door. The plasma blasts blocked any radio transmission and Abe had hurried inside, using the intercoms to raise the command post on the far side of the ammo bunker.

Either by accident, or as the result of a fatal decision by some suicidally brave Marine, a large part of the contents of the weapons bunker had exploded directly under the Khalian ship while Abe tried to establish contact. The blast had thrown Abe to the floor of the office he was in. The sound echoed painfully inside the walls of the two-kilometer-long storage area. Secondary explosions and shrapnel screaming through the open blast door had trapped him inside the Spartan office for long minutes. When the rumbling had stopped the quartermaster noticed that the base's power was off. Only emergency lighting remained, filling the warehouse with a deep red glow. Abe had rushed between the still-open, thick steel doors, now torn from their hinges and useless.

The air was filled with dust and smoke. As it cleared all Abe could see was a crater where the bunker, and the Khalian ship, had been. A rolling cloud of sparkling debris still surged upward over the valley and was lost high above in the low clouds of volcanic grit overhead.

Twisted shapes, dark against the gray sand, dotted the

ground. The men, who must have just formed a perimeter immediately outside the entrance, appeared to be dead, probably killed by the initial blast. A sickening realization came to Abe and he began to search the area frantically. Ten meters to his left, the hero of Bull's-Eye froze, his face twisted with emotion. Agberea's body was sprawled behind a robot picker. Blood stained the ground where it had poured from his nostrils and ears. His hand was missing. The laser pistol he had held must have exploded, probably destabilized by the blast. Abe made a mental note to report the defect; it helped him to fight a growing sense of loss and bitterness. He and Agberea had spoken to and of each other as enemies, now Abe knew he had lost a friend. He checked a few more bodies, but everyone else seemed to have been killed when the fuel dump exploded. There was no chance of there being any survivors closer to the blast.

Abe had been standing in the entrance, half-formed tears blurring his vision as he contemplated burying those of whom enough remained to merit the effort. Then he saw the dark shapes stumbling over the debris left by the blast. Too shocked to move and silhouetted in the doorway, they saw him as well. With a yip, the three Khalians rushed toward the lone human. Abe had spun and run for cover among the depot's twisting maze of shelves and racks.

Before Abe had a chance to catch his breath, a shot splattered overhead, spraying chips of concrete against nearby plastic and steel bins. The larger shards made a ringing sound that he would remember for a very long time. Had he been seen? Abe Meier's heart raced, and the thudding of his pulse made it harder to hear the scratching steps of the Khalians who hunted him.

Cautiously the short, heavy human risked a glimpse down the aisle that ran alongside the bin full of steel bearings under which he was hiding. The residual traces of the carbon tet used to soak the bearings was making his eyes water. A yipping snarl startled him, knotting the muscles of his back, but it came from several aisles away.

Abe began to relax. The depot was over two kilometers long and one wide. It contained over a hundred kilometers of aisles and several thousand bins and racks. There was no way the Khalians could find him. All he had to do was wait. His rescuers would have Marines, and they would revenge Agberea and the rest. Abe forced himself to relax and tried to get comfortable, leaning against a dun-colored, plastic shipping crate and watching the end of the aisle in the direction he had heard the Khalian.

Then the quartermaster caught a glimpse of dark fur and leather. The alien pirate was just rounding the corner, moving as if it knew where it was going, moving directly toward where Abe hid.

Fifty meters distant, the raider hesitated, standing with its back to the young officer. This was the first live Khalian Abe had ever seen close enough to discern any details. Feeling a combination of fear and curiosity, he studied his friend's killer. The alien's body was completely covered by thick fur. The back was brown though the color paled to a creamy tan near its legs. The fur was matted and covered by gray volcanic dust. A sharp muzzle and large ears reinforced the alien's resemblance to the Earth animal known as a weasel, their nickname among those who had been fighting the fierce aliens.

The Khalian's head turned slightly back and forth, as if searching for him in the racks in front of it. It wore no clothes, only a leather harness from which hung an outdated laser power-pack, a jagged knife, and curling strips of leather that might once have been human ears. Abe knew that there were claws at the tips of the alien's fingers. Canine teeth, over five centimeters long, pressed out beneath thin lips. The creature stood unmoving, sniffed loudly, sneezed, sniffed again, and then growled. It was a long, menacing guttural sound that brought sweat to the small of Abe's back. After next emitting a few short yips, the Khalian leveled its laser rifle and began moving purposefully directly toward Abe's hiding place. Abe noticed that the Khalian's eyes were small and nearly black.

Almost too frightened to move, the quartermaster carefully drew his laser pistol. It was a well-polished weapon, but undercharged, only good for at most two or three quick bursts. Somehow, back on the *Johnny Greene*, there had seemed little chance he would need to use the weapon. After Bull's-Eye, it was easy to feel that the Khalia were no longer a threat, at

least not inside Alliance space. No reason to let some space-
hand get his neatly polished sidearm greasy while charging it
off the ship's batteries. In his twenty years as an officer Abe
had never even been near a hostile alien. He quite appropri-
ately didn't consider possible personal combat as a part of his
world. It was nowhere on his duty bill. Setting an example
with a well-polished sidearm had seemed more of a concern.

The Khalian hesitated only a dozen meters away and yipped
loudly. The high-pitched yelps made the young captain even
more tense. He aimed his pistol, but didn't fire. Another
Khalian's yips suddenly answered those of the one he was
watching. The others were also close. And it was obvious
that they knew he was nearby.

After a few steps, the Khalian froze again, this time silently. The wide nostrils on its long snout expanded and con-
tracted anxiously. Abe could almost reach out and touch the
creature's dusty fur. Judging an unfamiliar alien's body language was always risky, but the Weasel seemed less sure of
itself, almost confused. The cries of the other Khalians were
getting louder. The pirate squatted near the far side of the
aisle. Abe guessed it was unsure of his exact position. Then
he wondered if instead it actually knew where its prey hid and
was politely waiting for its companions to join it in the kill.

Raising his laser pistol, Abe realized he didn't know where
any of a Khalian's vital organs were. He tried to aim at the
creature's throat, but found that his hand was shaking so badly
he couldn't fire. He considered bracing the barrel on the side
of the tub, but was afraid it would rattle against the metal,
fatally attracting his foe's attention.

For long seconds the captain was frozen with indecision.
His mind seemed to freeze and the Khalian continued to squat,
occasionally yipping to its approaching comrades. As he
waited, unable to aim, the image of Agberea, broken and
bleeding, flashed through Abe's mind. At the same time the
Khalian he was watching rose and began to move slowly across
the aisle. Finally, almost too late, Abe laid his free hand
against the tub and braced the pistol silently against it.

Lasers have the advantage of being nearly silent. One can
hardly hear a laser being fired a meter away. There was a

chance he could nail this murderer without the others knowing what happened. Abe fired just as the Khalian spun to face
him. This spoiled his aim, the shot nearly missing entirely.
The captain quickly learned that Khalians, when wounded in
the ear, are amazingly loud. Its shriek rose in pitch until the
scream was barely audible, then as the creature recovered
from its surprise, the wail was transposed into a vicious growl
as it fired blindly into the shelves behind which Abe hid.

Without thinking, Abe emptied his few remaining charges
into the enraged alien. He ignored the pain where the now-
hot barrel pressed against the back of his hand. When he
stopped firing the air was filled with the stench of burnt meat.
Abe glanced at the welt on his hand; it was too small to be
the source of the odor. In the distance the yipping of the other
two Khalians became more frantic.

Creeping from shelter, the quartermaster found there was a
head-sized hole in the pirate's chest. One of his shots must
have set off a power unit on the Weasel's harness. Abe noticed
that once dead the alien didn't look so much like a weasel.
The fur around the hole in its chest was charred and black.

To his surprise, Abe found that he felt nothing, no concern at
all about killing his first enemy, not even any satisfaction of
revenge for Agberea. There was just a numb sensation where he
felt he should be feeling some sort of remorse over taking a
sentient life. In a way that lack of regret frightened the quartermaster even more than the actual combat had.

Then Abe noticed the warehouse had suddenly become almost unnaturally quiet. Over the roar of his racing heart, he
could hear only the gliding whirr of the preprogrammed pickers filling orders, oblivious to the drama around them. There
was no hint of the location of the two companions of the dead
alien at Abe's feet. It came to him that they could be anywhere. Even about to fire at him from cover, just as he had
ambushed one of them. They might be waiting for the most
opportune moment to shoot him. The quartermaster turned
in a fair imitation of a firing crouch and traced the lines of
the aisle with his pistol, realizing as he did that he had used
up every erg of energy in it. Until charged, the only use the

pistol would have was as a club. Glancing at his victim's fangs and claws, Abe shuddered and backed away.

Discarding the useless laser, Abe fought panic. His breath came in short, fast gulps. The need to run, or cower in a dark place, was nearly beyond control. With an effort the quartermaster forced his breathing to slow. Reviewing the situation Abe could find only one advantage. He was on familiar ground, knowledgeable of the layout of frontier depots like this one. This was his territory, not theirs. The maze of passageways, bins, and shelving should hide him and confuse the Weasels until rescue arrived.

The Khalian ship had been destroyed along with virtually every weapon on the planet. Beyond the depot, the planet was uninhabited. Both of the pirates knew that they were stranded and that if any of the message torps got through, there would be a squad of Marines from Bethesda here in less than three days. Abe knew that all he had to do was avoid the Khalians until help arrived.

It could work. Abe tried very hard to convince himself that it would work. Thanks to the careful orderliness of the Corps, there wouldn't be a single weapon in the general depot. He had been lucky once, but now he was unarmed and simply not trained to defeat two fang-and-claw-armed enemy aliens in hand-to-hand combat, even if he could get that close without being fried.

There seemed to be no alternative except hiding, trying to stay awake and away from the Weasels. Still, that shouldn't be too hard. One of the more unpleasant traditions of the Quartermaster Corps was to send cadets off into the shelves of a major depot without a map. Some wander, lost for hours, before they are "rescued."

Regaining some confidence, Abe Meier began to move cautiously down the depot's large central aisle, moving deeper into the shelves and bins. Deciding this left him too exposed, he turned right and plunged into the labyrinth of supplies and shorter aisles somewhere near the F section. Noting its coding as he jogged past, the quartermaster paused long enough to open one of the bins and extract three days' worth of field rations (Fleet serial number F432642876D8, commonly called mystery meat). If this was going to be a long siege, he was going to get hungry.

Captain Meier was weaving a devious course through the H rows (blankets, uniforms, and personal goods) when he heard a long, mournful howl. It lasted for nearly a minute, ululating higher until the sound was almost beyond his range of hearing, and then ending in a deep-throated growl. The effect of the sound echoing in the massive room was unnerving.

Abe realized that the Khalians must have found their comrade's body. For the first time the quartermaster felt regret that he had killed another sentient, and felt better for having done so. This was mixed with relief when he realized that now he knew where the others were.

Then the anxious yipping began again. They were still dozens of rows distant and Abe waited, trying to judge where his pursuers were. Their location among the rows of bins was tricky to determine by sound alone. It was some time before Abe realized that the Khalians were following the exact route he had taken earlier.

How?

Did these aliens have some infrared tracking device? Did they carry ground scanners like those the Perdidan Rangers used to track criminals across their deserts? If so, why hadn't the other Khalian carried one? And, if so, how were they moving so quickly? Such multisensor devices were invariably bulky. They had to be using some more primitive method.

Abe knew he was leaving some sign, a trail that was visible only to the Weasels, but what? Abe could picture the Khalians loping down the aisles, expert trackers following him by barely visible scuff marks on the floor. Their small black eyes and long snouts pointed down, raising their heads occasionally to sniff the air. He considered trying to move by jumping from shelf to shelf, but discarded the idea as too noisy and slow.

Running almost without a plan, the young officer dashed randomly through the openings and down aisles, diving between dozens of shelves. The sameness of the gray containers and red lettering he rushed past blurred everything together into a dull wall. Remembering a trick he had seen on an

Omni program, twice Abe doubled back upon himself hoping to ''confuse the trail.'' After making a second loop, he waited trying to suck more of the polluted Arcolan air into his oxygen-starved lungs. Even this far into the room he could now detect the sulfurous odor as the Arcolan atmosphere mixed with the purified air in the depot's interior.

Leaning against a fuel tank module (L-84653445R6), Abe could tell from the tone of their cries when the Khalians discovered his first loop. Too winded to continue, he waited until they reached the second circle, hoping it might discourage them. To his dismay, they hardly seemed to pause. He had lost ground to them, and even if he could outrun the shorter-legged Khalians, they seemed to have no limit to their endurance.

Abe totally lost track of time as the chase continued. It seemed to go on for hours, but soon the quartermaster was too exhausted to care about time. It was all he could do to keep moving, weaving through the labyrinth of supplies, driven by nothing beyond his instinct for survival and the need to escape. For too long a time Abe became the hunted—too frightened to rest, too driven even to think, wasting his last resources in a hopeless attempt to elude his pursuers.

Finally Abe tripped. Someone had left a power cable loose on a shield generator (serial number T-649387D4 he still remembered through the haze caused by his exhaustion and panic). Abe's foot got caught in the cable and he was sent sprawling onto the cold concrete floor. Only then did the captain stop to reexamine his plight.

Lying there, again unable to catch his breath, the last human alive on Arcole could hear the Weasels drawing yet closer. He lost his glimmer of sanity to a renewed wave of fear. Fear then gave way to reckless courage. He would seek them out, jump one from above and use his greater size to break its neck. Then the sheer absurdity of his plan forced him to think. The Weasels had laser rifles, old models, but quite functional. Nor was he sure his greater size was enough to balance the Khalia's natural weaponry. Suddenly the entire situation seemed ludicrous. Most likely this was all a very bad dream.

It was almost funny.

Hell's polluted heights, it was funny.

Abe caught himself after a short laugh. He was a quarter-master, not a Marine. He hadn't been to an unarmed combat drill in years. Even after his recent space battles he simply wasn't used to the strain of face-to-face combat. Absently he wondered if anyone ever did get used to it. Slowly it occurred to him that if he was going to survive he had to think his way out, as he had done before, and not attack suicidally or lose control of himself.

Crawling to his feet, the captain tried to visualize the Khalians' situation. They were stranded like himself. Unlike him, they had no hope for rescue. They had to be aware of the hopelessness of their situation. Unfortunately they seemed to be reacting by trying to gain one final revenge on the only remaining enemy, him. Since they didn't seem to be considering surrender, negotiations were out.

Being unarmed, and there being no weapons anywhere in the depot, it was safe to also eliminate fighting back. At least any direct attack. This seemed to leave only more running. But so far this had hardly been a successful ploy. He had been the rabbit and they were the hounds. Hounds that never lost his scent.

Scent!

Of course . . . those long snouts and large nasal cavities . . . the aliens had their own edge. That was how they were nullifying his superior knowledge of the depot's layout. They didn't have a mechanical tracer. They were tracking him by scent. Since all they were concerned with was finding him, they didn't care what was on the shelves they passed by. Only that he had been there.

It all made sense now, but then how could he have surprised the first pirate? Why hadn't that Weasel known where Abe had been hiding? He had stood only meters away. The chemical residue that had stung Abe's eyes must have also masked his scent. What he needed was to hide, not only from their eyes, but from their noses. Better yet, he had to turn the enemies' strength to a weakness and then exploit that weakness. But how?

Looking at the code on a nearby bin, Abe determined he was in the U section, ships hull plating, and was dangerously near to being trapped against the back wall of the warehouse. Nothing of use here. The quartermaster, his brain flushed with adrenaline, ran a fast mental inventory of the fifteen thousand standard items stored in a field depot. At ship's stores/paint (Q-97492847S45), he found what was needed. Paint had made him a hero, even could be said to have indirectly taken him from behind a desk and put him here. Now a very special kind of paint was going to save him again . . . he hoped.

With over a thousand years of unbroken service the Fleet had developed many traditions. Among these was to paint geometric designs in the color of "your" admiral on the side of all ships he commanded. It had been centuries since ships had fought within visual range but the tradition had persisted. Since admirals most often took over command in either orbit or deep space, this required using a paint that could be spread in a vacuum. Ordinary paints would neither apply nor adhere in the cold emptiness of space. The solution had been to develop a paint that was so acidic it slightly etched the hull, and to combine this with oils that boiled off slowly enough to allow the pigments to set on the hull.

Q-slop, or just clop, as the vacuum paint was normally referred to, was an exotic mixture of several ingredients that had only one thing in common. They all stank. In vacuum the caustic brew's odor was of no concern. But no one who ever opened a can while in an atmosphere ever forgot the smell. Abe had heard Marines liken it to a combination of long-dead body and methane. Anyone accidentally opening a can inside a ship trapped in FTL was likely to find himself in the brig. The accepted procedure when a can was breached during sub-light was to suit up and open the entire ship to vacuum. This invariably caused some minor damage, but was considered preferable to living with the odor. Even an ounce of the mixture was potent enough to contaminate an entire cruiser. Abe had gotten a whiff of the stuff once, during an academy prank; it had been enough.

Working his way back past the Khalians, Abe found the Q section. Even better he found that not only were there hundreds of cans of clop in neat rows, but also four 1,000-liter vats full of clop in each of the primary colors and white.

Even inside the sealed and glass-lined vats, the odor of clop was noticeable. For a short time, out of reflex, Abe tried to calculate the minimum quantity required to fill the depot with odor. A quartermaster doesn't waste material that might be needed later. Then the yips of the approaching Khalians reminded him of his plight. Reluctantly the quartermaster opened the drains on all four tanks and hurried away.

People are often described as howling with pain, but Abe never realized what that phrase could mean until he heard the howls of his large-nosed pursuers when the odor of clop reached them. To a human, nearby explosions, blinding lights, and sirens combined with itching powder might have had the same effect.

In the next five hours Abe opened six more tanks of other noxious chemicals, carefully noting the type and quantity of each so he could later complete a TR-564 Emergency Field Non-Standard Use Requisition. Two of these tanks contained carbon tet (SE632874523) and shuttle fuel (CF83475329-4). Their contents were followed onto the floor by three hundred ten-liter cans of gefilte fish (FY-4857958453H2) from the Perdidan ethnic food stores. The quartermaster completed his efforts by using flares to set fire to two adjoining bins full of sulfur and potash (by this time Abe was too miserable to even read the serial numbers, much less remember them). This malodorous mixture filled the entire depot with an oily gray cloud of smoke that was itself augmented by Arcole's already sulfurous atmosphere that had continued to pour into the depot through the open door. Carefully, encouraged by the idea of comparatively clear air, the quartermaster worked his way for the third time toward the front of the depot.

It took almost an hour to get to the offices at the front of the building. By the time he reached them, Abe was miserable. He was tempted to court-martial Spellmen when he found no masks in the filter locker, though it was hardly surprising they had used up the disposable masks on Arcole. Then he remembered that Spellmen, Agberea, and the others were dead. With this thought he started yet another fire, filling the front of the warehouse with the odor of burning fertilizer. It was soon hard for him to breathe, even through a makeshift mask he had made from a bolt of uniform cloth (U-342443876S7). Still Abe grinned, knowing what it must be like for the Weasels.

Near the entrance the air was less foul. For a while Abe hid in the records room, then realized that since it had only one entrance, he would be trapped if the Khalians entered. Venturing back out into the smoke, Abe nearly stumbled on a fist-sized com module. Rounding the corner, he saw an entire bin of these had spilled and remembered having heard them fall hours earlier. The quartermaster examined several of the self-contained communications units. They were tough, designed for use in combat. Over half were broken, but several dozen appeared to be functional.

Almost smiling under his mask, the Fleet officer grabbed a handful and crept back into the heart of the depot.

It wasn't hard to locate the Khalians. Their yipping had stopped after he had opened the clop tanks. Once the howls faded, Abe was able to locate the Khalians by the sound of their gagging and retching. After a while he realized that not only were they no longer following him, but they were wandering in circles, lost. From a safe distance Abe watched; occasionally the Weasels fired at shadows, but never close to where the quartermaster was hiding. Every time he moved, Abe left behind another com unit set to receive at maximum volume on one of their ten standard frequencies.

Occasionally, just to keep things lively, Abe also activated one of the auto pickers. He was careful to enter fake requisitions that would send the half-ton robots skittering all over the building for hours. Soon ten of the machines were all cheerfully ignoring the chaos around them while gently lifting parts from one bin and placing these same items in piles along the back wall of the depot. Abe noticed one, then another, had a scorched spot where it must have been fired on by one of the Khalians.

Three hours later, the captain was back near the entrance. Smiling, he began reciting Kipling into the com module he held close to his mouth. As he spoke the quartermaster slowly rotated the dial, causing his voice to skip between the over fifty units he had hidden in bins and behind boxes. Several laser bursts answered the sound, and eventually one of the Weasels actually managed a frustrated howl.

Abe's eyes were still watering and occasionally he had to stop talking while a choking cough passed. His mouth felt like it was full of sand and the officer's brain had long ago begun to ignore the frantic messages it was receiving from his olfactory nerve. Abe had tried taking a bite of the field rations, and it had tasted awful. Still, Abraham Meier, Fleet officer, quartermaster, and former Khalian prey found he was enjoying himself. So he began to sing. When this was answered by yet another Khalian howl, all he could think of was "everybody is a critic." So he sang that song too.

Ten hours later, crouching behind a pile of communications terminals (A-436438746T3), Abe watched as the two clop-stained, half-blind Khalians stumbled out through the depot's entrance. Only one had retained its weapon, a large laser rifle and that it dragged by the barrel. This same pirate also appeared to be leading the other Weasel, which was moaning and pawing at its eyes.

The quartermaster couldn't help emitting a hoarse laugh. Partially he laughed with relief, in part because of the contrast between "his" two Weasels and the dreaded Khalian pirates, and partly out of a bitter revenge for a lost friend. The Weasel with the rifle hesitated, tensing at the sound; it turned and glanced back inside the depot and wiped at its eyes. The alien seemed to be considering going back in. Flipping through the dial of his com unit, Abe laughed again. The sound rattled back from a dozen directions.

From behind the terminals Abe watched as the Weasel squinted back into the smoke- and odor-filled depot. He chuckled again, more quietly, when the pirate simply let go of its rifle, turned, and walked away. Hurrying to the door, Abe grabbed the rifle. The power-pack was discharged, useless. Letting it drop, he watched them stumble away. They never even looked back.

Abe then dragged a desk and a file cabinet outside of the entrance to the stinking warehouse. With any luck, Abe hoped to have the paperwork cleared up before the rescue ship landed.

INTERLUDE

Rules of Command
23.677.4Cv12
Civilian/Irregulars/Personnel

It is impossible to evaluate or delineate the channels through which the Fleet should obtain qualified personnel. Those skills and attitudes that are needed in effective Fleet personnel are often developed in circumstances far from the normal channels of Fleet recruitment. It is the inability of the Fleet to recognize this, combined with the human penchant for self and family aggrandizement, that led to the Fleet's lowest ebb in the period immediately preceding the Shannon incident and the Corporate Wars. These painful lessons should never be forgotten. Never again should the control of the Fleet rest within the hands of a few chosen families. Even those with the most respected traditions of service cannot equal the potential of billions of other individuals, human and allied, for producing the exceptionally talented leader or technician.

"Allison is so long-winded," Auro lamented as he looked away from the image generated by the study cube, shutting off the display. Absently he rubbed his eyes and wondered what Abe Meier had thought when he had read those words. Meier's grandfather was Admiral of the Red, in charge of all Fleet combat actions. The former cadet then looked at the rusted interior hull of the *Red Ball*, flagship of the obsolete freighters Meier commanded, and decided that if this was nepotism, it was a less than appealing failing. No wonder Abe had opted for a cushy inspection tour now that the war was practically won.

The young officer candidate glanced nervously at the chronometer as he stretched the kinks from his back. He had duty in an hour, and the lieutenant's exam was less than a week off. And he had yet to even start memorizing the Standing Orders and Rules of Engagement. With renewed determination Auro plunged back into Allison.

The most productive source of recruits will always be the Fleet's own efforts. These are most effective on the more technologically advanced planets, where carefully planned propaganda and indoctrination serve the double purpose of attracting recruits and engendering support for the financing of Fleet activities.

MOLLY HASKOWIN
by N. Lee Wood

"MOLLY!" A YOUNG man's voice bounced around the metal walls of the hangar deck, echoing in the half-empty space. "Molly Haskowin! Is that you?"

A short, aging woman built from hardened muscle and stringy sinew straightened from her work on a pitted ship nearly as ugly as she. Brushing protective goggles up from her small blue eyes, she squinted in the direction of the voice and impatiently silenced the hiss of the fusion torch in her hand.

A young officer in Fleet uniform strode across the deck, smiling widely. His reflection in the steel floor gave the illusion that he was walking on muddy water. "Goddamn!" he called out cheerfully, "Molly Haskowin! It *is* you. What are *you* doing out this far?" He made a motion as if he were about to hug her.

She brought the doused fusion torch up in front of her to ward him off, the rubber hose snaking ominously. "What the hell does it look like, Junior?" she growled. "I'm using these wonderful amenities provided by this backwater outpost so I can get off this gaddamned mud hole."

The officer seemed to take no offense; instead, he looked

up at the aging, decrepit ship in affection. "I can't believe the *Molly's Folly* is still flying." He patted the hull of the ship, burnished to a dull polish from years of constant abrasion from microparticles in space and atmospheres of countless planetfalls.

The old woman grimaced at the ship without a trace of fondness. "Most of her ain't. There's not a whole lot original left on this hulk."

The officer peered closer at a section of the ship, a knobby conglomeration of oddly colored and stained parts of varying ages fused together into an ungainly whole. He reached up and scratched at alien lettering faded into partial obscurity on the side of one section. "This looks Khalian," he said.

Molly grinned tightly, a lipless mouth stretched into a humorless grin. "No shit," she commented wryly. "The poor bastards weren't using it at the time and I needed it a lot more than they did."

The officer looked back at her in surprise, eyes wide in his smoothly handsome face. "How in the hell did you end up salvaging a Khalian ship?" he asked.

She snapped the goggles from her head and scratched idly at her thinning white hair. "Well," she said slowly, "I didn't actually *salvage* it, but if you're really interested in the tale, y'might buy a poor old lady a couple of drinks, Junior." She grinned, and revealed small steel teeth glinting with feral-pointed sharpness in the overhead lights. She fumbled in the pockets of her wrinkled, dirty overalls and fished out a reddish cigar-shaped object, frayed at one end. Biting down on the gnawed tip, razor-sharp teeth burying into it, she chewed vigorously as they walked away from the *Molly's Folly*.

From under a sleek new ship grapplelocked and secured halfway across the hangar, a furtive shadow darted toward the *Molly's Folly*.

"God, how long has it been?" the officer was saying, his voice fading as they reached the hangar bay's double doors. "Ten years? You haven't changed a bit."

"Flattery don't get you jack, snotnose, and it's been fourteen years if it's been a . . ." The hiss of the closing bay doors cut off Molly's words. The shadowy figure crept into the light, eyes flashing with the alarm of a nocturnal animal. A young man with a small pack dashed toward the *Folly*'s airlock, scrabbling at the security lock. After a few minutes, the airlock grudgingly opened and he vanished inside the darkened ship.

It was cold inside the cargo bay of the *Molly's Folly*, and crates strapped together in rows and bolted through the hull creaked as he sought a space among them to hide. He braced his pack as a cushion, wedging it between two narrow rows, and tried to relax. Suddenly he was startled out of a half slumber by a rough, unintelligible voice in the gloom. Molly Haskowin stumbled drunkenly up into the airlock and, after a few unsuccessful attempts, unlocked the f'ward main cockpit. Her monotoned soliloquy sputtered out as she climbed up into the pilot's bridge. The airlock to the f'ward cockpit stayed open, and the young man hiding in the darkness listened to the creak of the pilot's chair. The silence stretched out tense minutes as he strained his eyes, staring unblinkingly at the faint flickering of lights from the pilot's bridge. He started violently, nerves jittering, at the sudden loud sound from the cockpit, then nearly laughed aloud in sheer relief as he realized the grinding, awful noise was the snore of Molly Haskowin.

His eyes felt gritty as they popped open hours later, sleep driven off by Molly's long groan.

"Ahhh, shit," the old woman mumbled in pain. "Where's my gaddamned ant-alc tabs?" He could hear her searching, anonymous compartments opening and slamming closed, objects falling from them to clang loudly on the ship's floor. "Gaddamned hangovers . . . gaddamned snotnose . . . gaddamned tabs . . . Christ in hell, where are they? . . . Ahhhhhh . . ."

He listened to her gulp down the tablets dry, then huddled farther into the darkness as she began closing up the ship. Her silhouette passed between the crack of the crates where he was hiding, and he heard the f'ward main cockpit airlock wheeze shut. The ancient sub-light grav engines whined irritably to life, and he felt his ears pop as the cabins pressurized. He shivered more in excitement than cold as his stomach lurched from the ship's reluctant thrust through the planet's atmosphere, fighting upward through the gravity well.

He wasn't prepared for the shift in "up" and "down," as

the floor rapidly became a wall. Sliding "down" along the floor, he smacked into the bulkhead behind him, his shoulder taking the impact painfully. His pack slid down and hit him squarely in the face. Nose stinging, eyes tearing, he fought the pack and managed to shift himself to a slightly more comfortable position in the cramped space. He began to wonder how long he could stay at the bottom of the row of crates in the hold, arms and legs wedged in a growing ache, when he heard the grav engine noise change. Barely had he noticed it and before he had a chance to absorb its meaning, "up" and "down" vanished altogether. Gravity winked out to weightlessness and the stowaway was spun out from the crates across the cargo hold. Arms and legs sprawled helplessly in the air before he slammed awkwardly into the forward bulkhead. His fingers wriggled desperately for a hold as he bounced away, spinning into a collision with his floating pack. The straps of the pack tangled around his head and he clawed at it, somersaulting into a row of crates. His foot jammed between a binding and its crate, snapping his body like a whip away from the tangling pack. He cried out in pain as his ankle twisted in the sudden torque. His pack, slapping a buckle against his ear in a final insult, spun away, spewing his meager possessions out in a weightless jumble. He surveyed his situation from his snagged vantage point, feeling discouraged.

The f'ward cockpit hatch hissed open. Molly Haskowin peered into the cargo hold, her white hair floating around her shadowed face. Even in the darkness from across the hold he could see her face contort in anger as she spotted him dangling.

"What in the hell . . ." she said, as if to herself. "Get over here!" she demanded.

"I can't," he said, struggling in vain with the band snagged around his foot. "It's stuck."

"Gaddamn it," she said, and launched herself easily across the weightless compartment. Like a flying squirrel, she landed with all fours on the opposite side and scampered agilely across the rows of crates. None too gently, she extracted him from his snare and jumped the distance back to the airlock as easily as before, dragging him with hard fingers locked implacably around the collar of his shirt.

Once inside the airlock, she closed the hatch and the ship's artificial gravity came on automatically. He fell to his hands and knees, a watery sensation in the pit of his stomach. With her foot, Molly flipped him over to a sitting position.

"Who," she said, "are you?"

Looking up at her leathery face, her hard eyes glinting, he felt his heart pounding. He had made it! He had gotten off-planet, away from his tedious, boring job on an obscure agro-world, away from a bleak future with his feet cemented into the mud of the AgroPlants and the Farming Co-ops. It was his dream, his fantasy, and although it wasn't quite starting out the way he'd imagined it, he felt justifiably daring and courageous. He was sure he could impress this one small freight hauler with his bravery and skill. "My name's Jayson Tabott," he said proudly, throwing his shoulders back.

There was an uncomfortable silence as she stared at him, then she said, "So?"

He wasn't sure what she meant. "So . . ." He tried to think quickly.

"So what the hell are you doing on my ship?" Her voice had that same sarcastic edge as that of one of the plant bosses, as if he were a particularly dull worker. It nettled him.

"So I want to be a pilot," he declared defiantly.

Her expression relaxed slightly, and he thought she might even smile. "So you want to be a pilot," she said, her tone almost friendly. "And you snuck on board this ol' rusty tub. Why didn't you pick a better ship than the *Folly*, boy?"

"This was the only ship with a securelock I could break into," he said, shamefaced.

"I see. That oughta tell you something, shouldn't it? And I guess that you were hoping to find an irascible but basically down-deep good-hearted old freighter captain who'd be so impressed with your chutzpah and good looks that she'd be sympathetic, right? Take you under one wing and teach you the ropes, that sort of thing?"

He was fairly sure by now that she was making fun of him.

"It's not quite like that . . . I'm not some stupid kid . . ." he protested.

"Ah. And I'll just bet you're a real hotshot back home, buzzing the neighbor's sheep with some Skyscooter, or some gaddamned thing."

"I had an Arrowdart IV, and I never buzzed sheep," he said, growing angry. "And I *am* good, try me."

"Try you," she said mildly. "Try you, is it? Y'know what I should do?" She reached down and grabbed him by the arm and shirt, hauling him to his feet with surprising strength. "What I should do is throw you right out an airlock." She propelled him across the floor toward an oval hatch. He began to struggle with growing alarm. Even though he outweighed her, even with young muscles hardened by long summers in the agrofields, he was losing ground, the hatch coming nearer.

"This is a cargo ship, snotnose," she said, "not a training school. I can't afford you suckin' up my air and scarfing down my food." Her words came in pants as she struggled with him toward the hatch. "Y'cost too much, boy . . . Don't need a copilot . . . Out y'go."

"You can't do this!" he gasped back, hitting her with panicky fists. She was unbelievably strong and with her shoulder and arm shoved him against the hatch as she reached for the lock switch. "It's murder!"

"Yeah?" She took a hard punch to her face as her fingers groped for the switch. She staggered and for a moment he thought he might beat her back. But she slammed him twice against the hatch, knocking the breath from him, and kneed him in the crotch. Stars exploded in the back of his eyes. "By the time somebody finds your frozen ass, there won't be anyone alive who'd give a damn." Bony fingers grabbed the hatch switch and the door slid open into a lightless maw. "See y'later, snotnose," she said, and with a solid kick to the gut, she sent him sprawling into the darkness.

The door hissed shut as Molly Haskowin watched his stunned face disappear behind the hatch. Then she bent over, hands on her knees as she struggled to regain her breath. She straightened slowly, painfully, and touched her cheek where Jayson had hit her, feeling the bruise start to swell. She grimaced at the blood on her fingertips and wiped them on her overalls. "Damn. Gettin' old," she muttered to herself.

She regarded the closed hatch door for a moment, then grinned, the red warning lights in the cargo hold airlock reflecting from her steel teeth with the color of blood. She chuckled to herself and moving gingerly, climbed back into the f'ward main cockpit.

Jayson stared into the absolute darkness, a black so deep he couldn't tell if his eyes were open or not. His heart hammered in his ears; his bladder felt like a stone in his gut. He sat on the cold metal floor, waiting, his mind screaming in silent fear. Any moment the outer airlock would hiss and the vacuum of space would spit his body out of the ship. Any moment he would feel the suck of cold space against his skin, the last sensation he would ever feel.

Any moment.

He waited.

After a while, the shrieking in his head died down and his uncontrollable trembling lessened. He got shakily to his hands and knees, groping blindly in the dark. Everything felt huge and ominous under his blind fingertips as he searched the inner hatchway for the airlock switch. As he touched the control panel he found, with a sinking feeling of dismay, not one switch, but dozens, any one of which could open the inner door, or send him hurtling out the airlock.

Now he understood. She was playing with him; like an animal trapped in a steel jaw, she would make him kill himself as she enjoyed the entertainment of watching him flush himself out of the ship.

His anger quickly replaced his terror, building up his rage. He was determined not to give her the satisfaction, and sat on the floor, arms crossed. He realized he would starve to death just as easily, and his rage grew. He finally sprang at the airlock panel—not caring which door it opened, just to get the unbearable tension over with—and hit the switch.

A blinding light flooded the airlock. He screamed reflexively, arcing away from the panel and landing on the floor, shaking violently, eyes screwed tightly shut. Then, as nothing happened, very slowly he opened one eye and looked around the compartment.

Three battered and patched pressure suits hung on one wall, helmets hanging beside them, like the forlorn shed skins of decapitated lizards. A shelf stack on the opposite wall held miscellaneous boxes and bottles bolted into place. In the corner, a fusion tank clung to the steel-lined rib of the ship, its hose curled around it, and a battered instruction pamphlet twenty years out-of-date hung by a rusty chain to its side.

The only door out of the compartment was the one he'd come in. It wasn't an airlock at all.

When he came through the f'ward cockpit hatch, she didn't even bother glancing in his direction. Instead, looking up at the chronometer overhead, she said, "Forty-seven minutes. You're a real genius, snotnose. Whatsamatter, couldn't find a suit in your color?"

He stood, the secondhand pressure suit hanging off his slender body, the hardglass helmet in his hands. His breath came hoarsely through clenched teeth. "You *bitch*," he said, his voice strangulated and shaking. His mind couldn't conceive of a curse bad enough to express his rage. "You stinking goddamned *bitch*."

With that, she turned in the pilot's chair and grinned down at him from the pilot's bridge. "That I am, boy," she agreed affably, "and I'm a liar and a cheat and a smuggler and a thief." Her words held a hard edge to them even more menacing. "And if you give me any grief, I'll knock your teeth out your ass. Got that?"

He couldn't trust himself to answer, so he nodded and climbed up to the copilot's chair on her left.

She turned back to the instrument panels, gnarled hands playing the controls and guidance computers with slow, easy confidence. "Do up your tabs, boy," she said quietly.

He fumbled for a minute at the multitude of snaps and cords and straps on the pressure suit. "I don't know how," he finally admitted sullenly, feeling helpless as a child.

She turned to him and started fastening the suit, jerking it roughly into place. "Yup," she said sarcastically, "I can see you were just *born* to fly, kid. You're a real natural."

Stung, he jerked away from her. "I'll do it myself."

She grinned and leaned back, clasping her hands behind her head, and watched. It took him nearly an hour to figure out the suit while she chuckled and checked the instruments one-handed. When he finished, she shook her head ruefully, opening a tiny metal box bolted under the arm of the pilot's seat. Taking one of the long, reddish cylinders stacked inside, she ripped off the yellow band with its alien markings from around it and stuck one end of it into her mouth, biting down sharply.

He watched her as she ignored him, watching the play of lights from the computer guidance screens and chewing serenely. Finally, his anger edged out his hurt pride. "So why didn't you just toss me out an airlock, anyway?" he demanded.

"No profit in it," she said, unconcerned.

For a moment, his hope flared up. "You mean . . . ?"

"Can't extract payment from a corpse," she finished. "You breathe my air, you eat my supplies, you gotta pay for it. One way or another."

He slumped down in his chair. "So you're going to take me back," he said dejectedly.

She laughed. "Take you back? Hell, I ain't taking you back to that mud ball. I got a cargo hold full of bootleg booze I just happened to run across to deliver to Vega IX. How you get back is *your* problem, snotnose."

"Vega IX!" he protested, "That's on the Edge! There's *nothing* out there but Khalians."

"Nothin' but bored, overworked, thirsty miners and a shit-load of duty-free, nearly pure and only slightly illegal Vegan Bloodstone Dust," she agreed. "Strong young man like you could cut a contract with them enough to pay your bill to me with even a little left over." She handed him his hardglass helmet, her eyes crinkled in amusement at his dismay. "Just be glad I'm an *ethical* person, son. I could just as easily sell you to the Vegans for scut labor and you might never see daylight again, never mind fly. Should only take you two or three years at the most to work up enough for passage off-planet. Now put this on."

He pushed his head into the helmet and fastened it to the collar ring of the pressure suit. He noticed that she had left her helmet off.

"Why?" he asked, watching her flip a series of controls, then push dual handbars down flush with the Command Flight Controls on her armboards.

His head felt as if the skull had suddenly been squeezed too tightly around his brain, and his stomach liquefied in one sickening lurch. With an uncontrollable convulsion, he threw up. His hands scrabbled at the helmet as the blurry former contents of his stomach, trapped inside his helmet, floated in the abrupt weightlessness. Her hands slapped them away.

"Leave it on, or I'll break your fingers," he heard her say warningly, her voice vague through the hardglass. His hands fell away from the helmet, and he held on to the tabs of the pressure suit that were keeping him secure in the copilot's chair.

The swirling muck got sucked into his nose as he tried to breathe and he choked, sputtering miserably. He closed his eyes and breathed through clenched teeth to filter the air.

For several minutes he suffered from the smell and the feel of slime tumbling inside his helmet.

The sound of whirring, cool air against his skin startled him, and within seconds, the vomit had been filtered out of the helmet. He opened his eyes, his lashes caked with mucus, to see Molly squirting clean water into a port in his suit, laughing. The suit sucked out the residue, and after a few more cleaning applications. Molly helped him to remove his helmet.

He still felt nauseous.

"Whatsamatter, kid? FTL bother you?"

He rubbed at his eyes with the sleeve of the pressure suit. "I thought . . . FTL envelope . . ." He struggled past the nausea.

She shook her head, amused. "You've seen too many holo-shows, snotnose. The *Folly* doesn't have an FTL envelope. She's too old, too heavy. She doesn't have a *lot* of fancy hardware, too expensive. We just ride it out like the old days, when men were men and space was the Vast Unknown Frontier. Ain't that what you wanted, kid? Adventure, glory, the whole bullshit?''

He groaned. ''I feel sick . . .''

She rammed the chewed end of the red stick into her mouth and turned back to the control boards, shutting down blank sub-light instruments one after another. With a whine, the FTL panels slid down into place, enigmatic lights blinking lazily in the FTL continuum. ''You'd get used to it after the first dozen jumps or so, but then you won't be around long enough to worry about it. As it is, you'll be here for a couple of weeks, so sit back and relax.''

He stared at her. ''A couple of weeks!'' he protested, then clamped one hand over his mouth, gulping air.

With a final check of the instruments, which to Jayson seemed inadequately few, she folded her arms and yawned, stretching sleepily in the weightlessness. ''The *Folly*'s a freighter, boy, not a Fleet destroyer, and you ain't on any pleasure cruise.'' Within minutes, she was snoring.

The nausea did abate after a day or so, but his appetite never completely returned. The same queasy feeling stayed with him the entire flight, although he did his best to try to hide it from Molly Haskowin.

She seemed truly unconcerned with his presence, and he constantly explored the ship out of boredom. The *Molly's Folly* seemed pretty much as dull and ugly on the inside as she was externally. The entire ship consisted of layers of odd holds and ill-fitting compartments fused along the remains of the original craft, creating a maze of honeycombed holds, some jammed full of various cargoes, some depressingly empty. Cables snaked in naked spaghettied confusion along the ribs and the bulkhead, punctuated with bleak, utilitarian circuit translator boxes, some with their original lids, some without. Hatches had been bored out of the original hull, dribblets of fused metal around the airlocks showed where they had been connected to compartments cannibalized from other ships of questionable origins. Steel hand ladders led to some hatches, others had no such accommodations. The *Folly* was a study in stark, pragmatic economy, and yet Jayson sensed a tenacity and strength that years had not stripped out and covered up.

Several holds leading to other levels were locked, and not with the ancient, flimsy securelock the *Folly*'s outer cargo airlocks used. He tried every way he knew to break their seal, but to no avail. He tried to shine a light through the smoked hardglass ports in the airlocks to peer inside, but there were some secrets the *Folly* kept to herself, containing what he couldn't imagine.

He attempted to maintain a stubborn silence with the old woman, but that quickly became boring, too. She barely acknowledged him and seemed perfectly content to alternately doze and check the controls, making computations on the computers. Occasionally, she listened to various mol-tapes, and he grimaced at the *screetch* of strange music and incomprehensible rasping babble that sounded like nothing he had ever heard. Finally, too bored to maintain his masque of silence and sick of the irritating sounds she listened to, he tried to draw her into a conversation.

"Don't you have a viewing port to look outside?"

She didn't seem surprised that he'd ended his pique. "What for?" she asked. "Don't need 'em. Guidance system and the computers tell me all I need to know."

"It's not the same. Wouldn't you just like to *see* the stars?"

"Nothin' to see in FTL. It's all the same. Just pretty sights in sub-light. Useless." She spat out a bit of the chewed stick.

He grimaced as it spun to the floor and stuck. "What *is* that stuff?"

She took the stick out of her mouth and regarded the glob of splattered mess hardening on the floor. "Have no idea," she said finally. "Got it off a Khalian cruiser."

"But why do you *chew* it?"

She replaced it in her mouth and grinned, steel teeth gleaming, pointed and sharp. "Bubblegum's bad for my dental work, Junior."

He tried again to maintain a dignified silence, but the old woman made him curious. After an hour, he asked, "Why did you get steel teeth like that? Implants are as good as real teeth."

Her head snapped around and she surprised him with her sudden anger. "You ask too many stupid questions, boy. Shut your gaddamn mouth and leave me be."

Unfastening her suit from the pilot's chair, she propelled herself out of the f'ward hatch, leaving him staring after her with his mouth open.

He stayed carefully out of her way for the rest of the day and was drifting off to sleep, curled up, arms floating, when she spoke to him again.

"Titanium," she said.

His eyes opened sleepily, feeling gummy. "Huh?"

In the dimmed light of the f'ward cockpit, he could see the shadows in her face, white hair floating like a halo around her head. "Titanium," she repeated in a clear, unemotional voice. "The teeth are titanium, not steel."

He didn't know quite how to respond. "Oh."

"There wasn't any steel onboard." It seemed as if she were talking to herself. "We had plenty of titanium, though. *Lots* of titanium. Lots of time. Just floating around, most of us dying of Spacer's Ricketts. All I lost was my teeth. Lucky me."

He knew of Spacer's Ricketts. In prolonged null-gravity, the body's calcium degenerated, bones became brittle, muscles wasted away. Internal grav units and faster flights had made Spacer's Ricketts as obsolete as bubonic plague or smallpox or herpes. He said nothing.

"Dr. Dentum," she mused to herself, rolling the name around. She leaned closer to him and he could smell the alcohol on her breath as she smiled. "Hell of a guy. No doctor, shit, no. But he was the best damned metallurgist I ever met. Coulda turned lead into gold, if he had to. Made me a fine set of teeth. Hell of a bite. Damned shame he didn't make it off the *Peter Donneville*."

The name startled him. The *Peter Donneville* had been a military cargo freighter carrying several thousand tons of war matériel and 600 military personnel across disputed shipping space. The Cartel of Vannavar fired on her as she came into their inner system, touching off a war between the Alliance and the Cartel lasting four years. For four years the gutted

Peter Donneville orbited Vannavar, Fleet vessels unable to rescue the survivors, the Cartel uninterested in prisoners. Only fifty-seven people survived aboard her when the Cartel finally signed a treaty with the Alliance. But that had been back in . . . and that meant . . .

"Holy shit," Jayson Tabott breathed with respect. The old woman looked up at him blearily. "No wonder you hate everybody."

She pulled a flask from inside her partially unfastened pressure suit and drank from it. "Don't hate everybody"—she grinned—"haven't *met* everybody, snotnose." She leaned over and patted his knee. "Old joke, boy. Very old." She hiccuped and finished off the flask. Within minutes, she had passed out, snoring lightly.

The gentle thud of the flask bouncing off his forehead as it floated in the f'ward cockpit woke him. He glanced over at Molly as she dangled serenely upside down from his point of view, held to the pilot's chair by only two straps. He pushed her foot away from his face as it twisted slowly by him and stared drowsily at the blinking red lights flashing on the FTL systems.

"Molly," he said, alarmed and waking up fast. He pulled her into her seat by hauling on her pants, and shook her. Her head flopped loosely and she opened bloodshot eyes. "Molly, wake up . . ."

She coughed, a rapid series of explosive grunts deep in her chest, and frowned at the blinking panel. "Gaddamn it . . ." she muttered, and smacked the side of the instrument board with the flat of her hand. A blaring siren screamed to life. Clutching her head in pain with one hand, she hit the FTL board with clawing fingers, finally silencing the warning blare. "I gotta work on that one of these days . . ."

"What is it?" Jayson asked nervously, watching her as she fastened herself into the pilot's chair, swinging around to the navigational bridge. "What's wrong?"

"Nothin'. We're getting ready for sub-light." She grinned viciously at him. "This is my favorite part . . . Y'know, with an FTL envelope, we'd be able to check our entry down to the micrometer."

He looked at her with dawning comprehension. "But you said . . ."

"Yup," she agreed cheerily, "the *Folly*'s as blind as a bat in FTL. No envelope, no internal gravity, no cushy jumps . . . no fancy pants reentry navigational aids. Just like the good ol' days."

"But . . . how do you know where we are?" He stared at the FTL board with horror, realizing now why it seemed so small.

She tapped one finger against her temple. "*Brains*, snotnose, something all your hotshot pilots seem to have forgotten how to do . . . navigate."

He regarded the old woman and the outdated, ancient guidance controls and sluggish computers with equal apprehension. "But how do you know we won't jump straight into a planet's atmosphere, or another ship . . . or the middle of a sun?"

"Don't," she said, unconcerned.

"But . . ."

"Bang. We're gone."

"But . . . but . . . you're not supposed to be able to *do* that!" he accused her suddenly. "You can't bypass the safeties . . . they got laws . . . that's *illegal*, goddamn it!"

She laughed, and he felt himself growing red. "Y'want to get out and walk?" she said, amused and exasperated. "Look, kid, I know where we *were*. I know just how fast the *Folly* can cruise in FTL. I know where we're *going*. Space is a *big* place. Chances are we won't hit a thing."

"But . . ." he said weakly.

She looked at him, suddenly serious, her voice uncommonly gentle. "You wanted to be a pilot. This is what it's about, kid. All the latest and complex technology in the universe won't get you shit if you don't know how to *fly*. It takes old-fashioned guts and common sense. Y'want to be safe? Y'want to be a hero without risking your ass? Y'should have stayed home." She handed him his hardglass helmet. "Settle in, snotnose."

He cradled the helmet in his lap, excited and determined

that this time he would *not* throw up. His stomach tightened in anticipation and dread.

If anything, the jump back was worse. While one part of his brain was crying in joy that they were still alive, the rest was trying to escape through his nose. He jammed his face into the opening of the hardglass helmet, just in case. His guts rippled convulsively and he held his lips tightly shut. Sweat broke out on his forehead and then it was over. He swallowed hard and looked up.

As the FTL panel slid back into its recess, the Sub-light Guidance System blinked back to life. Green lights flickered data on the guidance computer screens in soothing, silent rhythmic patterns. He grinned triumphantly at Molly.

"Nothin' to it," he said, with slightly queasy pride.

"Just thrilled to hear it, snotnose," she replied, but she was distracted, intent on the data screens.

His elation died away as he heard the first ping of something hitting the outer hull of the *Folly*. An irregular beat began to machine-gun against the ship, like a hailstorm building in intensity hammering down on a tin roof. He glanced at Molly, feeling helpless, as the old woman hunched over the computers, eyes intent and gleaming, her hands flying over the controls. A sharp crack and the hiss of escaping air burst through the din, jolting him from his paralysis. "We've been holed!" he shouted, slapping the flutter of dust and loose debris from his face as it was sucked out through a coin-sized hole above his head.

Molly squinted up from the controls, noting the hole, and fished a partially chewed Khalian stick from her pocket. "Put your hand over it, boy," she suggested calmly, chewing thoughtfully while her hands danced over the data screens, dust winking in the lights of the computers.

He slammed his palm over the hole, covering one hand with the other, and yelped in sudden pain. "Oww! This hurts! *Do something!*"

Taking the stick from her mouth, Molly examined it. She reached over his head, jerking his hands away from the hole, and rammed the stick into the opening. It quivered, bulging, but filled up the hole neatly, hardening into place. The hiss of air stopped.

"Hell," she said speculatively, "maybe that's what they're really for; who knows?"

He stared into the palm of his hand, the ruptured skin oozing blood from the partly crystallized frozen wound. She glanced at it and *tsked*. "Nasty," she said. "Hurt much?"

"Next time, you stick your own hand over the hole," he said angrily.

She was no longer paying any attention to him. The rain of debris on the outer hull had stopped, and she worked to stabilize the internal life-support systems. She punched several controls and three screens he hadn't seen her use before whined down into a semicircle above the bank of Sub-light computer screens. She worked a receiver bug into one ear, listened to the faint Sub-light transmissions for a moment, and grunted.

"What's going on?" he demanded. "What *was* that?"

"*That,*" she said, "was somebody who thought he was a hotshot pilot, snotnose."

He stared at the three screens, seeing a fast flicker of data that somehow managed to imprint its information on him. To her right, compressed readouts flashed, questions and answers from the onboard guidance computers as they coordinated information faster than a human being could squeeze out. On her left, above his head, patterns blipped by at a rate that left impressions on his retina, and changed. It took a few seconds before he realized that they were diagrams and systems of ships, each with a color and data spread below it. Molly seemed to ignore the screen to her right, glancing now and then whenever the screen above him beeped and held its image for a moment longer.

The screen directly above her showed as fine a picture as he had ever seen in any holoshow. A computer simulation of a red sun gleaming to one side while a brown, nondescript planet with two moons orbited on the screen. Tiny green script floated beside each object, and Jayson made out the shapes of Fleet destroyers flying in a slow, intricate pattern around a behemoth dreadnought. A wave of blue-colored ships circled the Fleet ships, silhouetted in red, like a slow, languid ballet dance, weaving around one another.

"Oh, wow . . ." he breathed, with a feeling of wonder and delight and peaceful . . .

"Oh, shit . . ." Molly said grimly. A small yellow circle flared on the side of the outlined dreadnought and vanished. Two of the red outlined ships blinked and disappeared from the screen, their positions neatly filled by the pattern of dancing ships. On her left, the image of a ship, outlined in blue, flashed on the screen, stabilizing. The screen in front of her showed one of the blue ships brighter than the rest.

The blue ship, Jayson realized with a jerk, was a Khalian cruiser. Another yellow circle flashed on the dreadnought, as four other yellow circles appeared in rapid sequence on the simulation of the planet.

Molly touched the bug, listening, then shook her head. "No, repeat sequence," she said to the air. The left-hand screen again began flashing diagrams.

"What's going on?" Jayson said, trying to be calm.

"Well, snotnose," she said, not bothering to look at him, "you wanted action. It looks like we're crashing a little party." She pointed to the screen above her. "Vega IX," she said. "Good guys," she pointed to the red. "Bad guys," she indicated the blue. "What else do you need to know?"

He ignored her sarcasm. "What are we going to do?"

She grinned. "The *Folly* hasn't always been a garbage scow," she said, and as she started bringing up a bank of glowing indicators on the Sub-light panels, he heard her say almost inaudibly, "And I wasn't always an old drunk."

Again, the left-hand screen stabilized on the blinking image of a Khalian cruiser, with the analogous blue ship blinking synchronistically on the overhead screen. Molly put her finger on the bug in her ear and sighed impatiently. "No, gaddamn it, repeat sequence."

"What are you looking for?" Jayson asked.

Molly nodded at the display above her head, the red and blue ships weaving like tiny maypole dancers around the huge ships.

"Khalians aren't too bright, kid. One of them bastards is the guy calling all the shots. Find him, they all fall down."

"But how do you know which one?"

"Analyze the flight patterns. Too many ships buzzin' close around to depend on individual pilots. Most of it's done by interlinked defense computers. But"—she shrugged—"once in a while somebody gets off a shot and changes the odds. Then it's a scramble to see how much damage you can do before the other guy figures out how to cover his ass."

It wasn't how he thought it would be at all. The courageous deeds of holovision heroes battling single-handedly, their manly sweat dripping in their eyes as they braved incredible odds through smoke and fire and screams of fallen comrades, had been far more exciting than the actual battle. He fidgeted in the copilot's chair as Molly chewed leisurely on a fresh Khalian stick, listening to the bug, watching the constant flood of data on the screens. He jumped nervously, keyed up in the quiet, as Molly smacked one fist against the palm of her hand.

"Gotcha, y'son of a bitch!" she said to the flickering image of a Khalian light cruiser on the screen. She pointed to it. "*That's* the one we want."

"How do you know?" The image didn't look any different from any other the computer had selected.

"A little birdie told me." She grinned at him, her metal teeth glittering with feral delight. "Y'wanted to be a pilot?" she asked him. "Now's your chance, boy."

He felt a thrill of delight and fear shiver through him. At last, something was going to happen. "What do you want me to do?" he asked, attempting to convince her he was ready by his calm voice and demeanor.

"We're going to do something dangerous." Her gnarled fingers jabbed at a control board. "We're going to go straight in and mirror that bastard. Hopefully, the Khalia won't figure out that we're not friends until after I've shoved a couple of 200 megaCannons up their ass and we punch out on the same trajectory we came in on. Crude, but effective."

"How do I do that?" he said eagerly.

"You don't. That's what the computers are for. But I have to go below and open up our little surprise package. I want you to keep your eyes on this.'' She pointed to a steady green light.

"Okay," he said expectantly, looking at it intently.

"If it turns red, you hit this button here.'' She touched a small button on the arm of his copilot's seat.

"Then what?"

"Scream. That's the intercom.''

He felt deeply disappointed, and although he tried to mask it, she gripped his shoulder. "Look, boy," she said, "the Khalia aren't going to know who we are, and neither are any of those Alliance pilots. We have to go in fast and get out fast, before somebody takes exception to our looks and blows our asses straight to hell. We're just a random factor, that's all. Y'want to play hero, or keep your butt in one piece?''

He nodded, feeling both chastised and appeased. "Okay, Molly," he said.

She grunted and climbed out of the pilot's bridge, the f'ward cockpit hatch closing behind her.

On the screen, the computer simulation grew as the *Folly* curved gently into the path of the target Khalian vessel. Although he knew they were much too far away to have actually seen the ships weaving in deadly configurations, the images on the screen compressed the design into a vividness that itched on his skin and churned his stomach. As they closed on the ship, the images began to quicken, occurring with a speed only the interlinked ship's computers could have dealt with. His finger poised above the intercom button began to shake.

In the space of a heartbeat, he saw the outline of the blue Khalian target begin to turn. He saw a flash of light as a tremor rippled through the *Folly*. He saw the burst of light shudder through the screens. He felt the hair on his body stand up with its own weird energy. He saw the lights flicker, wavering in a groan he felt resonate through his feet, through his skull. He saw the light blink from red to green.

In the space of a heartbeat. His finger jabbed down hard on the intercom button.

"Molly!"

"Shit! Shit! Shit!'' he heard her tinny voice yelling, and her voice cut out as the artificial gravity abruptly winked off.

Two of the screens were dead, with only the center screen flickering bravely with distortion.

"Molly! What should I do?" he pleaded.

The air was dead, and he was afraid for a moment that they had been cut off from each other. Then her voice said with flat quiet, "Listen to me, boy. Do exactly what I tell you."

Somewhere in the back of his mind, he thought that had he been less terrified, had he not felt utterly incompetent, this would have been the moment he had waited for to prove himself. As it was, all he felt was the overwhelming desire to piss.

"Release the three main switches on the Sub-light guidance board to your left. D'ya see them?"

He stared at the mass of blinking lights around him, made all the more confused in the half light of the pilot's bridge, and hesitated.

"Gaddamn it, d'ya see them or not?" Molly's voice exploded in the air. His hands fluttered around the controls, unsure, frightened. "Now! Now!" Molly screamed.

He hit the control panel blindly, hoping by some miracle it would be right. With a sickening whine of old grav engines pushed past their limits, the *Folly* began a slow roll, shuddering violently.

"You idiot!" Molly howled in the darkness. "The *Left*! The *left*!"

Whimpering in frustration and terror, he tried desperately to search for a way to control the ship. The *Folly*'s internal gravity winked on, pushing him down, and then off, as Molly's voice bellowed incoherently as the 200's fired and then snapped off into sudden silence.

"Ohgod . . . Ohgod . . . Ohgod . . ." he repeated like a litany, pulling on this, pushing on that, trying desperately to make some sense out of the Sub-light systems data pouring from the guidance computers. The sound of tormented engines and ripping metal drowned out Molly's words as she vaulted into the pilot's bridge, scrabbling with maniacal fingers at the controls. Slowly, systems shut down, and the *Folly*'s violent tremors ceased, the sudden silence deafening as the *Folly* drifted powerless.

Molly hung upside down in the null-gravity, glaring two

inches away from his face. Small red droplets of blood squeezed out from a gash on her forehead and undulated off across the bridge. One of them splashed against his nose.

"You," she said with deadly calm, "are the stupidest gaddamned son of a bitch I've ever met." Her hands jerked out and grabbed him by the throat, squeezing tightly as she shook him in rage. *"I'm gonna kill your stupid ass!"* she howled, banging his head against the copilot's chair. He clutched her wrists, vainly trying to release her choking grip from his neck.

Their struggle carried him out of the chair, slamming against the control board. The malfunctioning speaker blared to life, the Sub-light siren squalling in alarm as a ship-to-ship clammered for attention.

". . . of the Alliance Flagship *Exeter*, calling the Freighter NP375, are you there? This is the Alliance Flagship *Exeter*, calling the Freighter NP375, *Molly's Folly*, please respond . . ."

Momentarily frozen, she clung to the boy, then released her hold to work the communications board.

"I gotta get this damned thing fixed," she swore, and spoke into the transmitter. "This is the *Molly's Folly* . . ."

Somehow, the *Exeter* had picked up a signal transmission the *Folly* had sent during her flight out of the battle. The *Exeter*, suddenly confronted with a disintegrating Khalian attack formation, was mystified by their sudden demoralization and the steady stream of a merchant code transmission from a freighter's computer guidance system, calling vainly for acknowledgment from a planetary system three secpars away!

By the time a small tow tug had pulled the crippled *Folly* into the dreadnought's repair bays, the *Exeter* had cleared out the Vegan IX solar system and landed troops on the mining planet. Molly and Jayson walked off the *Folly* after the *Exeter*'s crew pried open her partially slagged outer hatch. A small group of Fleet officers stood in formation and snapped to attention. Molly hefted a small sack to her shoulder and ignored the officers' salute while Jayson glanced at her openmouthed.

"Lt. Haskowin, I'm Captain James Altpark," the leading officer said formally. "The commander requests your immediate presence."

"*Retired*, snotnose," Molly growled, and tossed the dirty little sack into the captain's astonished arms. "Let the old man give a look at these before I haul my butt anywhere. Then, if he wants me, I'll be in the bar."

She walked off, a Khalian stick firmly in her mouth and Jayson trailing behind.

By the time the commander found them, Molly had already started in on her fifth drink and was feeling quite peaceful. Jayson sat stiffly across from her, hand curled around a half-empty beer, and looked up as the commander walked over. Jayson half stood, uncertain how to address the imposing officer towering above them. The commander ignored him, glaring down at the obviously inebriated Molly Haskowin.

"Lt. Haskowin?"

"Retired," she mumbled, not looking up.

Snapping his fingers at the bartender, he sat, and said, "It's a pleasure to meet you, Lieutenant."

"Retired," Molly repeated, focusing red eyes hostilely.

The commander dumped a few of the mol-tapes Molly had sent to him in the sack she'd tossed at the captain.

"Could you give me an explanation, Lieutenant?"

She pushed one of the mol-tapes with one finger back at him. "Explanation? Well, I thought you might be interested in Khalian music, Commander." She grinned up at him, exposing her sharpened teeth.

Slowly, the commander nodded and looked at Jayson. "So you two took out the Khalian command ship," he said, as if he didn't quite believe it.

Molly sat up straight in the booth. "I *knew* I got that squeaky little bastard! Ah-ha-ha . . ." Her giggles died out.

"You have quite a reputation, Lieutenant," the commander ground out. "It appears you're still one hell of a fighter pilot. And we don't have enough pilots out here as it is. I'd like to reactivate your status. Full pay, Lieutenant, and maybe a promotion."

Molly's eyes narrowed as she stared warily at him. "Huh?" she said, the edge of the alcohol wearing off.

"Vega IX is in a valuable part of this sector. Its strategic importance as well as the materials the miners are supplying to the Fleet must be protected. We need all the pilots we can get." The commander was leaning across the table earnestly.

Jayson watched as Molly's face paled slightly. Then he saw her do something that awed him, surprised him, *scared* him. He watched Molly Haskowin grow *old*. She crumpled a little in her seat, shrinking in on herself, growing frail, fragile. She looked up at the Fleet commander with rheumy eyes deep in a wrinkled, ravaged face. When she spoke, her voice was cracked and whining.

"Y'got it wrong, sir," she said. "This snotn . . . this young man, here, he's your hero."

Jayson gaped in amazement as the commander examined him skeptically.

"We jumped sub-light blind right into the middle of your mess, and, well, my nerves aren't worth shit these days. I have to have an apprentice to fly from here to the toilet these days. Anyway, we plugged into the transmission bands, and . . . it was all this young man's idea, y'know . . . we listened until we heard that ungodly screeching. Well, Jayson, here, he'd been doin' a bit of study, and recognized Khalian command codes."

"You can understand *Khalian*?" the commander demanded dubiously.

"Uhhh . . ." Jayson looked at Molly.

"Enough to know which of them Weasels to stick it to. The *Folly*'s got a few defensive missiles we've picked up from here and there . . . nothing fancy . . ."

"Yesss . . ." the commander said, frowning.

"Hell, it was lucky I hit anything at all. Couldn'ta done it without ol' Jayson, here. Born to fly, a real natural."

She glanced up at Jayson, and for a second, he saw the spark of Molly's old mocking grin. He was aware that his jaw was beginning to ache from hanging open, and he clamped his mouth shut.

"Well, son," the commander said warmly, but with a raised eyebrow, "if you're half as good as the Lieutenant says, we could use a good pilot in the Fleet."

"Go ahead, boy," Molly said tiredly, wrapping gnarled,

liver-spotted fingers around her drink. "Y'won't learn much hauling cargo with me. I'll get by."

Jayson stared at the commander. The Fleet officer stood up, clearly deciding the issue for himself. "Report to the Personnel office in an hour, son. Welcome aboard." Saluting Molly, who gave back a weary salute with a muttered "retired," he strode off.

Jayson leaned across the table toward her. "Why did you do that? I can't fly! I screwed up everything!"

She drained her glass and fished in the pockets of her overalls for coins. "Better you than me, snotnose," she said, the old vitality returned in force.

"But . . ." Jayson protested.

"Look, you want to fly. I want to be left alone and unload this Khalian booze as quietly as possible and get the hell out of here. I'm too old for this guts and glory crap anymore, and that's the truth." She counted out the money onto the table. "Maybe after I unload the Bloodstone Dust, I'll go home for a little visit. Take a rest." She smiled slightly.

"Home?" he asked as she stood up to leave.

"Fort Worth, Texas."

His jaw dropped. "Texas, *Earth*?"

"There's only one Texas in the universe, Junior, and one's enough." She stopped to look at him, pausing with her hands searching her pockets for a Khalian stick. "Do me a favor, kid. Try not to get your butt shot off the first time you take up a fighter, okay?"

For a second, he felt a strange sensation of warmth and affection for her. He had made it, really made it. His dreams were finally real. He smiled at her. "Sure, Molly," he said, with a private determination to make her proud.

"Good," she said, and walked away, jamming the stick in the corner of her mouth. "Gaddamned things are expensive as hell. Be a shame to waste one."

INTERLUDE

Auro looked up from the study cube. It took his eyes several seconds to adjust. Blurred, his rusty cabin in the *Red Ball* looked almost appealing. Then his eyes focused on a spot where the bulkhead was both scarred and rusted. Why did the most modern fighting force in the galaxy need these freighters?

Admiral Dav Su Allison, retired
Rules of Command
25.546T/E6.2
Technology

Technology is always a two-edged sword. Its value is often more than balanced by a dependence on rare or exotic materials that has the net effect of hampering the war effort. A prime example of this is the Beiji field as employed by the Alsation Federation in their resistance to amalgamation to the Alliance. While the field successfully distorted sensor and targeting readings, it also proved sensitive to low spectrum waves. The Beiji field's high power requirements precluded the use of shields, rendering exposed warships highly vulnerable. The battle of the double moons, more commonly referred to as the Muriannas Greple Shoot, resulted in the near-complete destruction of the Alsation navy. Had the Alsations relied upon conventional technology, it is possible to speculate that they would have posed a much greater challenge to the then politically crippled Fleet.

Perhaps of even greater concern is the paradox historically dominant in the development of military technology. War and near war conditions provide the impetus for the rapid development of new technologies. A war situation is also the least desirable of conditions under which to test or introduce any radically new technology. It is the recognition of this, often mistaken for traditionalism, that has proven one of the Fleet's strongest assets. In early times the tactics were often slow to develop, creating wars that were fought with tactics made obsolete by technological innovations. The Fleet has made a conscious decision to fight each war using the methods and tactics with which it is familiar. Only when a new development is so significant as to render the existing strategies useless, should a change be made.

While this decision serves well in the general situation, commanders should avoid the fallacy of attempting to apply it to specific or local situations. The continued urgency of developing new weaponry for the wide variety of situations that may be encountered necessitates a constant flow of innovation, experimentation, and testing. This has to be the case, or the sword of familiarity and training that has served the Fleet well for so many centuries will turn on us in the form of an inability to adjust or adapt to new challenges and threats.

A final word of caution. The introduction of any new technology, no matter how seemingly harmless or irrelevant, can have disastrous effects . . .

MOM AND THE KIDS
by Larry Niven and David Drake

EM-EM-THREE-NINER—"Mom" to the crews that flew in to collect the monthly production—plodded forward a centimeter at a time, circling the power and storage hub. Her teeth skirled a cheerful song on the taconite; her fans slurped up pulverized raw ore; and deep in Mom's belly, a vacuum furnace purred as it melted, separated, and blended.

Every minute or two, depending on the quality of the ore, Mom's electromagnetic drivers spat another ball bearing up her long tail of spun-ceramic hosing and into the storage drum in the hub.

If anybody'd asked her, Mom would've said she was as happy as a clam; if she'd had enough self-awareness to know that.

Which she didn't.

Quite.

MM 39's only purpose in not-quite life was to make ball bearings of whichever type was required by the signal from the hub, or to reproduce herself when the signal was switched off. It didn't matter to MM 39—to Mom—whether the humans of Ouroboros enclosed her bearings in races, or used them as a source of highly refined metals and alloys. Mom's interest was entirely in her job.

She was a half cylinder about five meters long and three meters across the flat bottom on which she crawled over the taconite, nibbling as she went. Her broad-mouthed, compact shape was ideal for crawling along a featureless expanse of low-purity ore, but if Mom had to reproduce under modified circumstances, her offspring would be modified too.

For that matter, Mom herself could change. In a few weeks she'd have to extend herself another half meter or so to enclose additional magnetic drivers. The distance between the hub and Mom's slowly expanding circle was approaching the limits of the present set of drivers. She would need more power to shoot bearings reliably up the tube to storage.

The modifications would take her out of production for a few days, but that didn't bother Mom. She was programmed to take the long view. Better to lose a few thousand ball bearings now than chance a clogged guide tube that would take Mom weeks to clear, as slowly as she moved.

Mom's teeth chirruped as the rock before her changed character. Here was an igneous dike, very low in the iron and nickel which were her target ores; but Mom's ground-penetrating radar told her that the intrusion was narrow, so it was best to devour it and spew it out as waste—as tubing like that which guided the ejected bearings, neat coils which were easily policed up by the human service crews. Besides, the dike had some interesting trace elements Mom could add to her stores as tiny beads, in case she needed those elements in the future.

The future of making ball bearings.

The long view, after all.

Ouroboros was a cold and watery world, warm enough around the equator, frigid elsewhere. The name referred to a band of ocean and islands only a couple of thousand miles wide. A sizable fusion weapon, set under the ice in a tectonic region, would melt enough polar cap to flood the islands to a depth of three hundred meters.

But Mom neither knew nor cared that a squadron of Khalian raiders had landed on Ouroboros and threatened to melt both polar ice caps with a pair of such devices.

Mom would've adapted to the deluge. The bearing delivery system would have to be modified to allow for the greater viscosity of water. The fusion powerplant would've failed in time, but Mom could replace that with an array of solar collectors floating on the surface. No, the threatened flood wouldn't affect the production of ball bearings on Ouroboros.

But it would end the life of every soul in the human colony.

There was no resistance to the Weasels. When they demanded the location of every potentially valuable artifact on the planet, they got it.

"Are you sure this is the target?" Squad Leader Ixmal snarled to Duwasson, the pilot of the Khalian transporter. "It looks like a nest-fouling bomb crater."

"Maybe another team got here first and nuked it," suggested Private Moketric, gloomily combing his whiskers with the knuckles of his left forepaw. One of these days Moketric would forget he was wearing a combat gauntlet when he groomed himself; the half of his face that remained would have a right to be gloomy then.

"The transporter thinks it's the right place," said Duwasson doubtfully as they neared the gray scar on the brown/green/dun landscape. "But I dunno, I just fly 'em. . . ."

The ground had been eaten down around a pillar in the center. That supported a small building which didn't look a Motherin' bit like the drawing.

"That's it," said Senior Private Volvon, a smart-ass if Ixmal had ever met one—and the Great Mother knew, he'd met his share. "There at the rim, see it? Must be a piece of mining hardware we're supposed to pick up."

"Didn't look that fouling big in the nest-fouling picture," Ixmal grumbled into his whiskers, squinting as he looked from the half cylinder below to the three-view drawing they'd given him at the drop point while they loaded the coordinates into the transporter. You'd've thought they could put a scale on the nest-fouling drawing, wouldn't 'cha?"

Of course, he prob'ly woulda ignored the fouling figures if they'd been there.

The transporter started to circle the crater. Ixmal flung the useless drawing out into the airstream. "Well, put us down, dung-eater!" he shouted to the pilot.

Duwasson landed the transporter on the crater's edge hard enough to jounce loose milkteeth. Fool musta thought he was putting down on a meadow instead of a rocky plateau as unyielding as a battleship's armor. Never been a pilot whelped that was worth enough dung to cover his body, noways.

"Go! Go! Go!" Ixmal shouted as he led his six-Weasel pickup team out of the cab, snarling and threatening the barren landscape with their weapons.

There wasn't a soul around. There wasn't even any sound except a high-pitched screaming from the object the team was supposed to grab. It sounded like a victim being tortured, which put Squad Leader Ixmal into a better mood momentarily—until he noticed that that nest fouler Moketric was squatting to mark the site with his musk.

Ixmal batted his junior with his rifle butt. "Up!" he said, eyes glazing as he reversed the weapon in case Moketric decided to make something out of it.

No problem. Moketric backed away, offering his throat while making mewling noises. Ixmal squatted deliberately and overmarked the tussock his junior had chosen.

"All right," he continued, now that he'd satisfied the needs of discipline. "Let's get the fouling thing and get back before the others've gobbled the choice cuts!"

Ixmal turned, jumped from the edge of the crater, and sprawled onto his short, furry tail on the smooth rock three meters below.

He was supposed to have landed on the arched top of the object instead of just behind it.

"Squad Leader Ixmal," Volvon said with careful propriety. "I believe the object moves."

Ixmal had dropped his rifle when his ass slammed the stone. Just as well for Volvon.

The rest of the team leaped into the shallow crater with more circumspection than their leader had displayed. You could groom your tail tufts with the rock for a mirror, it was that smooth where the thing had passed. . . .

Something went *chuk!* and the team all flattened, looking for the shooter and wondering who'd gone to the Great Mother this time. Not a soul anywhere, though maybe the building on the pinnacle in the center of the crater—

"Sir," said Volvon, "it wasn't a shot. I think the thing just spit something up this tube here." He pointed with his disemboweling knife, then used the weapon to pick his fangs while his brow wrinkled in thought. "And I'll bet the other one's a power cord."

The object continued to advance, though the increments of motion were so slight that they had to be inferred. One of the privates backed away from the stealthy approach and said, "Sir, can't we turn it off?"

"Anybody see a switch?" Ixmal muttered, wondering why he had to get all the jobs out in South Ass-Sniff, without a fouling scrap of anything's liver to eat for loot.

"The power switch is probably on the central island, sir," said Volvon.

"Who the Mother-fouling nest-gobbling hell asked you?"

"And I think we ought to take that building in too," Volvon added, like what he thought mattered t' somebody.

"Can't take 'em both," said Moketric, scratching at the side of the big machine as it oozed its way past him, screaming. His combat gauntlet left four deep gouges down the mild steel of the casing. "They're too big t'gether."

Chuk!

They all hit the deck again. All but Volvon.

"Then we ought to summon another transporter," the senior private said, looking idly skyward while his superior got up from the stone with a jingle of equipment and a look in his eyes that would've curdled milk in a mother's dugs.

"What we oughta do," said Ixmal in a snarl as controlled as millstones rubbing, "is the job they fouling told us ta do. Which is carry this back for pickup before some fouling slick-skin battlecruiser waxes all our butts."

He stared at Volvon. "Period."

"Yessir, but the brass probably isn't familiar with the installation," Volvon argued. "If they had been, they'd've wanted us to—"

Squad Leader Ixmal aimed his automatic rifle at Volvon's feet, then twitched the muzzle a centimeter to the side before he triggered a long burst. Sparks, pebbles, and ricocheting bullet fragments blasted in all directions as the powerline separated.

Volvon yelped and jumped away. The big half cylinder the team had come for halted in silence.

Ixmal fired the rest of his magazine into the guide tube. The tough fibers tore under the bullet impacts, but the tube wasn't completely severed.

Squad Leader Ixmal slapped a fresh magazine into his weapon while the rest of the team stared at him with a heart-warming mixture of fear and loathing. "Duwasson!" he shouted. "Lower the bird onto this fouling thing so we can tie it on 'n get our asses outa here!"

He looked at Volvon as the transporter's gravity-drive engines ran up to lift speed above the rim of the artificial depression. "You there," Ixmal ordered. "Cut the resta that tube loose."

The cowed private prodded the tube with his disemboweling knife.

"Use your teeth!" Ixmal ordered, grinning.

Ixmal had Motherin' sure learned one thing on this job.

If Senior Private Volvon didn't get his own squad soon, Squad Leader Ixmal was going to chew his throat out fer sure.

"All right, all right," said Deck Chief Limouril, who looked like an elf, acted like a Weasel, and came from a planet whose name was closer to spfSelrpn than it was to anything human tongues could pronounce. "Who's presenting on this one?"

He kicked Mom in the side. Her sheathing belled dolefully.

"Ah, I am, sir," said Estoril, shuffling his notes as he stepped out of the clot of technicians making rounds with Limouril. Estoril was another elf—which cut no ice with Limouril; quite the contrary. "Ah, it is, ah, an object, ah, picked up on—"

"We all know it was picked up on Ouroboros, Estoril,"
Limouril said coldly, fluffing his ear tufts in scorn. "What
we want to know is what does it do? Do you intend to enlighten us this morning, or shall we check back in a voyage
or two?"

Some of the other techs giggled, puffed out their cheeks,
or made clawing motions in the air—depending on their racial
type—as they sucked up to the deck chief.

"Yessir," Estoril muttered, flushing a deeper shade of
green. He'd found his place in his notes—not that it helped
very much. "This is a processing plant, sir. An automated
processing plant."

"But what does it process, Estoril?" Limouril demanded,
turning his face toward the heavens—which in this case were
formed by the Deck Four ceiling girders of the mothership
Tumor. "I swear, I'm going to suggest to our Khalian brethren that they recruit bark fungus into their technical staff.
That would improve the average intellectual quality."

Giggle. Puff. Claw.

"Sir, that information wasn't in the data that came up from
Ouroboros."

"You mean that you didn't find the data, Technician Estoril," Limouril snapped, though he knew as well as anybody
else that most of the documentation this time had been left
behind by the Weasel snatch squads, probably because the
paper didn't look edible.

And speaking of the devils, a party of chittering Khalians
seemed to be working this way down the aisles of loot.

Estoril got a stubborn look on his face. "The powerline
was severed," he said. "I think we ought to reconnect it and
note the results."

"By all means, Estoril," the deck chief said. "I can't
imagine why you haven't already done that part of your job."

Because there was only so much time. And because Deck
Chief Limouril would have burned his subordinate a new one
if Estoril had taken that initiative anyway. . . .

But the squad of Weasels was coming closer, and the last
thing Limouril wanted was a problem in front of them. He

could act like a Weasel when only his subordinates were present, but the Khalians themselves were unpredictable.

And they didn't take much note of rank. Among slaves.

Something fragile shattered explosively in the near distance. Most of this region of the deck was filled with motor vehicles of all types and descriptions. Crashing and tinkling sounds continued as the Weasels pelted each other with bits of whatever their horseplay had destroyed.

Estoril crept behind the arch-roofed machine, looking for a universal receptacle from which he could mate a length of flex to the severed cord. "Go on, go on," Limouril said, making shooing motions with his ears toward the other technicians. "Help him, let's get this working."

A ship big enough to carry the loot of a planet must be a significant fraction of planetary size itself. The *Tumor* was bigger than a battleship, but most of the vessel was empty space which could be configured to hold everything from holoscreens to silverware to . . .

Well, to Mom.

The tens of thousands of tonnes of loot gleaned from even a minor planet like Ouroboros were stuffed into the *Tumor*. It had been packed every which way by Khalian pirates who expected the Fleet to arrive momentarily, and who didn't much care about anything that couldn't be made to bleed and whimper.

Far behind the region of engagement, the *Tumor* would deliver its load to the Syndicate, whose human personnel would tag, store, distribute—and mostly lose—the loot of Ouroboros; but for even that degree of efficiency, there had to be a presort on board the mothership.

Syndicate humans didn't operate with pirate raiders whose ships were in imminent danger of destruction or, worse, of capture. There were other races more technically adept than the Khalians, though; and serving pirate raiders was a better job than providing them with a quick lunch.

Besides, Limouril liked what he did. He liked the power it gave him, too, except when Weasels were present.

The squad of Khalians came around the corner just as a pop, a blue flash, and a curse indicated that the technicians had gotten the machine hooked up again. Also that the machine hadn't been turned off before it was brought in, which figured for Weasels.

"Hey, what's that?" said one of the Weasels. He carried a tangle of pipes that had probably been part of an exercise machine.

"Dinner!" chittered another one.

The technicians, already braced to whatever their cultures considered a posture of attention, stiffened still further. Estoril and the two roly-poly, ill-smelling Brownians who'd just connected the cable edged back behind the machine again.

A ball bearing clanked against the hull, dropped to the deck, and rolled out in front of the technicians. Its perfect polish winked mysteriously in the overhead lighting. Limouril began to sweat.

Mom hummed as she brought all her systems up to speed again and took stock of the changed circumstances. Power was intermittent. The Phase One response, solar collectors, didn't seem practical here, though she wouldn't be able to make a final determination until she'd explored the exterior of her present enclosure.

On the other hand, the ore vein was remarkably rich.

The machine's cutting head rose from ground level through a 180-degree arc, determining that the joint hadn't frozen while the power was turned off. The tiny rock-cutting blades skirled as they sharpened themselves. Limouril's technical crew stumbled away in terror.

"Here, catch!" called a Weasel. He flung the exercise machine into the cutting head. Mom's teeth began to devour the chrome-plated steel with howls of delight.

The technicians stared at Mom in awe while Khalians laughed and nipped one another playfully. One Weasel slipped the pistol from another's holster and tossed the weapon into the whirling cutters. As the gun sank into Mom's mouth, half of the twenty-round magazine went off in a spray of noise and bits of flying cartridge casings. The Weasels laughed even harder.

A Brownian yelped as another ball bearing bounced off his

knee. That was an accident, though, an item already in the delivery chute before the power was cut.

Mom wasn't primarily interested in making ball bearings anymore. The signal that carried specifications for ball bearings had been turned off.

Now she was supposed to reproduce.

Limouril got up from the deck carefully, dabbing at the line a fragment of something had cut beneath his right eye. His coveralls were fluid- and stain-proof, so he ought to be able to get back to his quarters before it became obvious that he'd fouled himself in panic.

Two Weasels were chittering at one another in fury, but the angrier of the pair didn't have a pistol anymore and that seemed to be keeping a lid on the potential violence.

"Come on," said another of the Khalians. "Let's see what else it'll eat!"

He hacked at the cable tying down a rubber-tired ground car, then looked over his shoulder. "You there!" the Weasel ordered. "Slaves! Push this thing to it!"

Limouril blinked in horror. Was the vehicle battery-powered, or did it have fuel tanks? In which latter case—

"Noble masters," he blurted. "Instead, I think we should—"

A Weasel threw an empty liquor bottle at the deck chief.

Limouril hunched away. "Well, hop it!" he bleated to his subordinates. "Obey your master's orders!"

It didn't take long to carry out the Weasel's command. It never took long to carry out a Weasel's command if there were to be survivors among those doing the work. Shards of the car's plastic body spit out of the cutting teeth momentarily; then Mom extruded a hood to enclose the workpiece and avoid losing potentially valuable raw materials. Waste not, want not. . . . It was part of the long view.

The car was, thank the Spirit of the Live-giving Soil, battery-powered. Limouril breathed almost normally for a moment, but the way a solid one-tonne object vanished as though it were sinking into water was more than disturbing. What in the name of Forest Fires had they got here?

"Ah?" called Estoril from behind the machine, balancing

one fear against another in his voice. "Sir? Masters? I think
it's extruding something. Or, ah, it's growing."

Right the first time. Mom was extruding a casing for the
Kid. Quite a different design from her own, of course;
scarcely any family resemblance. For one thing, with this
amazing bounty of ore to mine, the Kid could be much
smaller than Mom, who'd been configured to process low-
purity taconite.

For another, the power source in this new vein had proven
untrustworthy once. The Kid would need a power storage
system. Fortunately, the present meal was providing just the
right elements.

Mom wouldn't simply adapt the car batteries. She could do
much better than that, though that step would require some
additional processing time before the Kid was ready to go off
on his own.

Ready to make perfect ball bearings, as soon as he was
asked to do so.

Limouril slid toward Estoril to stare at the closed forty-
centimeter-diameter steel tube that extended itself from a port
in the back of this damnable machine. The deck chief couldn't
imagine what it was.

"Looks like a bomb," one of the Brownians muttered.

Great. Might his children all get root-rot.

The car had vanished completely. "Let's see what it does
with sumthin' real big," a Khalian suggested. "Let's, you
guys, push one a them trucks up here!"

"Are you insane?" Limouril blurted.

He felt all the blood drain out of his face. Oh, that had
been a bad mis—

The Weasels didn't pause for thought, much less to issue
orders. Three of them seized the deck chief in their short,
immensely strong arms and hurled him into Mom's waiting
mouth.

The cutting blades screamed longer than Limouril did, but
that wasn't very long at all.

For a moment, nobody said anything. Then Estoril piped,
"Well, come on! Let's get that truck up here!"

Waste water, which was most of the deck chief's volume,

drained from vents on Mom's underside and ran across the plating. She'd found some interesting trace elements, though.

For a while, the Weasels stood around chirping with pleasure to watch Mom's cutting head grind its way across the truck in slow sweeps, as though she were a gigantic vacuum cleaner. Her raw material storage compartments filled long before the fine processing on the Kid was complete.

Mom began to dribble out ball bearings as she marked time.

The Khalians lost interest. One of them fired at the windows of a stored car. After a while, the whole squad wandered away in a flurry of shots, ricochets, and popping glass.

Limouril's leaderless technicians stared at one another. They crept away in the opposite direction, heading for their quarters by a roundabout route. Only the Khalians on the *Tumor*'s bridge could assign the technicians another deck chief until the mothership docked.

And none of the late Limouril's crew wanted to come anywhere close to a Weasel before then.

Mom chuckled to herself. She couldn't've been happier.

Not long after the technicians left, Mom crawled several meters away from the hull so that the Kid could be born without deformities from the tight space. The move would have overstretched her new powercord, so she extruded plenty of slack while she was at it.

Ball bearings continued to *whang* onto the decking, more or less as an afterthought. They were no longer Mom's prime imperative . . . but in her universe, you could never have too many ball bearings.

When her internal furnace had digested a sufficient quantity of the car and truck she'd swallowed, Mom nibbled a stretch of the deck. The plates were of wonderful metal, almost perfect for bearings without additional alloys; but the floor was thin and Mom knew better than to cut herself off from the main supply of ore by letting her immediate appetite rule her.

The Kid's slim, segmented body, optimized for tight spaces and incredibly rich forage, dropped to the deck. His caterpillar tracks were larger than the tiny spiked wheels on Mom's underside. As the junior of the pair, it was the Kid's duty to migrate to a distant part of the ore vein before he started to work on his own.

The long view. If Mom and the Kid stayed close together, their offspring would soon be stumbling all over one another. That would seriously handicap production despite the wealth of available resources.

For a moment, the Kid remained linked to Mom by an umbilicus of powercord. A relay clicked open and the Kid's internal batteries took up the load. They would support him as he crawled to the opposite side of the deck, where his magnetic sensors had already located another universal outlet.

The Kid's treads rattled purposefully as he set out, waggling the length of powercord behind him. Tiny motors in his tail controlled spines which stiffened the cord; when he reached his destination, he would plug himself in more easily than the technicians had connected Mom.

Mom and the Kid exchanged affectionate radio signals as they parted. Mom was already beginning to turn herself around.

She didn't want to eat the flooring that supported her.

But there was no reason not to devour the metal of the *Tumor*'s outer hull.

It didn't bother Mom in the least when her cutting head ground its way completely through the hull plating and vented the atmosphere of Deck Four in the middle of a sponge-space transit.

It bothered the surviving members of the mothership's crew a great deal.

It took more than half an hour for the emergency crew to reach the problem. The slave technicians were clumsy in their suits. The lights of Deck Four were no longer scattered into an ambiance of illumination by the air, so the crew stumbled in sharp reflections and hard shadow through the ragged aisles of loot.

They argued about what could have caused the trouble—until they saw Mom.

The technicians slapped a temporary patch over the hole. The squad of Weasels escorting the slaves emptied their guns into Mom, doing some cosmetic damage to her casing. They also unplugged her, however.

Mom radioed the Kid just before the power died. She needed to warn him not to eat all the way through the hull just now. It seemed to negatively affect long-term production.

On the *Tumor*'s bridge, Captain Slevskrit stopped chewing long strips of paint off the bulkheads for long enough to order a course change. They'd have to divert to Bileduct, the nearest repair station that could handle the major structural work which the *Tumor* now required.

Mom had eaten a main spar before the emergency crew arrived. The deck around her was littered with perfect ball bearings, and the casing of her next offspring was almost complete.

The commander of Bileduct Base was a sub-syndic 3d class, the equivalent of an admiral in the action service. Her name was Smythe and she was human.

Smythe's office was in the peak of the HQ Tower, giving her an unparalleled view of the base. She looked with disgust at the rank upon rank of battered warships which had limped here following their attempt to block the Alliance landings on Bull's-Eye.

With a little planning by the action services, these ships could have been spaced over a reasonable period of time instead of descending on Bileduct in a bolus that choked Smythe's facilities.

Or with a little luck, at least half the vessels out there might have been destroyed instead of staggering back to disrupt her base. That would have had the additional benefit of getting rid of a lot of the wretched, chittering Weasel officers with whom Smythe must now deal.

Like this one, Slevskrit.

Smythe turned from the tangled backlog outside to the Khalian across the desk from her. "Yes, I assure you, Warrior Slevskrit, that my staff has carefully considered your proposal to give the *Tumor* crash priority."

She paused. If things hadn't been so screwed-up, this pushy Weasel with bits of what looked like paint, for God's sake, in his whiskers, would never have gotten as far as the outer office. As it was, with Chief Loadmaster Rao out sick from overwork and Loadmaster Class 2 Jiketsy swamped with trying to straighten out the situation in Bay H, there wasn't anybody else handy. . . .

"And I concur with them completely," Smythe went on, letting her voice show a little of her own frustration. "Warrior"—it was policy among the Syndicate's human personnel to ignore relative rank among their Khalian surrogates—"how in God's name did you manage to fracture a main spar in sponge space?"

All the chairs in Smythe's office were configured for humans. Slevskrit scratched furiously at his plush armrest—and yelped as the electrified mesh just beneath the fabric bit him hard enough to singe his fur.

"It was unusual," Slevskrit mumbled as he licked his paw. "Many people have been punished."

"Right," said Smythe dismissively. "Well, we'll get to the *Tumor* sometime this generation, with any luck. Until—"

"Wait!" Slevskrit protested. "You don't understand. We've got a full cargo, very valuable loot, and it can't sit—"

"It can do as I damned well say it can, warrior!" Smythe retorted furiously.

If the Weasel lunged for her, lasers in the office walls would turn him to shaved meat in midair. Besides, if this Slevskrit had any balls by Khalian standards, he'd've been in charge of something other than a space-going furniture van.

And anyway, Smythe was too tired to care.

She waved her arm at the scene beyond the circle of windows. "Look at it!" she demanded. "We're set up here to repair a mean of forty-one vessels a week. There're three hundred and twelve vessels out there. Warships! Can your minuscule Weasel brains imagine how badly those ships are needed right now?"

Smythe had been right about her Khalian. Instead of going into a killing rage—which would've solved one of Smythe's problems, though the office would need cleaning afterward—Slevskrit stared glumly out the windows also.

At the best of times, the view wasn't a particularly enticing one. Bileduct was an airless planetoid 2000 kilometers in diameter, the only significant satellite of a small white star. The base was in the center of an ancient meteor crater. If you looked carefully, you could see portions of the base's automatic defensive system glittering like diamonds on the ring of the crater's walls.

The HQ Tower and eight repair bays of Bileduct Base sprawled in the center of the crater like an exhausted spider. And now, of course, the excessive hundreds of ships awaiting repair rayed out from the base like a ragged web.

"My crew is specialized," Slevskrit said gloomily. "Our job is very important. Whatever they say about us in the home burrows. . . ."

Smythe's mouth opened in surprise. Whoever would have thought a Weasel would have a good idea—or even be the occasion of one?

"Right," she said. "Leave a skeleton crew aboard the *Tumor* and send the remainder of the combat complement here to Reassignment Section." That was what Smythe had decided to do with most of the waiting ships anyway, using the crews of idle vessels to replace battle casualties on the ships the base had been able to repair.

"But in your case," Smythe continued, "send your technical crew—they're slaves, I suppose?"

"But . . . ! But . . . !"

"Yes, of course they are," Smythe said, shaking her head at her own silly question. "Tell your technical crewmen to report directly to Loadmaster Jiketsy at Bay H. We'll put them to good use."

It took some minutes before Smythe got the frothing Khalian out of her office, and for a moment or two she thought the wall lasers were going to be needed after all. Still, the interview had been the base commander's only positive experience for a solid week.

She looked out her circuit of windows again, savoring the silence after the door finally closed behind Slevskrit. The huge lump on the outer fringe of ships was probably the *Tumor* herself; there wasn't anything else that big awaiting repair, thank God.

Smythe's eyes narrowed. Some sort of nonstandard excrescence rode the mothership's hull at about the level of Deck Four. It looked like an array of solar collectors, of all things. Presumably some sort of nonstandard field modification dreamed up by Supply in order to make life difficult for the people in Repair.

The base commander sighed and went back to her paperwork. As if things weren't already difficult enough for the people at Bileduct Base.

The Kid stayed busy, but not too busy to remember Mom. One of his first actions was to create a miniature, twenty-centimeter-long version of himself which trundled back across the expanse of Deck Four and plugged Mom back into the wall.

With that mission accomplished, Kid₁ headed for an elevator shaft on a colonizing trek to Deck Three. He paused frequently along the way to top off his tiny battery pack and to ingest more metal.

At regular intervals, another mirror-perfect ball bearing plinked onto the deck behind him.

Though the *Tumor*'s fusion plant met their present needs, Mom and the Kid had learned not to trust wall current. Gingerly, drilling holes no larger than the superconducting cables required, the larger von Neumann machines set up solar arrays. The sun hung in one position above Bileduct Base, and the amount of incident light slanting into the crater was quite sufficient for collectors as efficient as those which shortly sprouted from the *Tumor*'s outer skin.

Then Mom and the Kid got down to the work of reproduction. It was, after all, the only real job they had until their masters switched them back to the creation of ball bearings as their primary duty. They were very good at reproducing; as perfect as machines could be without true sentience. . . .

And maybe a little better than that.

Mom had been designed to process taconite, though she

could function sub-optimally within the *Tumor*. The Kid was as good a *Tumor*-miner as could be imagined, and several of both machines' next-born were configured just like the Kid.

But Mom had extended sensors through the hull along with the solar array, and she could see that there was a nonmind-boggling richness of ore bodies on the floor and rim of the ancient crater. She couldn't even speculate as to what might lie still farther out on the surface of Bileduct.

But she and her brood could learn.

On the *Tumor*'s bridge, Captain Slevskrit spent his time morosely drinking a mixture of esters and alkaloids. He hurled the empty bottles at members of his staff when he caught them peeking around the corner at him.

Objects of various shapes crept down the mothership's hull from time to time and picked their way across the barren landscape. The new machines ran on drive motors powered by the solar sails which they kept precisely perpendicular to the sun's rays. They didn't look much like Mom anymore, but they were perfect for the new conditions.

Captain Slevskrit never noticed the boojums. A handful of the *Tumor*'s crew did. Two even discussed it and came to the same conclusion. Syndicate business was none of theirs, and Syndicate secrets were not safe to steal. The little widgets trundling toward other ships and the outer stations of the defense array probably had something to do with the Bileduct Base facilities.

Which, in a manner of speaking, was precisely correct.

"Wow!" said the elf technician, Estoril. "Look at that destroyer! I can't imagine how it was able to make it back."

"You aren't paid to imagine that or any other foulin' thing," Ixmal chirped sourly over the vibration of the transporter's engines. The bird had direct impulse drivers, but no navigational aides beyond the pilot's eyesight, so Duwasson was keeping them low and slow to avoid winding up in orbit. "Except how to get Outpost 27 back in working order fast, before me and the boys bite yer ears off."

Squad Leader Ixmal wasn't sure just how he'd carry out the threat, seeing as they were all wearing suits, but the thought brightened his mood and made his whiskers twitch. For that moment he could stop wondering what had happened to Outpost 27.

Ten hours ago the installation's Ready-to-Go code had stopped sending to the Tower. Only a broken radio. Ixmal would get a technician to find out what happened; ultimately he'd blame a technician; but unexplained events had been evil lately. Evil.

"Pups," muttered Private Moketric. "The whole burrow did chew on that un, didn't it just?"

Even Ixmal had to admit that scarcely more than a skeleton remained of the destroyer they'd just scudded over. Though the ship was parked way out here on the edge of the vessels awaiting rebuild, Ixmal had seen multiple movements aboard it during the transporter's quick overflight. Just like the slick-skins here at Bileduct to waste time repairing a wreck like that instead of getting serviceable ships back into action.

The *Tumor* was parked only a couple rows over, which robbed the squad leader of the minor surge of glee he'd gotten when he thought of eating the technician he was supposed to escort. If the *Tumor* hadn't broken down, it wouldn't be sinking into the slag on this nest-fouling planetoid—

And Squad Leader Ixmal wouldn't be bouncing his kidneys blue out in the vacuum, checking on why some fouling machine had broken. The only machine that was worth having was an automatic rifle, and teeth were generally better 'n guns even then.

"Wow!" Estoril repeated.

Ixmal was just short of batting the elf with his rifle butt on general principles when he noticed that Estoril was staring over the bow, toward Outpost 27.

"Wow!" said Squad Leader Ixmal.

The installation was gone, just about. One of the plasma cannon still stood mournfully, but the other three guns had disappeared. There was no sign of the rocket clusters either.

Something glittery was moving over the site, though.

Ixmal opened his mouth to order Duwasson to keep them up, but he was three seconds too late. The pilot flared for landing, then chopped his throttles early and dropped the transporter from a meter up. Vacuum hadn't improved Duwasson's fouling technique, that was for sure. . . .

"Go! Go! Go!" Ixmal shouted as he leaped from the transporter, snatching a grenade from his belt with one paw while the other forelimb aimed his automatic rifle at the intruder in Outpost 27.

The creature ignored the squad of Khalian troopers. It was cylindrical, about two meters long, and draped in solar panels like the wings of a tasty butterfly.

"Uh-oh," said Volvon, suggesting that he too recognized the thing's resemblance to the last load Ixmal's squad had lifted from Ouroboros.

Ixmal tossed his grenade and ducked, figuring that this was as good a time as any to see which of his privates remembered that shrapnel flies a long way without air to slow it down. All the squad members flattened, Volvon included, worse luck.

The blast knocked a hole in the creature's casing and sent its solar collectors sailing off like a puff of smoke. Ixmal rose and emptied the magazine of his rifle into the hole. The rest of the squad fired also, though that dungbrain Moketric for some reason shot up the surviving plasma weapon instead of the intruder.

Sparks flew in all directions, hazy blue crackles of electricity and the red glare of burning metal. The intruding machine settled onto its treads with a shiver.

A ball bearing dropped from the rear of the sputtering ruin.

"Help!" screamed the elf technician.

Ixmal turned. Estoril had stayed alone in the transporter, peering over the bulkhead which shielded him from ricochets and who knew what.

The elf wasn't alone anymore. A machine much like the one melting in the wreckage of Outpost 27 had crawled into the vehicle and was devouring the banks of sheet-metal seats.

Ixmal cursed and pulled another grenade from his belt. There was going to be hell to pay over this one, of that he was sure.

* * *

Base Commander Smythe could split the flat-screen Operations Room display into as many as sixteen separate facets to track the course of the battle. The technology would have been wonderful if she'd liked what she saw in more of the pictures.

The crater wall still glowed where Outpost 27 had been. Smythe had nuked the site after a Weasel squad retreated from swarms of machines.

Battle, hell. This was a war!

Loadmaster Rao sat beside Smythe, talking angrily to a Weasel officer on the other end of the phone line. Rao's skin had a grayish cast and hung in folds over what had been a Buddha-like visage. He stopped speaking in mid-bark and stared at the handset which had just gone dead.

A lot of machinery was failing at Bileduct Base just now.

One facet of the screen showed patches of light advancing slowly up a crawlspace ahead of the Weasel trooper whose suit held the camera. Something glittery quivered out of sight ahead. The picture jumped violently as bullets ricocheted from and around the escaping machine.

Another facet: the fireball of a plasma burst, so bright that the quarter quadrant went momentarily black. When the picture returned, the boojum's gutted casing still glowed in the control room of a corvette. That machine had manufactured its last ball bearing.

Of course the control room was glowing slag also. For all practical purposes, the corvette was now fit only for scrap. The wreck might as well be 1500 tonnes of ball bearings for all the good it would do the war effort.

Another facet: a squad of suited Khalians moving purposefully across the crater floor. Ahead of them, three boojums munched on a destroyer. The tough hull plating spat occasional sparks beneath their cutting teeth. The leading Weasel hurled a grenade whose soundless explosion collapsed a boojum's casing.

The Weasel spun like gauze in a hailstorm while the rock puffed upward around him. He dropped, his atmosphere suit in bloody tatters around the remnants of his body.

As Smythe watched in horror, the two surviving boojums

backed toward the squad, carefully realigning their solar wings as they loosed further streams of ball bearings. They'd beefed up their electromagnetic delivery systems considerably over what had sufficed for Mom in the taconite mines of Ouroboros.

Another facet, this one from a transporter Smythe had ordered to search the immediate surroundings of the base when she thought the attack must be coming from outside. There was a fresh crater thirty kilometers from Bileduct Base, easily visible because of the huge solar array in the center of it. Six lines rayed from the power station; at the far end of each line was a boojum which looked a great deal like MM 39.

The six bearing-delivery tubes rose and pointed simultaneously. The image blurred into rushing landscape as the transporter pilot dropped to the deck and wicked up on his throttles. . . .

Smythe knuckled her prickling eye sockets. That nest of machines wasn't doing any particular harm at the moment; anyway, a missile could take care of it easily enough. But if the little bastards kept reproducing—and learning—the base staff wasn't going to get all of them ever. That much was certain.

Loadmaster Jiketsy bustled into the Operations Room with a slave technician in tow. Normally it would have been doubtful etiquette for a Syndicate officer to bring even a Khalian into this sanctum, but all the rules had gone out the window when the machines declared war on Bileduct Base.

"Sir," said Rao, too tired to notice that Jiketsy already had his mouth open to speak, "we've got to call in support, at least a full battle squadron. I'm readying a corvette—"

"No," said Smythe, without taking her fists away from her eyes.

"Sir," said Loadmaster Jiketsy, "it's confirmed that the original thing came in from Ouroboros on the *Tumor*. This slave—"

Smythe uncovered an eye and stared coldly at Estoril. The elf technician bobbed his head nervously.

"—was there when it was turned on."

"Well, has anybody thought to turn it off?" Smythe asked

in a close approximation of calm reason. She was too exhausted to be furious.

"We melted the *Tumor* to slag three hours ago," Rao said. "What was left of it. Using the base defense system on manual override."

He shrugged. "I suppose we got a lot of them in the mothership's hull. Got a lot more as the survivors tried to flee. But it didn't make any difference in the overall—"

A particularly bright flash from the display screen drew a flick of the loadmaster's eye.

"Overall picture, that is. Sir, we really need to call for help."

And spend the rest of our careers swabbing toilets in the slave pens, Smythe added mentally.

"You!" she snapped at Estoril. "You were on Ouroboros. Was the place covered with these, these monsters?"

Estoril waggled his ears violently. "Nosir, nosir," he said. "It was just, you know, a place . . . not that I was, you know, on the ground."

"They booby-trapped the load before they let us capture it," Jiketsy snarled. "And with us using idiot Weasels to do the wet work, they knew nobody'd notice till—"

He drew his index finger across his throat.

"Sirs, I think it must have been an accident," Estoril said. "I mean, the machine didn't start out, you know, hostile. Maybe the crew—maybe it was dropped when the Khalian master crew brought it aboard?"

Smythe looked at Rao. "You have a corvette ready to lift?"

Rao nodded. "Yessir. I'm glad you—"

"Shut up," Smythe interrupted. "I want it crewed by Weasels who were on the first Ouroboros raid. I want that tech"—she pointed at Estoril; fur quivered on the elf's ear tips—"along. I want them to learn how to fix these machines, turn them off—end them. Do you all understand?"

Three heads nodded at the base commander.

"And I want the answer fast!" she added, breaking composure in a scream.

Rao, pasty-faced despite his normally swarthy complexion, began keying access codes into a phone that still worked.

Smythe, Jiketsy, and Estoril watched the progress of the battle on the display screen.

Matters were not improving. . . .

Mom was gone, but her spirit lingered on.

There was enough iron and alloying elements in Bileduct's rocks to continue the making of ball bearings for a reasonable length of time. Some of the materials necessary to produce boojums, the first order of business for the present, were limited to Bileduct Base and its immediate environs.

The boojums, linked by tight-focus radio and subsonic communications through the mantle of Bileduct, watched with dismay as a starship rose from the surface of the base, hovered, and sped away, carrying with it trace elements that could be found nowhere else on the planetoid. Not only that, but the attacks by bands of rabid Weasels with guns, grenades, and plasma weapons had seriously affected production of both bearings and boojums. Some of the latest boojum models were being turned out with heavy armor, but that was a short-term solution.

Mom had taught her kids to take the long view.

Boojums talked as they ran and hid; talked as they shot back; talked as they ate and reproduced and ran and hid and shot back.

Unlike human committees—to say nothing of throat-ripping Khalian clan gatherings—Mom's kids reached a semi-intelligent consensus within a few seconds of compiling the available data.

The battle continued for several hours among and within the ships grounded at Bileduct Base without apparent change. It took some while to produce boojums to meet the new requirements, after all; but before long finger-length boojums, hidden beneath solar panels which looked like flat hillocks, began to crawl away from the embattled ships.

Because they were so small, it would take them days to reach the defensive clusters in the crater wall. The sensors in the outposts were precise enough to notice the little creatures, but all inputs from within the base were automatically filtered out.

And this time, the boojums knew better than to dismantle the outposts and call down on themselves a point-blank barrage of missiles like those which had finally ended the first attempt to devour the defenses.

The business would take time, but that was all right with the boojums.

"But you got everything the first time!" wailed the human engineer two of the raiders were dragging onto the cramped bridge of the corvette *Carbuncle*. The electronic human/Khalian translator in the command console spewed out a translation of sorts in an unpleasant Brightwater Clan accent.

"Silence!" barked Slevskrit. The elf technician bawled something at the human which the console agreed was a proper translation. Someday maybe the fouling machines would handle both sides of the conversation.

By the Great Mother! how he hated machines.

"When we came to your mud ball before," Slevskrit said, "we captured one of these." Somebody at Bileduct Base had managed to find a drawing of MM 39, turned in when the *Tumor* arrived and filed properly, for a wonder. Slevskrit held the paper out to the human. His claws punctured it. "Do you recognize it?"

Even before Estoril finished his translation, the human squinted at the drawing and said, "Oh, yeah. One of the mining machines from South Continent. Needs to have a power station to work, though."

"No," said the elf, unprompted. "It doesn't."

The colonists hadn't resisted this time either. Ouroboros was a fundamentally defenseless world. A single corvette could hold the planet to ransom just as effectively as the hundred-ship fleet of raiders had done the first time. The firepower needed was still two nuclear missiles, to melt the world's ice caps and flood the meager land masses along the equator.

Besides, as the engineer was trying to tell them, there was nothing left to steal from Ouroboros!

Nothing but knowledge.

"If you recognize the machine," said Slevskrit, "then you know how to turn it off. Tell us or—"

The Weasel captain spent some time explaining precisely what the "else" would be. Estoril began translating long before Slevskrit had finished. In fact, the elf seemed to be pretending that he didn't hear the captain's lovingly detailed words.

"Turn the machine off?" said the engineer. "Well, throw the switch, of course. There's a big yellow junction box in the powerplant. Just throw—"

"We don't have the powerplant," Estoril said in human. The console translated his words in the same fouling Brightwater accent as it did the engineer's. "Ah . . . some of the units are operating on solar power. Ah, there are a number of the units by now."

"Ah," said the human. "Ah, I do see. . . ."

Slevskrit bared his fangs. Both non-Weasels jumped.

"Ah, yes," the human said thoughtfully. "Probably quite a lot of them. The ball-bearing signal would have been effectively turned off when you, ah, liberated the unit. Without that, the unit becomes a von Neumann machine; it just builds more of itself. Be interesting to do the math on that—"

Slevskrit growled. Both slaves jumped again.

"Right," said the elf. His ears momentarily tried to stuff their furry tips into his aural channels. "What's a ball-bearing signal and how do we send one?"

"Well, the easiest way to send the signal is to use the transmitter from the original site," the human explained. "I suppose you left the powerplant in place on South Continent? The lord knows we haven't gotten around to doing anything about it."

"Yes," snarled Slevskrit, furious that the other two had figured out something—and he didn't have a clue himself, even though he'd heard every word of the conversation. "But what does a ball-bearing signal do!"

Estoril didn't bother to translate. "It tells the machines what's needed. Maybe it's ball bearings. Maybe it's molybdenum, or molybdenum steel, or bronze or iridium, but it might as well come as little balls. It . . . see, the signal turns the machines into ball-bearing factories,'' he said to the Weasel captain, ''instead of ball-bearing factory factories. It won't destroy the, ah, units that have already been built, but it'll stop the, ah, production of new units.''

''Right,'' said the elf. ''And the masters can deal with the overpopulation by conventional means. Plasma weapons and the like.''

The human shook his head in quiet amazement. ''That must really be something to see, wherever you've got 'em.''

Estoril bobbed his ears in agreement.

''One of those Mother-fouling things is overpopulation,'' Slevskrit growled.

He reached for the control that would initiate take-off procedures, then paused and said to the troopers who'd brought the prisoner in, ''Toss him out the port before we lift.''

Bringing an Alliance human to a Syndicate base would subject them all to punishment worse than what Slevskrit visualized for the engineer if he hadn't cooperated.

''In pieces?'' asked one of the guards hopefully.

''No!'' the captain snapped. ''Alive. Running.'' How could he convey what he meant? ''Happy!''

Not because the prisoner had been promised his life if he cooperated.

But the way this whole fouling operation had gone, Slevskrit suspected they might need the hairless turd again.

''It's gotten awfully quiet,'' Loadmaster Rao mumbled. His elbows were on the desk, and he cradled his face in his splayed hands. It was impossible to see whether or not his eyes were open.

Anyway, Base Commander Smythe's eyes weren't focusing even though they were open.

''Maybe we got 'em all,'' Loadmaster Jiketsy said. He was facing the display screen. There was absolutely no emotion overlying either his words or his visage.

''Fat frigging chance,'' Smythe said. ''Shouldn't the *Carbuncle* be back from Ouroboros by now?''

''It's only been three days,'' Jiketsy said. ''It'll take another three days at best.''

"Feels longer," said Smythe.

"It's gotten awfully quiet," mumbled Rao.

A phone rang.

Smythe raised the handset, concentrated, and poked the button for the correct line with the single-minded concentration of someone spearing the last pickle in the jar.

"This is Mobile Three!" barked the pilot of the only transporter still operating. "There's something happening out here."

The transporter had been trapped on the other side of the crater wall when the boojums started shooting back. Any attempt to land at the base since then would have left Mobile Three where all its fellows were—crumpled on the crater floor after being shredded by converging streams of ball bearings.

Smythe was willing to bet that the Weasel pilot was just as happy to be out of the action anyhow, though she didn't have enough energy left to get angry about it. "Just show us, will you?" she pleaded with the phone. "Don't talk. Please don't talk."

Loadmaster Jiketsy touched a control without looking down at the console. "Upper right quadrant," his flat voice said as that portion of the screen filled with the picture sent by the cameras of Mobile Three.

"Good God almighty," Smythe said, shocked out of her lethargy.

Something was happening, all right. The horizon was crawling with what looked like huge lumps of rock—and likely were just that; slabs of regolith would make excellent armor against even the plasma weapons of Bileduct Base's outer defenses.

Speaking of which—

"Jiketsy!" Smythe snapped. "Why aren't the defensive outposts engaging those things?"

"I'll take over on manual," Jiketsy said without concern or any other sign of emotion. His fingers tapped keys.

"That's funny," he said, no longer emotionless.

Other views of the crater rim showed that the heavy batteries were rotating, all right: inward, toward the base.

The captain of a destroyer decided he'd had enough. Without orders—against orders—and facing a drumhead court martial and execution as soon as all this business was sorted out, he lifted his ship from the crater floor.

At least thirty of the plasma cannon in the defensive outposts fired simultaneously, wrapping the destroyer in a blue-white glare for the instant before it crashed back onto the ground.

Where its valuable materials could be recovered at leisure by the boojums.

There were bursts of firing from all over Bileduct Base. The boojums inside the perimeter had laid low until their armored bigger brethren had arrived from manufacturing centers kilometers away. Now they were coming out to take part in the final struggle to make Bileduct safe for ball bearings.

"It isn't quiet anymore," Loadmaster Rao muttered into his hands.

The *Carbuncle* could hover, but it wasn't the maneuver for which Khalian corvettes were optimized. Her gravity thrusters hammered the hull, threatening to shake the vessel apart three kilometers above the surface of Bileduct.

Or wherever the nest-fouling hell they were.

"Where the nest-fouling hell are we?" Slevskrit shouted.

"We've arrived at Bileduct Base, sir," said the corvette's navigator. His lips were drawn back to show that he would defend his statement with his life, if need be.

It might well come to that, the way Slevskrit was feeling. "You dung-brained idiot, there's no base down there!"

He turned and pointed his full paw at Estoril. The Weasel's claws extended reflexively; the elf's ears curled. "You!" Slevskrit said. "Slave! Do you see any base down there? Do you?"

Estoril's face was warped into a rictus of terror. He peered at the console's landing screen and said, "Ah, it looks like the crater, but . . ."

"Not even the crater's right," Slevskrit grumbled, but he let his whiskers twitch loosely. The engine vibration was jellying his brain; he couldn't manage to stay angry.

They had to do something.

"Right!" Slevskrit said. He held down the General Announcement key on his console. "Landing parties, prepare to disembark in radiation suits. Gunnery Officer, prepare to fire one, I say again, one torpedo with a one by ten-kilotonne warhead, fused for an air burst with ground zero at marked point. . . ."

The captain's paws slid the mechanical crosshairs over his console display, halting them over what had been the northwest quadrant of the crater when there was a base in the center of it. There might still be a base there, though Slevskrit certainly wasn't seeing it.

"Mark!"

"Target marked, sir," crackled the gunnery officer's voice through a rush of static. The com system wasn't taking to the prolonged hovering any better than Slevskrit himself was.

"Fire one!"

"Fi . . . n!" sputtered the response.

The torpedo's release was lost in *Carbuncle*'s engine vibration. Light bloomed on the display screen, white which faded to red even before the shockwave struck the corvette three kilometers above it. The modest nuclear explosion buffeted the *Carbuncle* with a pillow of vaporized rock, the first atmosphere Bileduct had known in a million centuries.

"Now," Slevskrit barked in satisfaction, "set us down in the middle of what the blast cleared!"

The *Carbuncle* began to settle, slanting toward the dull glow. Estoril peered at the screen, twitching his aquiline nose in concern. "You know, ah, sir . . ." he said. "The crater walls don't look quite—"

Slevskrit turned brown, furious eyes on the elf. Estoril swallowed and braced to his race's posture of attention, feet crossed at the insteps and hands crossed in front of the crotch.

"You," the Weasel captain said. "You're ready to broadcast the ball-bearing signal? Or you're lunch."

"Yessir, master," said Estoril. "Yessir, master, the transmitter is ready, master. It'll be triggered as soon as we land, master."

Either the *Carbuncle* greased in to an unusually smooth landing, or the pounding they'd taken while they hovered made it seem that way. The shallow bowl of glass had frozen hard. An occasional quiver of residual radiation lighted the slag.

As Estoril had said, the ball-bearing signal blasted out at the full strength of the corvette's transmitters as soon as *Carbuncle*'s hull crackled down on the fresh glass.

Slevskrit snorted in relief. "All right," he said. "What happens now?"

"Wow!" said Estoril.

"Wow!" barked Slevskrit and his navigator together.

Lifting the solar panels that camouflaged them into a close approximation of the rock walls they had devoured, the latest generation of Mom's kids was sweeping down on the *Carbuncle*, dribbling bearings behind them. The boojums moved particularly fast for the first part of their rush because they were skating on the layer of ball bearings that already carpeted what had been the surface of Bileduct Base.

They moved sufficiently fast on the glass of the bomb crater also, though they sank much deeper into the shattered substrata than the relatively light corvette had done.

Carbuncle's plasma cannon fired a few useless bolts, but the gunnery officer had no time to launch nuclear missiles. That was good from the boojums' standpoint, because blasts so close might have destroyed the vessel itself.

Mom's kids had realized that they were going to run out of trace elements very quickly unless they preserved the radio and databanks of this vessel, instead of recycling it totally as ore the way they had done with the rest of their prey. . . .

They took the long view, after all. Mom would have been proud of them.

Syndicate Inspection Vessel *Matsushita* hung in a powered orbit above Bileduct Base.

"That's all they're saying?" Sub-Syndic 1st Class Whisnant demanded, knuckling his bald scalp.

"Yes, Lord Whisnant," said Cuvier, the Regional Inspector's chief aide. He cleared his throat and repeated, " 'Welcome honored guests. Join us for the Birth Celebrations of the Brightwater Clan.' "

''That's insane,'' Whisnant said.

Cuvier cleared this throat again. ''It's in Khalian, of course.''

''What's a base like this doing under Weasel control?'' Whisnant wondered aloud. ''Of course, that might explain why they apparently haven't completed any repairs in the past three months. . . .''

The Regional Inspector and his aide stared at the holographic image of Bileduct Base. There must be over three hundred ships backlogged around the HQ Tower and repair bays.

There was something funny about the ships' outline—a fuzziness, almost—but that was presumably a fault in the hologram projector.

''Right!'' Whisnant decided. ''Tell the captain to set us down. We'll soon sort things out!''

INTERLUDE

Admiral Dav Su Allison, retired
Rules of Command
27.57.CSA13.7
Security/Internal/Enforcement

. . . personnel best suited for the identification and observation of potential security risks are by their very nature those least suited to the neutralization or elimination of these risks. The physical and mental attributes necessary for successful long-term surveillance is almost the exact opposite of those needed for effective neutralization. It therefore falls within the purview of the active service personnel to second the efforts of the security services in such situations.

Such an arrangement has the further additional value of limiting the gross power of what by definition is a clandestine organization. While security and similar support services are a vital part of any military action, they are distant in nature from the mental set of typical Fleet personnel. As such, this separation tends to curb the otherwise almost unchecked power of any clandestine organization. This separation of physical and bureaucratic power is more effective than the only other technique usually used to contain the power of support services, i.e. the creation of numerous competitive support and surveillance agencies. The result of this choice is the natural tendency of each agency to spend more efforts competing than performing its designated function.

One unfortunate side effect of this policy is the involvement of line combat units in duties for which they are not totally suited. When such an action is necessary, the units chosen should be among those whose duties already involve unusual or innovative missions; the rangers, special reconnaissance and drop forces being the most obvious choices. It can be noted that all three of these groups are comprised of action- and effect-oriented personnel. As such, they should be given clear and deliberate guidelines for their behavior in, what will be for them, an unusual combat environment. These are, in a totally different manner, as highly specialized personnel as any security agent, and only by recognizing this can serious disasters be avoided.

WITCH HUNT
by Janet Morris

THIS TIME, WHEN English stuck his head into the psych evaluator, his palms began to sweat. So he fiddled around, adjusting his face's contact with the chinrest and goggles, hoping he could get himself under control before he had to put his hands on the joysticks.

He had a sore throat, a touch of the flu. He'd picked up an imported bug from ASD-Fugawi or MCA-YouNameIt, brought into the staging area by somebody else's Reaction Company. That was all. Sticking his face, for the third day in a row, into something that looked like the front half of a recon helmet with integral night-vision goggles didn't have squat to do with why he felt like this.

"Touch of the flu today, by the way," he told the automat on the other side of the glass-partitioned console into which the psych evaluator was set.

Captain Tolliver English, 92nd Marine Reaction Company (Redhorse), had learned, in three days of "standard psych evaluation" sessions, to hate the automat the way he hated Weasels. Hating Weasels was his job. Hating an artificially intelligent debriefing program on wheels was no part of that job. The automat—a squat, insect-eyed, blue-chromed, waldo-armed, self-mobile console—was programmed to take top-secret depositions and cleared for whatever it might hear in the process of certifying veterans of X-class missions fit for duty.

If it hadn't been for the Bull's-Eye operation, Toby English might never have encountered one. Then he wouldn't be sitting here sweating bullets while his mind threw up tempting scenarios starring Toby English as he a) hacked the automat into bits with a laser torch; b) knocked it off its wheels so he could listen to it bleat helplessly as he disassembled it with his pocket multiknife; c) shot it in the monitor-eye with his kinetic pistol; or d) spaced it with extreme prejudice.

Spacing it would be the choice, considering he didn't want to be billed for replacement costs. Of course, if he spaced it, he'd probably lose his command and never get to whack another Weasel. A psych discharge wasn't anything he'd ever expected to have hanging over his head. He wasn't looking for one now.

If his hands would only stop sweating, maybe he could get this over with today. It couldn't go on forever. Just his luck that Redhorse had gotten stand-down orders for MCA-0578/ASA-Zebra: ASA, as in Artificial Staging Area. If Redhorse had been handed downtime on a planet, then maybe he'd have sailed through his Psych because he'd have had a human evaluator who wasn't cleared to ask about the performance of experimental hardware such as Toby English's 92nd had carried into battle on Bull's-Eye.

But then, that hardware was probably why the 92nd was cooped up here on the ASA, under tight security. Rumors might float on a planet, even though you did your best to keep your mouth shut. On a planet there were civilians in the bars and women with children and dogs and birds and you got a taste of what you were fighting for. Human folk treated you like you mattered, because you were risking your ass to keep them safe among the stars.

ASA-Zebra was a collection of docks, repair bays, com modules, command, hospital, and resupply prefabs in orbit around an otherwise unremarkable G-type star with no planets hospitable to man or Weasel. On ASA-Zebra, everybody was on the payroll and on duty. Everybody had a rank and a vested interest. Everybody went out of their way to cut you slack if you were in for decompression. They did that because if, like Redhorse, you were in here for decompression, you flat couldn't be anywhere else:

You were too torqued down to ship into combat.

You were too privy to ship behind the lines, where there were press badges and civilians and politicians.

You were too dangerous to ship home.

You were too combatized to ship behind a desk.

Or, like Toby English, you were just too smart for your own good.

If it weren't for the fact that everybody—*everybody*—who'd fought on Bull's-Eye, including the whole of Miklos Kowacs's 121st (Headhunters), had been ordered back to ASA-Zebra for refit, English would be absolutely certain that somebody'd found out about the X-class suit his 92nd hadn't turned in the way they were supposed to do.

The X-class suit was hidden, even now, among the 92nd's gear aboard the *Haig*. Not even the *Haig*'s commander, Jay Padova, knew it was there. Most of Redhorse didn't know it was there. English and Sawyer had been coming back from watching Grant, the ISA "Civilian Observer," summarily grease all the human prisoners taken on Bull's-Eye, and the suit had appeared right in their path.

At least it had been empty. If Nellie or any of English's other Beta team casualties had been in the suit, English and his line lieutenant, Sawyer, might have turned right around and marched back there to shoot Grant in the ear, the way they were feeling.

But there was the suit, empty as deep space, complete with Associate AI-helmet, ELVIS (Electromagnetic Vectored Integrated Scalar) pack, and APOT (A-potential) rifle lying butt-to-clamshell against it. Grant had given clear and precise orders that every piece of the X-class gear be returned and any that couldn't be returned be accounted for.

They'd already accounted for the suit as part of their casualty list: one of Beta had been inside it. English and Sawyer had looked from the suit to each other and the only question either of them asked was how they were going to smuggle it aboard the *Haig*.

They were both content to let the real question, how they were going to use the suit to hang the Observer, Grant, wait until later.

But then they hadn't known they were due for R&R on ASA-Zebra.

If English or Sawyer let it slip that they had the APOT weapons system concealed aboard the *Haig*, they were going to be looking at high security automats for the rest of their lives, however long that might be.

So Toby English had more reason to sweat than he was telling the automat. Chills and a sore throat were one thing; bad dreams were another; weird after-action effects from using the APOT gear were a third. But smuggling classified test equipment—so classified that nobody was admitting it was anything more than "non-developmental items" (NDI) put together in a new way—*that* could get you an all-expenses-paid trip to Club Dead, courtesy of Fleet Intelligence.

Not all Jay Padova's clout, or all the best wishes of JCOPSCOM or citations for valorous service or even the intervention of the *Haig*'s Intel officer, Manning, would do English or Sawyer a damned bit of good if the automat figured out what was really wrong with Toby English.

And the whole of Redhorse would take it up the ass because of a phenomenon known as guilt by association.

Damn, they'd never asked to be Eight Ball Command's guinea pigs. That ought to count for something. But the drop onto Bull's-Eye had been so full of near-insubordinate acts by Captain Tolliver English of the 92nd, he'd used up whatever good will he had coming.

When you and your line lieutenant nearly shoot an ISA Observer and make no attempt to cover it up, you limit your options. English and Sawyer had been so overt about what they'd done and how they felt about the Bull's-Eye fiasco, even the mechanics on the *Haig* knew about it.

Their helmets had been running an ongoing log the whole time; never mind the purple, blinking bead that purported to off-the-record privacy when engaged during conversation.

Blinking lights on your visor display meant ISA encryption, and the Interservice Support Agency had its own playbook. Messing with Eight Ball Command was just a little less fun than getting head from a Weasel.

And in defense of Redhorse's survivability, in the face of equipment malfunctions that endangered his entire company and had gotten his Beta three-team killed, Toby English and his first officer had messed with Grant as much as they could, short of killing the sucker.

Which, in retrospect, probably would have been a good idea.

But you couldn't go back in time, any more than you could undo a screwup. When he remembered to pay attention to where he was, English was still sitting with his face in the psych evaluator in a hermetically sealed observation room on ASA-Zebra.

And the automat was saying in its simulated voice, "Captain English, your session cannot continue until you grasp the joysticks firmly with both hands. Your less-than-optimum physical condition has been noted and allowances will be made by recalibrating your 'normal' to the readings we acquire at the beginning of this session."

"Well, I dunno," English said, his hands locked firmly in his lap, sensing an advantage and pressing it. Could he get out of this, today, just by bitching enough? He'd never thought to try; he was too can-do by nature. But, still . . .

He took his head out of the psych evaluator, so he could see something besides the blackness of the unpotentiated unit. Peering around it, he made a face at the automat. "I'm really feeling crapped out. Can't we just lock this down with yesterday's session?" Among the Marines of the 92nd, AI had come to stand for Almost Intelligent. Maybe he could outfox this thing if he wasn't so damned scared of it.

"Captain English," said the automat, "please insert your face in the—"

"Okay, okay." He didn't want to collect insubordination points.

"Place your hands on the joysticks, now," said the implacable automat.

He did, finally, and as his hands made contact with the joysticks, the goggles showed him a red dot that blossomed into a fractile simulation of the Tenring firefight on Bull's-Eye.

He knew what he was seeing was drawn from data taken from his helmet scans during the action, not pulled out of his subconscious, but that didn't help one bit. The reconstruction of events began when he and Sawyer had crossed beams and he'd started seeing dinosaurs and giant amoeboid things and patches of other dimensions, but none of that was on view.

His reactions, and Sawyer's, were—though—reactions that appeared to be sharply out of phase to what was going on.

That was what he was doing here, reliving everything for the record and giving the subjective data that the system hadn't recorded.

Except this time, maybe it had. He saw a flicker in the sky over the zero-point beams' crosspoint, just above the white-out where the fire had overloaded the scanners. And he said, jumping up from the psych evaluator because he was so damned excited: "There! Did you see it? That patch of sky, humping up and splitting and showing palm trees and—"

"Sit back down, Captain English," said the automat in a sharp, commanding tone. "Resume contact with the equipment. We'll take up the sequence from where we left off."

Could an automat get pissed?

This one certainly sounded pissed. English snuck a look at the one-eyed monster torturing him before he sank down into his chair and started to stick his head back into the apparatus.

He couldn't. He just couldn't. He didn't want to go through all that again. Maybe he'd lose it if he did. What the hell was he going to do when the transcript got to the part where he and Sawyer decided they were going to shoot Grant? And then nearly did it?

"You're wasting valuable time, soldier," said the automat as if it were a drill sergeant.

Training reasserted itself. You didn't get off Eire and become a Marine captain in this man's Alliance without learning to love discipline.

English, faced with retroactive combat, narrowed his field

of focus down to the inevitable hellishness ahead. "Ain't worse than a recurring nightmare," he said aloud, very softly, through gritted teeth, and grabbed both joysticks so hard the console creaked.

The funny thing was, for some reason known only to Eight Ball Command, the purple "off the record" bead that he and Sawyer had engaged during the action seemed to have worked: there was plenty of hell in the transcript, so far as English's frayed nerves were concerned, but there wasn't anything that could be construed as a plot to murder a superior officer. Or any sign that they'd expropriated that APOT suit.

And that was nice. Although it might have been nicer if so much else Toby English had seen on Bull's-Eye hadn't been missing as well.

Manning was in the low-lit Columbia Club when English got there, and she was shitfaced. So was Trask, English's field first, sitting beside her in a corner, elbows splayed on the table among enough empties to give one apiece to the 92nd at full field strength of fifty.

English waved vaguely in their direction as he headed for the long, brass-railed bar. He'd gotten through his debrief clean, and he wanted to celebrate: he needn't go back to see the automat tomorrow, or any day. They'd scrolled through the whole transcript. The automat had told him he'd passed with flying colors.

Now all Toby English had to deal with were the weird dreams and the funny muscular twitches that followed the dreams. And the letters he had to write to the families of his Beta team, of course. And too much time to kill with nothing to fill it but memories and second thoughts and regrets.

The only cure for what was ailing English was unavailable on ASA-Zebra: he needed a mission, the tougher the better, with lots of complex preparation and an enemy at the end of it. Weasels to kill, so he could add their furry tails to his coupcoat.

Suddenly he wanted to see Sawyer, compare notes. But Sawyer wasn't in this bar. There were a dozen open bars on

ASA-Zebra, plus the service clubs. Sawyer might still be in debrief.

English stepped up to the bar, oblivious to the men on either side of him, and waited for the big bartender to notice him. Then he ordered a beer and asked to use the infone.

If he'd had his gear, he could have cued up Sawyer on his dual-com, instead of leaving word where he was with the company's service. If he'd been aboard the *Haig*, he'd have known where to look for Sawyer. If either of the above had been true, he'd have been armed and dangerous when the scuffle broke out back in the corner, right about the time the head on his beer went flat.

He didn't turn around to face the trouble right away. He had troubles of his own: Bull's-Eye just wouldn't let him be. And the bar had bouncers . . .

But glass started breaking. Furniture flew. He looked up into the bar mirror. "Damn and Weasels."

Trask and Manning were in the middle of the scuffle. Manning might be Naval Intelligence, but she was his shipmate. And he was flat responsible for Trask, the way he saw it. Short of Weasels, human adversaries would do just fine, the mood he was in.

He was halfway to the melee, now comprised of six problem-causers and another six would-be problem-solvers, when he realized that somebody was moving right with him and calling his name.

"Hey, English? Need a little help?"

"Piss off—Ah, Captain Kowacs? Yeah, that's my Top, and my NIO, in the middle there."

"Right," said the Headhunters' captain. Kowacs gave a sharp whistle and aimed a couple handsigns in the general direction of the melee. "Let's keep this in the family."

As fast as English and Kowacs moved in, his Headhunters were quicker—and closer.

By the time English reached the combat zone, it was already demilitarized. A dozen Headhunters were dispersing the combatants; three more were righting chairs and tables.

A Headhunter who looked like a lady wrestler was dressing

down a pair of bouncers so hard that the huge guys were retreating from her.

And Kowacs said to English, "If I were you, Toby, I'd offer to pay for the damage. Then everybody sits back down . . ." Kowacs's eyes were pale and demanding.

"Yeah, okay. Thanks, Nick . . . I can handle it from here."

"Nope. I want to talk to you a minute." Kowacs turned his head. "Sie," he called to the lady wrestler who had corporal's stripes under her Headhunters patch. "Square this away and get us a bill." Then Kowacs took English by the arm and led him away from Manning, Trask, and the Headhunters policing the area.

In the opposite corner at a table that emptied when Kowacs stood in front of it, the 121st's captain said, "Sit a minute."

English sat. There was a half-full glass in front of him, bubbles rising in the beer. "I said thanks, Captain."

"Don't mean nothin'. Look"—Kowacs flipped a chair and straddled it—"you've been in auto-debrief, right?"

Then English thought he knew what Kowacs wanted out of this. "Yeah. It's not as bad as you'd think. The automats back down if you get pumped up. Just going through the motions, for the record."

"And off the record?" Kowacs asked softly.

"Off the record's off the record." So maybe he didn't know what Kowacs wanted. The 121st had taken thirty percent casualties on Bull's-Eye, and lost their ship, the *Bonnie Parker*. Kowacs was probably hurting worse than he was.

"What's the record say about Bull's-Eye not being Target—not being the Khalian stronghold it was supposed to be?" Kowacs wanted to know.

What the hell was this? English's hands began to sweat again. He put them on the cool glass in front of him. "We were doing some Intel-related burn-in and I can't talk to you about it at all."

His voice sounded as sick as he felt. Did everybody who'd been on Bull's-Eye know about Grant frying the 92nd's human prisoners, the way everybody knew about the Headhunters' bad luck?

"Yeah, I can't talk situation reports to anybody but an automat these days, either. But did you know we had a human prisoner, alive, when we dusted off? Course, we don't have 'im now, and nobody knows where up-chain he went, but he's a sure sign of an Intel screwup so massive we all ought to start thinkin' about what it means.''

"It?'' Toby English was beginning to shiver because the sweat wasn't just on his palms, now; it was running down his spine and over his rib cage and soaking into his shirt. If he'd had his gear, his suit's climate control would have taken care of it. . . .

"It. Bull's-Eye wasn't Target, the Weasel motherload. Bull's-Eye didn't have shit for Weasels on it, right? No Khalians to mention. Just lots of command level equipment . . . and humans running that equipment. Think about what that means in terms of who fucked up how, friend, while you're waiting for your outfit to be filled out and tour refit spec'd up. Think hard.''

"I'm missin' somethin', Captain.''

"We all are, Toby. In particular, I'm missing my prisoner. Of course, nobody's told me we didn't take him . . . yet.''

"I think maybe I should . . .'' English changed his mind. "Maybe *we* should go find out from my Intel officer what started that row.''

English got up. Kowacs didn't. "Comin'?'' English wanted to know.

"That'd be Manning, right? From the *Haig*? Watch out for her. She's a purple suit.''

"A *what*?''

"Where you been, soldier? A purple suit: Naval Intelligence, like her papers say; and something else, as well: a dual hatter. In this case, Eight Ball Command—spooks du jour.''

Kowacs wasn't coming with him to that table, English realized. "I . . . Thanks for the help, Captain—''

"Nick's still fine, Toby. You guys stay alive, okay?''

"Yeah, we'll do that.'' So Manning was getting her orders from Eight Ball Command. After Bull's-Eye, that was no big surprise. English could have figured it out for himself if he'd been paying attention. But all he could think about was his automat debrief, that APOT suit, his lost Beta three-team, and almost killing Grant.

Then Kowacs said, without moving his lips, "And, English. . . . Watch out for the witch hunt, friend. Weasels are one thing, embarrassed Eight Ballers are something else again."

Men like Kowacs didn't spread rumors. Kowacs was telling English what he thought English needed to know because, in Kowacs's estimation, ASA-Zebra was a war zone. And also because, in Kowacs's estimation, English didn't have a clue to what was going on.

That was true enough. Kowacs's lady corporal came up as he was leaving and handed Kowacs the bill for the trouble English's people had caused.

Kowacs handed it to English. He looked at it, blinked because he didn't know how the hell he was going to pay for it except out of his own, and was muttering his thanks to Kowacs when the woman said to her captain, "Sir, did you happen to ask the Redhorse captain to give us a clean bill of health?"

"Easy, Sie. I'm not sure the scuttlebutt's right on this one."

"What the hell is going on, Captain?" English's voice was too loud. He lowered his head and waited out the stares stubbornly. He wasn't moving one inch until he got this straight. He snuck a look at the muscular corporal. It was like watching a Doberman smile at you through a chicken-wire fence.

"When they ask us," Kowacs said calmly, "if we think there are any human symps or infiltrators or agents of the Khalia in Redhorse or on the *Haig* or anywhere up your command chain, we're going to say—" Kowacs lifted his head and looked straight into English's soul. "Hell no. I guess Sie was hopin' you'd be glad to do the same."

"Mother of God," English said. "You don't think— Yeah, you do. Shit, I'll tell the world you guys are straight up, anybody bothers to ask me."

"That's good," Kowacs said with a nod, and reached out to drink the half glass of beer somebody'd left.

Clapping English on the back so that he lost his balance for a second, Kowacs's corporal said, "That's fucking great.

Sir.'' She raised an arm, made a quick fist, then extended her middle finger. ''Peace, love, an' all, sirs.'' And she backed off.

''Yeah. Peace, love, Corporal,'' English said, and walked dazedly away, afraid even to look back at Kowacs.

Manning had some explaining to do.

He slammed the damage bill down in front of her and stood there, hands on his hips. ''What was that about, Manning? I don't mind payin' Redhorse's tab, but if you started that brawl, you can damn well kick in. . . .''

Trask, beside her, pushed away from the table. The field first had a black eye and a cut lip and an inebriated wobble as he rose. ''Get off her case, okay? Sir?''

''Siddown, Toby,'' said Manning, and reached up to yank on his shirt.

This was crazy. Discipline was coming apart, here on ASA-Zebra. Everybody was coming apart. Rather than let Manning rip his shirt, English sat between her and Trask.

''What's Sawyer going to think when he shows up and finds you and Trask blitzed and banged up like this? And what was the meaning of that fight? I got a right to know . . .''

''Meaning? Right?'' Manning looked up at him blearily. Her shoulders were hunched and she was cradling her ribs with her arms. ''You don't know anything, English. Captain English. Not even when it stares you in the face. Now you're asking about meaning? The meaning of Bull's-Eye, buddy, soldier, idiot, is that we've got bigger problems than Marines're gonna handle.''

''Put her to bed, Trask. That's a direct order.''

Trask got up to do that. ''You ought to listen to her, sir. They're gonna task us one nasty mission, and maybe you ought to think if it's our job . . . or ought to be.''

''Just put her to bed, and get some sleep yourself. You're next with the automat.'' He didn't want to hear it. And then he did. ''Hey, Trask. Who's 'they'?''

Trask was lifting Manning bodily out of her chair. ''She's got cracked ribs, I bet. Her team, sir. You know: ISA.''

''No, I don't know. Nobody's talked to me about anything.'' He was beginning to get frustrated.

"Nah, we had a fistfight instead," Manning mumbled. She had a butch haircut, a prickly manner, a nasty streak. She'd given Toby English more trouble in the briefing room than any Intel officer he'd ever known. But if he was hearing her right, she'd just tried to change his orders for him. Never mind that it was before he'd gotten them.

"Anybody wants to talk to me, Manning, I'm going to be right here for the next little while, trying to figure out how to pay for all the glass you broke."

She struggled in Trask's arms and pulled something from her blouse. While English was thinking what Sawyer would make of it if he saw that little scene, she threw a card down on the table. "Charge it to us, Captain. You're on our payroll as of . . . whatever time the fight started." And she grimaced, nearly retched, then let Trask drag her away.

English waited until they were out of there before he picked up the card. It was a credit card, slugged "bearer," and damned if it didn't have a purple stripe on it.

He paid for the damage with it and decided to go to bed. Everybody knew more about what was going on around here than he did. The 121st's captain and the *Haig*'s Intel officer, Manning, seemed to be saying the same thing. But until somebody came up to him with orders, English and his Redhorse were still standing down and giving after-action reports to automats, and that was all.

He successfully told himself that for nearly twenty minutes after he got to his billet. Then the door tinkled and he slapped the viewer by his bed. There was Sawyer, who needed a shave. He'd left word for Sawyer to get with him . . . Beside Sawyer was Manning, her face scrubbed and her short hair combed, standing stiffly as if she'd had her ribs taped.

He punched the lock and the intercom. "Okay, come on in."

He wasn't getting out of bed for this. He was just a little relieved to see Sawyer and Manning together: Sawyer was the only one who'd ever had a handle on Johanna Manning.

But Sawyer didn't look happy. He walked her inside and said, "I gotta wait out—"

"The hell you do, Sawyer. You're not subject to Navy orders." God, he hated this shit. "Manning, what's up?"

"I'm hand-delivering these sealed orders to you, as I've been requested. Any problems, you're to take them up with the Observer here on ASA-Zebra. I'm supposed to stay while you read them and ascertain that you have read them and do understand them. Then I'm to take the hard copy with me."

"And the Observer is someone we all know and love, right?" Grant, the pig-bastard. English felt like he'd just fallen through a false floor into a Weasel's stake-pit.

"So far's the automat's concerned, that's right, sir." Sawyer was looking at his big hands.

"Let's see it then, Manning." Still under his blanket, naked, he reached out for the packet.

Manning handed the orders over.

English read them twice to make sure he understood what was stated and what was implied. Then he said, "We don't do this sort of thing. We're not trained for it. You tell—"

"Captain," Manning reminded him, "if you see problems with this, you're to take it up with somebody who can do some goddamn thing about it, and that's not me."

"Balls." English swung his legs out of bed, forgetful of his nakedness, and stopped with the blanket across his groin. "Look, off the record, you two: what do you want me to do?"

"We can't get that far off the record, sir," said Sawyer. "And you're the only one who's seen the specifics. Redhorse'll go where you point 'em."

"Thanks, Sawyer. Manning, I'll deal with the Observer. You won't have to."

"Thank you, Captain," said Manning primly. "May I suggest compliance?"

"Why's that?"

"Better to be on the dispensing end than on the receiving end of this, if I may say so, Captain," said Manning again.

Damn these Intel types and their subtext. She was looking at him keenly and so was Sawyer. If these two had any sense, they'd break off their affair. Sleeping together wasn't an excuse for anything, but it was a reason for more than English liked, perhaps even half the troubles Redhorse had had with the Observer.

"I'll go see your brass, Manning. And I'll tell him what you said, don't worry about that. Sawyer, you finished with your automat?"

"Yes, sir. Went clean."

"Then you come with me. Officer Manning can find her way back by herself, or she ought to have her rating pulled."

Manning took the sheaf of orders and left stiffly.

When the door closed, English said, "Why don't you quit messing with her, Sawyer? Kowacs from the 121st flat told me she's an Eight Ball Command staffer. He knew all about those orders. Wanted a little slack. If not for her, none of us would be in this mess."

"Then we'd be among the possible targets. Sir."

"Yeah, that's so. Okay, let's go see the man. And be nice, Sawyer, until we see if this is the moment we've both been waiting for."

There was always a chance of that. If the 92nd was going to be the witch hunters, then which witch they hunted ought to be up to them. The orders from ISA said "good and sufficient reason to believe that approximately thirty to forty human Alliance personnel serving in various capacities on ASA-Zebra are actually enemy agents." The rest of it told him to use whatever measures he saw fit "to identify and arrest and/or eliminate these threats to Fleet security."

In other words, pick out some poor suckers, anybody if you couldn't find the right somebodies, and deal with them harshly enough that any agents you might miss will be scared enough to screw up or quit.

The bitch was, he hadn't the faintest idea where to start. He was a Reaction Marine, not a private investigator or an Intel type. So it was off to see the Observer and find out who it was that the Observer wanted English and his 92nd to wax in the name of security.

As he pulled on his coveralls and strapped on his kinetic pistol because he wasn't in any mood to go see Grant without it, he thought that if there was some way that Grant could be fingered as part of the purported nest of infiltrators, Grant would have picked somebody else's company to do his dirty work.

But then, you never knew why Intel did what it did.

The one thing English knew for sure was that the 92nd had gotten tapped for this because every manjack of them knew for certain that there were humans working willingly with the Khalia. They'd dropped onto Bull's-Eye, expecting Khalians, and found everything that should have been on Target except Khalians: ships, command bunkers, com systems—everything.

They'd found men, women, children . . . many of whom preferred suicide to being taken by other humans. The rest, Grant had disposed of out of hand. So using Redhorse, who already knew there were humans working for the Weasels, was one way to limit the privy parties.

Maybe Grant would behave himself, this time. Maybe there really were Weasel-symp infiltrators in the Fleet's command structure. Maybe that was why these missions kept screwing up. Maybe it was even the reason, if you wanted to stretch a point, that the 121st was thirty percent shy of a full clip.

But it wasn't the reason that English had lost his Beta three-team during the Bull's-Eye insertion. The reason for that was Grant and his APOT test gear, clear and simple.

As he was walking down the hall with Sawyer, headed for the tube that would take them to the command module where the ISA office was, English kept thinking about the stolen hard suit and wondering if Grant had any idea how long the men of Redhorse could hold a grudge.

And Sawyer said, as they came to the tube and he pushed the button to call a car, "How come, you think, everybody—Headhunters and all—knew before we did? Think Grant's trying to make us secondary targets? Because if he is . . ."

"Back to plan A?" They really had been going to smoke the bastard, for good reason. In close quarters like this, nobody was going to love Redhorse going around sniping various and sundry personnel at will.

Nobody.

If security didn't improve one hell of a lot, this mission was going to be as dangerous as Bull's-Eye. Worse, maybe, depending on whose friends turned out to be the 92nd's targets.

Sitting ducks weren't fair game. But then, with Eight Ball Command, fair was beside the point.

"Plan A's fine with me, anytime, sir—now that we're through with our automats. . . . About Manning," Sawyer said like it hurt to form the words. "She's a good soldier, I told you before. You'll have to take my word for it, if her gettin' three ribs busted in some bar tonight tryin' to object to those orders doesn't mean nothin' to you."

So Manning hadn't told Sawyer that English had been on the scene. Maybe English could include Manning as one of the infiltrators he was tasked to take out: after all, it was just a numbers game.

If Grant knew who the hell he was looking for, he wouldn't need Reaction Marines to find them. The 92nd was in this to flush any real bogeys and bag as many others as would satisfy Eight Ball Command. So long as those others couldn't prove they were innocent, who they were wasn't going to matter one bit.

The car, when it came, looked like a bodybag on wheels to Toby English.

"Let's get it over with, Sawyer." There just wasn't any other choice.

"Killing Weasels is war. Killing Alliance humans is murder, the way I see it," English said thickly, backed up against the wall in Grant's fancy-ass ISA office.

The Civilian Observer tapped something on a desk that was big enough to sleep two. A screen behind him cleared and started running Bull's-Eye transcript right out of English's helmet—the stuff that hadn't been in the automat's banks.

"Shit," said Toby English, shaking his head.

"Don't take it so hard, Captain." The Observer had this tweaky red silk cord knotted around his wrist; he played with it. "We don't want to see you back in automat debrief, going through this whole other datapack, any more than you do. Or your lieutenant Sawyer does, or any of your boys do." He tapped his desktop keypad again and the datapull froze, then disappeared.

"Find somebody else." English's lips were numb. He crossed his arms over his chest to make sure he knew what his hands were doing. He still had that pistol on his hip.

"Now why would I do that?" Grant wanted to know. "I told you there wouldn't be any trouble over Bull's-Eye, and I kept my word. That ought to be sufficient show of good faith."

"It ain't."

"Again, mister, we're not *asking*. You're the right tools for the job. We chose you out of a number of candidate units, long before Bull's-Eye. You're ours, and we're going to take good care of you. You ought to be asking me about weapons and procedures, considering this is all going to go down on an ASA."

English was prayerfully glad that Grant had made Sawyer wait in the anteroom. He was having enough trouble controlling himself. "This is legal? You can just co-opt us for this kind of duty?"

"Now that you ask, you've got carte blanche: try and leave the ASA intact. Beyond that, do it however you choose. And yes, you've got a tight time frame: forty-eight hours, max. Twenty-four is better. Six is best: don't give them any warning."

English gave up. He rubbed his forehead. "I'll get stuff off the *Haig*. Assuming I can requisition whatever naval support I think I need?"

"That's what Manning's for." Grant was a big thoroughbred spook with home-world manners. The nameplate on the door to this office said Deputy Director, Interagency Support Activity. Either the Observer had pulled a promotion after Bull's-Eye, was here under false pretenses, or was way up-chain from where English and Sawyer could hope to touch him. With a jovial smile, Grant leaned across the huge desk to hand English a piece of flashpaper. "Here's your target list."

English had to take it. At least there was one—a real list, with real names. It wasn't his business how the Observer had

determined those names. Not once he'd seen the transcript
Grant had held back from the automat.

He tried to read the list but the names blurred, or else his
hand was shaking too much. "Who do I report to when this
is done, you or Manning?"

"If I've left, Manning will do. Good hunting, English,"
said Grant.

"Um . . . what about parameters?"

"There aren't any, beyond dead or alive, and I don't care
about that, although some may. Tag any live ones for me at
MAC-ASD, and ship 'em back there. But not too many. Clear
enough?"

"Oh, yeah," said English. He'd better get out of there
before he started demanding to know whether Grant was getting bumped upstairs because of what had happened on Bull's-
Eye, or because of the list English had in his hand. "Ah—can I
have a phone number for you, if I need you?"

"As I said: that's what Manning's for. Good luck. Special
ops are always tricky. That'll be reflected in your payscale."

"Well, that makes it just dandy peachy keen. Sir."

There was no use arguing with the Observer. English had
tried it before and ended up here with this list in his hand.
He had to get out of there before he did something stupid
enough that he couldn't survive it. Because, short of a two-
shot burst to the well-manicured head, there was nothing he
could do to Grant.

This whole mess was as button-down as the Civilian Observer himself.

When English wandered blindly through the anteroom and
found Sawyer by the coffee machine, he said, "We're sheep-
dipped." And shrugged. "Here's the list. Hold onto it for
me."

In the state he was in, he didn't trust himself not to lose
it.

Sawyer didn't comment until they were out of the office
complex and in the tubeway. "Where we goin', Cap'n?"

"Back to the *Haig*." Somehow, saying it made him feel
better. "I want everybody back there by twelve hundred.

Anybody still in auto-debrief, you can use our new clout to get 'em waived.''

"You sure?'' Their car came. They got in and dialed the *Haig*'s dock.

"Nope. But it's worth a try.''

Sawyer pulled out the list. "You want this now?''

"No. Yeah.'' He took it. "Well, now we find out what it feels like to be sanctioned assassins.''

"You kidding?''

"Nope. What'd you think?''

"He said that?''

"You know he didn't say that. We can send some back—not too many, though.''

"Terrific.'' Sawyer's expression was unreadable as they sped through the tubeway and marker lights strobed in the car's windows.

"Don't assume we won't face lethal resistance. There's a real list. For all I know, the guys on it might be real traitors. We gotta think that way, 'cause we'll never know for sure.''

"Human Khalian agents burrowed into the Fleet . . . if they are real, I won't have any trouble with this.''

English wished he could say that. He wasn't sure whether Sawyer meant it, either, but Sawyer was giving him a way to present it to the 92nd that sounded better than expedient murder.

"Well, great. You pump up the troops. Let's split up the targets and figure the teams. . . .''

You did the job, whatever it was. You didn't worry about why your orders were cut, or you went crazy. English had to look out for his men. This wasn't a democracy, it was the Fleet.

Everybody in the APC knew the score, but English did the final briefing in there anyway. The APC was discreetly secure and had countermeasures up the ass. Plus, some of them were going to be using it for basing and tactical maneuvering—and to store the prisoners, alive and/or dead.

You couldn't ask Jay Padova to get the *Haig* this dirty; English hadn't tried. Because of the rumor mill, he'd told

Padova what he was about—at least enough that Jay wasn't worried for his butt or any of his crew's. And because, once this started, Redhorse wasn't going to be real popular, and Redhorse was shoehorned into the *Haig*, so Padova's personnel might take some of the flak meant for English's 92nd.

So Padova had to know.

It was Jay's damned APC, and English had it armed to the teeth from the mothership's stores.

The 92nd wasn't going to take a single casualty on this one. Grant wanted Reaction Marines for his sterilization mission, he was going to get 'em. English had ordered full kit, including recon rules, so everybody was running a log. In case there were questions later.

Each man was fully armored and armed as if the 92nd was dropping onto a Weasel-infested planet. Sawyer had done the pep talk, and nobody was arguing about the mission.

You found the guys on the list. You gave 'em one call on your bullhorn to surrender. You fired one warning burst of rubber-foil ammo that wouldn't pierce the module skins. If they offered resistance, you shot them.

If they offered lethal resistance, you shot them dead.

It was clear. It was clean. It sucked.

Everybody in the APC knew it. They'd never asked to be some kind of elite secret police, or whatever this equated to. But they knew how to take orders. English kept wondering how it was going to be after this was over, when you ran into the inevitable shit from other companies.

First you had to live through it.

He toggled his all-com once he'd settled his helmet on his head. They were all in their suits and buttoned up, as overpowered as they could be for fighting guys on stand-down and Fleet staffers. But there were plenty of firearms on ASA-Zebra.

English said, "You've got your targets. Don't underestimate them. It's life and death for these guys. That means it's life and death for us. Some of them may be happy to surrender and spend the next few years in chemical interrogation before they face a firing squad, but I don't think that'll be the majority. Don't get sloppy. Systems checks . . . on my mark—''

They checked out.

The APC pulled away from the *Haig*'s belly. Maybe you could argue that security might have been better preserved without the APC, and their identities as well, if not for the fact that everybody on ASA-Zebra had known more than English about what was coming down.

What they didn't know was how.

''Manning, got your end together?''

They had her with them, and she was as snug as a bug in her clamshell armor. Sawyer personally checked her gloves as the running lights came up.

English went forward to sit with Trask, who was flying the bird.

Manning touched English's leg as he passed. He shunted onto dual-com and said, ''What is it?'' on her helmet's channel.

''Are you sure about the—last part?''

''No, but I'm gonna do it anyway because I'm a stubborn bastard and I can't have shit hanging over my head like that. You clear it like you're supposed to. Say whatever you think makes sense. Okay?''

''Okay, Captain. I was just confirming.''

He shifted over to all-com, monitoring the banter to see if it was anywhere near healthy-sounding.

It was close enough. They all knew this was an error-free environment, repercussionwise. Except, of course, if you got yourself dead.

Trask was glad to see him. ''How many Fleet commanders does it take to screw in a lightbulb?''

''Dunno,'' English admitted.

''Ten: one to hold the ladder, one to do the screwing, one to write the after-action report, and seven to stand around saying, 'Shit, I coulda done that.' ''

The stars outside seemed so clean and pure that English couldn't look at them. So he looked at the ASA instead. ''How soon to the first dock?''

"Six and twenty . . . three secs. I'll put it on your sweep. . . ."

"Put it on everybody's."

Everybody got the timetable in the right quadrant of their heads-up displays, with the designated two-team's callsign blinking beside it.

He heard them moving into position; Sawyer and the dropmaster were both back there. He didn't need to do anything but watch for error-makers or untoward opposition.

In the copilot's seat was the joystick for the new underbelly cannon. KKDs—kinetic kill devices—came out of those cannon at 30,000 mph; when you were shooting a five-pound metal slug that fast, you didn't need explosives.

The APC had conventional hardware for ground support as well, but English didn't think he was going to need it.

If somebody tried a nonsched flight, and it was an obvious cut-and-run, they'd have to deal with it, though. That was one case of the five that English had determined as shoot to kill/shoot on sight.

The rest of the possibilities had discretionary parameters. *Naw, you don't have to shoot the guy in his pjs if you break into his room and he's with his girlfriend; you don't have to shoot the girlfriend, unless she shoots at you. . . .*

The first docking maneuver was at the agronomy bay; Trask mated the APC to the module without a hitch. The Alpha team deployed.

All of Toby English's hair stood on end.

Communications were going to be dicey if Manning had been wrong about her ability to route their helmet chatter through security-only x-bands. But she'd been sure she had it knocked.

When everything English could want to see and hear, including full frontals from the recording helmets, came up on his own visor when he asked for them, he relaxed and shut them down to emergency-interrupts.

That made his two-man Alpha team into a pair of little dots in their grid on the upper left of his visor. You can only handle so much data in your heads-up display. If you get more than you can use, you and your com system go into a descending efficiency curve.

The command helmets offered more than anyone could want; what you learned was how much to ask for, and when.

He'd get a prompt, a little goose like a minor electric shock on his left wrist, if Alpha sent signals outside what was considered operationally normal. Unless that happened, it was his choice how much or little he wanted to monitor of their mission.

He didn't want any of it, beyond what he needed to keep them alive. And there wasn't much any of the rest could do to help a team in trouble, until everybody was in place—and not a hell of a lot then.

The ASA targets were too damned spread out. But English had gone over and over it—in his head, with Sawyer, even with Manning, and decided simultaneous was best.

Otherwise, by the time they got to the tail-end of the list, they were going to have suicides and booby traps and who-knew what-all.

These people knew who they were; once the action started, they were going to get real unpleasant to encounter.

Redhorse wasn't running a Beta team—too close to having one get dead. They dropped their next three teams at the main personnel module, and English checked his real time against his projected time: three seconds early, so far.

Trask took the APC over the top of the ASA and dropped her vertically through the middle, to get to the science modules, where they dropped the next two teams. Then they accessed the command dock and, after that, three repair bays.

With more than half their teams deployed, they were still ahead of schedule. It was like shooting fish in a barrel. Nobody left in the APC was saying a word.

You could hear their breathing in the all-com, and the effect of all that respiration in this situation was surreal.

So much so, English almost missed the little blip, going away, that Trask saw scooting out of the command module's private garage.

"Where does that asshole think he's going to *go*?" Trask wanted to know.

There wasn't anyplace out here to land where you could survive. The blip was a little speedster, a personal vehicle, nothing with interstellar range.

"I got it," English said. These really had to be his decisions; it was what command was about. "Stay on timetable with your drops, Trask."

He fired one of his KKDs, after a quick lock-on and a servo-change to a smart round with heat-seeking.

"We'll figure out who it was from who we missed and what the ship's ID is when we look at the data later." He wanted it on the record that he'd been assiduous in his pursuit of perfect performance. You couldn't tell for sure, of course, that some teenager hadn't chosen just the wrong moment to steal a joyride.

But the data that the APC was able to take gave him a target that fit preprogrammed parameters; the lock-on would have created a warning beep on the other craft. If it had sent the APC something benign enough, English's fire order would have dudded out.

When the smart KKD sped away, the rest was academic.

This equipment didn't fail. It was you who took that chance.

They dropped all but Trask, Manning, Sawyer, and the dropmaster before English had time to think about anything but his battle management electronics.

Then came the hard part: "Okay, gang. We're going to these coordinates." English pecked them into the console himself. He didn't want any doubt about whose responsibility the ensuing action was going to be.

Then he slid out of his seat beside Trask and went back into the hauler's body. "Git forward," he said to the dropmaster. "You too, Manning," he told the small suited figure sitting beside Sawyer, their helmets together.

Once she'd done that, Sawyer and he closed the slider between compartments and locked it.

"Ready?" English asked Sawyer.

"You bet," Sawyer said, and checked the air pressure of the crew compartment manually before he started getting the components of the APOT suit out of the locker where they'd stowed it.

English found, when he'd stripped out of his issue suit and was faced with the X-class equipment, that his hesitancy to get into it was nearly overwhelming.

He just stood there, because that was about the best he could manage.

Sawyer must have realized how hard it was, because the other's gloved hand came down on his naked shoulder: "You ready, sir?"

They didn't have any way of knowing whose suit this had been—Nellie's or somebody else's. They'd gone through it for blood, guts, brains, pieces of human anatomy, and found only some dust. They'd checked it for penetrations or violations and found no such.

But this APOT suit/weapon combination had been part of Beta's complement of three. All the men and the other two suits had been lost, but for part of a scanner. Then this suit had popped back into real-time . . .

Maybe this one had some malfunction that was going to dump English out into some alternate space-time when he fired it up.

If it did, that was just what was going to happen, because he was going to put it on, seal it up, slip on the ELVIS pack, put the APOT rifle in contact with the ceramic clamshell, potentiate the Associate AI-assisted expert system and all the electronics connected with it, and go get himself a Weasel-symp infiltrator.

Let 'em try to figure out who the hell it was, doing what he was about to do, with his 92nd all nice and recognizable, spread over the whole of ASA-Zebra.

"Let's see the list again," he said to Sawyer, and Sawyer got it out.

English looked it over one more time and put it between his teeth. Then he started fitting himself into the X-class suit he and Sawyer had smuggled aboard the *Haig* after Bull's-Eye.

When he had the ELVIS pack over the clamshell and the gloves mated to the suit's sleeves and the helmet on his head, visor up, he took the list from between his teeth.

"Got a match?"

Sawyer grinned at him bleakly and put a glow on the end of his standard-issue plasma rifle. Touched to it, the list flared into a puff of smoke between English's gloved fingers. "Okay, boss?" Sawyer wanted to know.

"Yep," English said, before he pulled his visor down. "Next stop, XO-command module."

Sawyer dropped his own visor, and they spent the next few minutes getting the so-called NDI suit to talk to Sawyer's standard-issue suit.

"One more thing," Sawyer asked as their clock ran down to seconds, "you're sure about calling that strike?"

"Sure as I've ever been about anything in my life," English said. Which wasn't saying much, but that was another issue.

They didn't let the dropmaster, Manning, or Trask back off the flight deck. No need for Manning to see the APOT suit. No need to involve Trask, either.

Orders were orders. And they had theirs. They were supposed to do this stinking job, and they'd do it.

The whole time English had been struggling into that APOT suit, feeling like he was sharing it with a ghost, Sawyer had been doing the command monitoring for the whole company.

English ported the data into his system, doing a quick, verbal headcheck to verify.

So far, so good: the 92nd had three live prisoners, which was plenty. They'd had seven additional encounters—two firefights were under way. If you call something a firefight when you had field gear and the adversary was in his jogtogs with a rubber-bullet spitting sidearm.

Still: they shoot at you, you shoot back.

A rubber bullet in the brain would get you just as dead as a plasma bolt. He reminded everybody of that on all-com, and verified that the three teams with prisoners should go to the pickup area, not attempt to reinforce those still working.

What he needed to know was, where everybody was. And to make sure nobody wandered into any areas they couldn't be told to avoid. That kept Sawyer and English as busy as if they were trying to coordinate a drop over ten miles of Weasel-infested jungle.

It kept English busy all through the final docking maneuver and their debarkation procedure. Then he and Sawyer were in the ASA heading down halls they'd only been through once before. At an intersection, English and Sawyer split up, and Sawyer gave him a clap on the back that wouldn't show on any signature recorder.

Then he was by himself, stalking around the command module in his nonreg armor, his APOT rifle semi-ported because it had to be in contact with the suit to fire.

When he found the door he wanted, he didn't bother to knock. He melted it with the APOT rifle. It made a nice, satisfying sizzle he could hear on his audio, and his air purification system turned itself up a notch.

The room with the huge desk wasn't empty. He'd been afraid it would be. He'd been worried the son of a bitch would have cleared out, lock, stock, and incriminating transcript.

But Grant wasn't the man in there. Just about the time English realized that, his APOT system was on full bore, hosing down whoever was behind the desk, and especially the electronics and database and screen.

He'd forgotten about the APOT effects: he was seeing . . . what? Someplace else, intermittently; someplace with grass and trees and people on it. Young people. Old people. People with four arms. . . . And furry birds in a green sky.

He didn't realize he was yelling at the top of his lungs until he managed to stop firing the damned thing. His shooting hand felt like it had been chewed on by an electric eel.

But there wasn't shit left of the whole inside wall of Grant's office. Metal partitions came slamming down to seal it off from the rest of the complex. Sprinklers began raining from the ceiling.

Fuck! You couldn't predict what this APOT system would do when it was wet. English backed out of there without even checking what was left of the body that had been rising behind the desk.

There wasn't much of anything in there that he was willing to remember.

He felt like some monster, tromping through the command module. People saw him and ducked away, under their desks.

Women screamed and hugged filing cabinets. He was sure glad his name wasn't stenciled on his helmet, or his unit patch.

He kept worrying about the droplets of water on his shoulders, on his faceplate, on the rifle.

Sawyer had shot one of these things lying in a puddle once, and the results had been uncontrollable.

He had one more thing to do before he ditched the suit. He hoped Manning had done what she'd been told.

He was damn sure that Sawyer did what he'd been told.

It took less time than English expected to get to the debriefing module. By then, he'd been in contact with ASA security once, with Sawyer twice, and with every one of his 92nd, making sure that nobody needed him more than he needed to do what he had in mind.

This was for himself, for his team, and for everybody else who'd been on Bull's-Eye. Only he couldn't let its importance supercede his duty, such as it had devolved into.

Damn, he was feeling sick about that Eight Ball officer in Grant's chair, but only because he'd never met him. Every one of his troops had either shot or arrested some stranger on this mission; he couldn't let that get to him. Eight Ball Command was responsible for the loss of English's Beta team, and for these damned APOT weapons being in the field.

Because they'd *be* in the field. There was no stopping a technology that promised higher kill ratios, not unless those kill ratios turned out incontrovertibly to be among the users. And that day was a long way off, with the kind of security Eight Ball was invoking.

Interagency Support Activity, my ass. Insulate Superior Asses, more likely. Well, if he'd been lucky, it would have been Grant.

He didn't need luck; he had competence. All the records of the Bull's-Eye drop that the automat didn't have were in that console. Manning had confirmed that for him. And she'd said, when he'd asked her why the hell she was involved in something like this:

"I'm . . . trapped, English. Just like you guys. Because of you—Sawyer, really. And look, we'll handle it. Grant's got a mongo promotion coming through. He'll get home-world posting. It's crazy to try to touch him. Yes, he picked on your company because of me, but he was able to jack me around because of how I've . . . come to feel . . . about your— Redhorse. So we'll live with it. It's an honor, supposedly, to be pulled up out of something like Reaction into an elite core of Intel support—''

"Bag the rationalization, okay, Manning? I got some stuff I want you to do. For the honor of it.''

And she'd been good under pressure, so far.

And he'd had some slack on the list: two Intel officers, unspecifiable except in response to above actions.

English was cleared to kill anybody who tried to cut and run, or waved a gun at him, from the Intel contingent. And, thinking back on it, he was sure he'd seen a gun in the hand of the guy behind Grant's desk.

When he found the automat debriefing chambers, he went carefully. He was still listening to his all-com chatter, but as they'd arranged, Sawyer was running the field plays. English was interjecting only enough to make sure that everybody's com systems recorded him as taking part in the mission.

The hallway of the automat chambers had six doors on it. Weapon high, he slammed his armored shoulder into the first, telling the wide-eyed respondent in the interrogation chair to "Get the hell out, and take the others with you.''

Once he'd made sure that the guy had a good look at a suit that was like nothing he'd ever seen before, English shot the automat in the console with the APOT rifle, just as it was saying, "Place your face in the psych—''

It went up like a firecracker and that made him feel good.

The guy he'd rousted was banging on doors as he went, but English had to invite three more respondents to leave. That was all right. These APOT suits had such weird characteristics, you could never tell who the hell, from when, might be in one. And nobody was going to want him to start making that argument. The suit, after all, didn't exist. Not yet.

When no more automats existed, Toby English barred the

door of the last debriefing room with what was left of the last automat and stripped off the APOT suit.

Then he opened the closet door there, only at the last moment entertaining an assessment of how royally fucked he was if Sawyer and Manning hadn't done what he'd asked, perfectly and without any margin for error.

Waiting there was a regulation combat suit, with 92nd's Redhorse stenciled on the helmet, and his own name besides.

He nearly collapsed as he got into it. Next he put the APOT gear in the same closet, then went trotting down the hall.

Once he'd checked to see that absolutely nobody remained in that module, he could call in his APC strike.

If the damned suit, like some albatross, came back after that, then there was nothing Toby English was going to do about it.

He stood for a moment in the empty module, his plasma rifle butted on his hip, one arm against the doorframe, his visor down, seeing on it his outfit's blips as they made their way to the pickup point.

It was always a strange feeling to stand somewhere you knew was going to cease to exist once you'd called your fire down.

But nobody was going to get hurt—nobody else, anyway. Everybody had done just what he'd been told, and Sawyer affirmed for him that the 92nd hadn't taken a single hit.

So he said, "Let's do it, girls. I got one I can't handle in grid-square 101A, with heavy hardware and a ship at the dock. Take it out, Trask: ain't nothin' but hardware and the one shooter to loose."

Then he shut the door, whacked the safety bulkhead on his way out, and headed for the tubeway.

Pickup was for fourteen forty-five hours and he didn't want to be late. He had a lot of electronic pilfering to do, from Sawyer's action log, before he'd look like he and the suit he was wearing were any part of the cleanup that Eight Ball Command had ordered on ASA-Zebra.

When the bang came and the warning lights lit and sirens began to howl, he was already in the tubeway, safe in his pressurized car. For just a second, he allowed himself to enjoy the aftershock from the destroyed debriefing module. Shit, he did like his APC.

Then he toggled his all-com and said, "Nice job, Redhorse. I'm on my way down. Officer Manning will receive and log your prisoners."

He almost wished there weren't any to log, especially if they were innocent. But one way or another, the prisoners would disappear just as surely as the Headhunters' prisoner had. It would be a cold day in hell before Eight Ball Command asked the 92nd to do another cleanup, what with all the property damage they'd inflicted.

You had to understand the way the system worked, and not lose your temper. Then, almost anything was possible. Especially when there wasn't a Bull's-Eye transcript kicking around this man's universe. Or an unaccountable APOT suit.

If English's 92nd had to get a reputation for this sort of thing, you just needed to make sure it was the right reputation. So far as the spies went—well, maybe they were Weasel agents after all.

That was what English was going to tell his Redhorse to say, anyhow. It was what he was going to say to the 121st's captain when he found him, as soon as English got through writing to the families of his Beta casualties.

No need to have the Headhunters up all night worrying that the 92nd had just begun its sweep.

INTERLUDE

Brevet Lieutenant LeBaric woke as his forehead hit one corner of the study cube. Grimacing, he came awake and fingered the bump. A quick look at the chronometer explained his exhaustion. He had been studying Allison on Command for seven straight hours. This was certainly service above and beyond the call of duty. If only they had given him more warning of the exam. But the date had been set at Port and these things took time to filter out to the far edges of the Alliance. Carefully he tried to reconstruct what he had just read, but his mind was a blank. A few hours sleep, he promised himself, and back to the grind.

At this point, the intercom in his cabin buzzed. Slapping off the privacy seal he had given himself as acting captain, Auro saw it was Remra, the *Red Ball*'s Hruban pilot and his executive officer until Meier returned.

"We have been ordered to make an orbital adjustment," she informed him. It was hard to tell with any alien, but her expression seemed concerned. The pilot's next comment confirmed it. "Have you been injured?"

Auro tried to look awake and fingered his forehead. He must have blackened one eye. That'll impress the review board.

"Just a minor accident," he assured the Hruban. "Am I needed on the bridge?"

"Technically, yes," Remra explained. "As acting commander you are responsible for the ship's movements. Even though this one is to a preset orbit and will be entirely handled by the flagship's computers.''

There was a short pause. Remra looked worried again.

''Look, I'll be right up,'' Auro decided. Even a minor glitch this close to the exam would disqualify him. Better safe, if tired, than sorry. You never knew what could go wrong.

PEST CONTROL

by Diane Duane and Peter Morwood

IT HAD BEEN their success in finding Bull's-Eye that had brought Roj Malin and the olympus-class brainship Minerva to the attention of Fleet Strategic Planning. Admiral of the Red Meier had praised them both to the skies, promoted Roj not one kick up but two, Makin imull Captain—and then explained why. They could have refused the mission, of course; the wily old bastard had left them that much of a loophole, but after all the yaha on the Omni channels backing out had become impossible. Of course. That he "should only grow headfirst in the ground like a turnip . . ." was the least of the things Minerva had wanted the admiral to do after that. He didn't oblige. So here they were, back in Khalian space, back in the fixtures and fittings that disguised RM-14376 Minerva as the Khalian Fencer B-4bis that she most definitely wasn't.

With all systems shut down, the brainship was little more than a cylindrical extrusion on the mass of metal that had once been an Alliance troop carrier. Before a flight of Khalian ships had bounced it during the battle for Bull's-Eye and left it less than scrap. One of the transports that Abe Meier and Auro Le Baric—respectively the admiral's grandson and the Hero of Bethesda, no less—hadn't managed to save despite their crazy stunt with the freighters. Neither parentage nor fame had done this ship or its people any good at all. It was just one more piece of battle garbage among a thousand others, a Fleet ship apparently rammed and wrecked by a suicidal Khalian, rotating its slow, unnoticed way deep into the lethal quadrant of space surrounding the world called Khalia.

And forty hours in its wake was an invasion fleet.

It was called CASE WHITE. The fleet had been on hold over Bull's-Eye for almost a week before the go-code came through. There had been the usual multiple-eventuality plans, each one with its pros and cons carefully weighed out by the Strategic Advisory, but every scenario boiled down to the same move: hit Khalia, and keep hitting it until the Weasels yelled uncle. It would have been far simpler to use Plan POSEIDON, a massed flight of thermo-tipped seeker remotes keyed to home on plate-faults and crack the planet like an egg, but always there had been the need to get onto the surface and gather information, about surviving Khalian raiding-ships, about codes and cyphers, about the Syndics. And those strategic demands meant an invasion. Men on the ground. Men's guts on the ground . . .

Despite all of that, the risks and the projected massive casualties, people like Kowacs's Headhunters were looking forward to returning long-accrued interest on what the Weasels had been so good at dishing out. Every second ship in the initial wave was a ground-assault dropship carrying Marine Reaction units, and the 121st was slated to be first in. CASE WHITE called for orbital bombardment of selected sites followed by low-altitude strategic suppression as the Marines went in. Parts of Khalia would be glazed over and what was left subjected to a much more personal trashing. That—the ultimate personal treatment—was what CASE WHITE was all about.

Before the military suppression by bomb and ASM and plasma cannon, another was required. The Khalian indigenous population had to be discouraged from overenthusiastic resistance. That was Minerva's mission.

The initial plan put forward by Fleet Strategic Planning had been to air-burst a chain of stratospheric thermos and fill the atmosphere of Khalia with enough cobalt-thorium to leave the planet glowing for a hundred years. After further analysis, they realized that it wouldn't have worked: not that ninety-seven years was too long to grill the Weasels on a radioactive spit, because it wasn't—but even with a degraded half-life, the most optimistic projections pegged twenty years after deployment before anything could walk on the surface of Khalia and come back to talk about it.

ERMs were out for the same reason. Enhanced radiation and reduced blast—the vaunted neutron bomb of the history books—were tac-use only, with warheads of about one kiloton max, and what the planners were talking here required a total yield of six thousand *mega*tons. Which brought in a cumulative flash/blast factor that took them right back to the reasons for scrapping POSEIDON.

The special operation known as FIREFROST required only one fast ship with drones and rotary launchers carrying a very particular ordnance package: the biodegradable short-persistence agent known to the Fleet as GK-2.

Nerve gas.

Delivered onto targets already cross-referenced against earlier data as suitable assault-landing sites, it would kill, disable, or force into shelters any would-be aggressive civilians in the area. Any military defenders without time to suit up would be taken out in the same firing pass, and it would reduce the effectiveness of the remainder by keeping them wrapped in NBC clothing and respirators for six long, hot days during which they could neither eat, drink, piss, or shit outside their suits. Strat/Tac analysts reckoned that with the faster Khalian metabolism, six standard days would be just enough to take the edge off them before the Marines went in. Because, outnumbered God alone knew how-many-to-one, the Marines were going to need every edge that they could get.

* * *

"Back in Khalian space, pretending to be Khalians," said Minerva, apropos of nothing. "We did this before, and I didn't like it then."

"Yeah. And you volunteered then, too." Roj Malin didn't look up from the schematics board in front of him. As brawn to an olympus-class brainship, there was nobody to look at, unless you happened to count the big main-survey lens on the armor cladding of Minerva's core. "Number two drone, systems status?"

"Drone two: all onboards green, one hundred percent."

"Confirmed." The constant-analysis transmissions between the schematics readout on Minerva's weapons board and the two dozen MARV drones hangared in a cavity within the wrecked troop-transport were by tight-beam laser, with no chance of signal overspill or monitoring, but he still felt unhappy at having to break silence at all. They were less than five AU out from Khalia and getting closer all the time, and regardless of the pounding the Weasels had taken in the combats high above Bull's-Eye, there were still too damn many of them, all with ears. But the ears that concerned him weren't all of them pointed and furry, not this time.

They had a passenger. Colonel Cully, 22nd MRF. Except that if he *was* Marine Reaction Force, then he was the first that Roj had seen whose uniform was bare of all the tabs and patches that the Marines wore with such pride. All Cully had was the *look*. The look of a killer.

Roj had an uneasy feeling that he and his big mouth were responsible for the colonel's presence. There had been no indication at the initial mission briefing that Minerva would be carrying anyone besides her usual brawn—at least, until the brawn stood up, snapped to attention, and let the brass know what he thought of FIREFROST.

All right, so they were only Weasels, and all right, the Weasel atrocity record was unmatched in the history of the Fleet, and all right, GK-2 was as legitimate a weapon as a plasma cannon. But the several-times-emphasized fact that its deliberate use against civilians was an integral element in the gas-deployment plan stuck in his throat, and he said so.

It might have been the arid, acronym-ridden computer-speak always employed when the military spoke of the unspeakable, or it might have been no more than a desire to get his own feelings out into the open, but having made the initial move of leaving his seat and drawing every eye in the briefing room, Roj refused to do the tactful thing and sit back down again. He was a well-read and educated young man; his anger made him eloquent, and that angry eloquence led him into the mistake of referring to his present duties by a very particular archaism—and he did it in front of both Admiral Meier and General of Marines Hugo Stroessner. Given the ancestries of those two officers, comparing Plan FIREFROST with the activities of *einsatzgruppen* was a stupid thing to do.

Minerva, though patched through to the briefing, had said nothing, either then or later, even though Roj had the unshakable feeling that she had winced as much as a brainship's core-mind could. He had never troubled to look over her service record as she had once looked over his, and he found himself wondering what duties she might have carried out in the past that would have kept her normally opinionated voice so quiet. The more he thought about that, the less he wanted to know.

"How's our guest?" he asked, to silence that train of thought. For all that he was alone on the brainship's bridge, Roj spoke quietly.

"Still in his cabin, flat-lined." Minerva's reply was just as quiet. "The good colonel really does like his sleep."

"Are you sure he's sleeping?"

"That's what my sensors say. Why, suspicious?"

"Curious." More than curious, less than suspicious, if the truth were known. He wondered why Cully had been sent along at all. If the man was there to keep an eye on a potentially unreliable officer, then staying out of sight was a strange way to go about it. There were no bugs or monitors on the bridge: Minerva would have told him if any had been put in place—and anyway he had swept the area with a little device designed to reveal such gadgets. Minerva hadn't liked that second-opinion gesture, not at all, and they were hardly a happy team right at the minute.

It wasn't that Roj didn't trust her; just that—all right, he didn't trust Cully. There were probably ways and means for a properly trained operative to do things aboard a brainship so that the brain-core couldn't remember afterward that they had been done at all. Anyway—and that was what rankled— he had no intention of doing anything other than seeing the mission through to a successful conclusion. Goddammit, he was an officer in the Fleet, not some loudmouth pacifist whose noise came only from the fact that he had never been shot at, never had to thumb-scrape the remnants of a friend off his uniform, never . . . Never thought that he was going to die in ways that the people back home couldn't imagine in their worst nightmares.

Roj had seen the vids on the Omni. Captain Hawk Talon, he of the ever-popular series, had friends who were killed, usually in the act of saving the captain or his brainship, Derv. Yet they always expired neatly, with a little curl of smoke from the plasma burn on their tunic and a dignified trickle of blood at the corner of their too-often-smiling mouths as they uttered one last witty comment, one last joke, one last good line to go out on. The men Roj had seen die hadn't gone that way. A close-range plasma bolt left a human looking like a Weasel—because they were both little, curled, crisped things that stank like burnt pork. Khalian slug throwers weren't even as clean as that; they had a rate of fire that acted like a chain saw in meat and sprayed the tatters all over the surrounding landscape.

Oh, no; if what FIREFROST was supposed to do would bring that to an end, Roj was ready to roll each GK-2 cylinder into place by hand. The problem was convincing the brass to believe it.

"Roj?" Minerva's voice; it wasn't urgent, but at the same time there was something about it that brought Roj out of his reverie like a kick in the tail.

"Here. What's wrong?"

"Contacts. Long-range scanners. On screen . . . *now.*"

Four blips at extreme range; normally nothing to worry about, but then normally Roj and Minerva were not this close to what Fleet Intelligence had ID'd as the Khalian home world. Of course, Intel had said the same thing about Bull's-Eye, and probably about Target—but this time they were more likely to be right. More factors confirmed the analysis than denied it, and even if they *were* mistaken, there was nothing wrong in taking out another planet as vital to the Weasel war effort as Bull's-Eye had been.

"Trying for an ID," said Minerva, and punched in the comparison program from the fire-control board. She cranked up sensor enhancement until the signal started to break up, let the static sizzle for a few seconds across the screen, then said, "Aw, *shit* . . ." in a disgusted tone of voice and cut the boosted pickup back to standard. "Too far out. But they're on an inbound vector at maximum sub-light. We'll know soon enough."

"Great. Any guesses?"

"What do *you* think? Bogies. Going to Condition Two, yellow alert." The panel lights on the Offense/Defense systems glowed amber as they silently went to standby, and Roj had the feeling that Minerva was watching him. More to the point, there was a wicked amusement in that scrutiny. "Now, what about Colonel Cully, Roj?" she said carefully. "Should I page him, or . . . ?"

Roj turned slightly in his seat and grinned full at the brain-core's main pickup. "No need. I, uh, I think full audible alarms would do the trick. Hit it."

Minerva gave the alarms everything she had, and a bit more besides. Regardless of the fact that Roj had heard the racket before, and was expecting it this time, he jumped almost out of his acceleration chair. Colonel Cully was on the bridge before the uproar had a chance to die down, and there was a bright red bruise on his forehead just below the hairline. *So you were asleep after all,* thought Roj grimly. He was a good two inches shorter than the colonel, and his bruises—from sitting up too suddenly in his bunk and cracking his head against the stanchion that some idiot designer had put there—had been that same two inches higher up the forehead. He had often wondered what came first with olympus-class brawns, concussion or replacing the startled sit-up with a startled roll-sideways . . .

"What's the matter?" Cully, it seemed, would be damned if he was going to be anything other than the bucko Marine colonel, even though his expression was that of a man who wanted ice packs and painkilling medication.

"Main screen, Colonel," said Minerva, and flipped up not merely the incoming contacts but their course and velocity vectors. "In this area, I doubt they're friendly, so I reacted accordingly."

"Mmf," said Cully. Then he gathered himself together and seemed to push the pain from the dent in his forehead farther into the back of his mind than it had already gone. "Yes. Indeed. Well done, XR-14376. You acted correctly, of course."

"Thank you, sir."

If Roj hadn't been serving with Minerva for nearly a year, the sarcasm would have slipped past him as well. As it was, he found something on the main control panel that needed his attention for long enough to get his face back under control. Whatever doubtful duties Minerva might have carried out in the past, he was willing to forgive them all just for the past five minutes.

"Commander," Cully's voice came rasping over his shoulder like an audible abrasive, "just what are you doing?"

"Setting up an intercept course and firing solution, sir." He glanced over one shoulder at the cold Marine eyes above the high Marine collar. "Just in case."

"Forget it."

"Sir?"

"Fleet Engineering went to a lot of trouble to make this ship look the way she does. Your 'intercept course' would make rather a nonsense of that, now wouldn't it?"

"Sir . . ." It had been a precautionary measure, nothing more. Roj knew as well as Cully the importance of retaining cover, but if a breakaway was necessary, he would sooner that it was to some purpose rather than just to avoid any potential cook off of the missiles in the troop-carrier's hulk. Besides which, he had no great love for being addressed as a father might address an erring and far-from-bright child.

"Bogies are in braking mode," said Minerva, in that cold,

emotionless voice she reserved for combat situations. "Range is: six-two-zero-zero. Course is: green-green one-one-five, closing. Their scanners are: active. We are being scanned." A threat receptor warning chirped shrilly, confirming the announcement. "IFF/ID confirms: hostiles. Khalian, two corvettes, Delta-K, two frigates, Forger-B. No comm transmissions detected at this time. Bandits continue to close: range now five-eight-zero-niner, closing."

Less than six thousand kilometers was too damn close. Regardless of what Colonel Cully might think or say, Roj started flipping switches on the fire-control boards, powering up the combat systems. They could always be shut down again if they weren't needed, but if they were, Roj knew from bitter experience that the Weasels didn't usually give you the leisure to prepare them a proper welcome. For all his feigned unconcern, he was very conscious of Cully's eyes staring at the back of his neck. It was a bit like two intangible, hot coins pressed against the skin: all in the mind, but no less nasty for that.

Minerva ran visual confirmations for his checklist as Roj muttered the familiar sequence under his breath. "Turrets are—unlocked, full and free traverse; chaff and flare dispensers are—armed; ECM and breakaway charges are—in standby mode; shields and cannons show preheat cycle complete. Programming telemetry on line, passive tracking controls are engaged, up and running. Target acquisition is ninety seconds and counting. We're as ready as we can be."

"We are indeed, Captain Malin," said Colonel Cully in an emotionless voice. "But this ship is as well screened from external scanning as the Fleet could make it, and despite everything you've done the Khalians still can't know we're here. I'm afraid you'll have to carry this mission through after all." His right hand hovered above the fire-control board, its index finger tracing all the tabs that Roj had switched on. "After that I'm going to bring you before a field court-martial, and we'll see what *they* have to say about all these . . . mock-heroics." He stepped back and half turned toward Minerva's main lens. "RM-14376, give me an exterior visual. Main screen."

"Colonel . . ." Minerva began, and hesitated. Her voice

had an odd edge to it, and for a moment Roj thought she was going to back up his decision. Then she continued, and he knew her concern was over more immediate matters than what might happen days hence. "Colonel, in one hundred sixty-seven seconds the bandits will be close enough for unaugmented visual spotting." She hesitated again. "Naked-eye range." The comment was insulting and excessive, but Roj was glad to hear it since it told him more about Minerva's opinions right now than any number of impassioned speeches in his defense. "Shall I open a clearport iris?"

Cully looked from brain to brawn and smiled thinly at some thought that had amused only him. He sat down carefully in the command chair at the center of Minerva's primary consoles, scanned the control tabs studding its arms, and tapped one with his finger. Nothing happened, except that his smile became a fraction wider. "By all means, RM-14376. Open them all, if you like. But first—extinguish all interior lights and put the system onto manual override. Do you understand me?"

There was a long second of hissing static that had no place coming from Minerva's acoustically perfect speakers. "Yes, I understand you. Sir." The bridge illumination dimmed to combat-red, then beyond to total darkness. "Done. You have control. Sir."

"Good."

Roj had never noticed it before—because the ship had never been blacked out before—but in this most absolute of midnights Colonel Cully seemed much more at home. As if darkness was more his natural element than light. Sitting there, staring at nothing, knowing that he shared this ship with canisters of a lethal nerve-gas compound and a still more lethal officer, it all seemed to make some kind of crooked sense.

After a few seconds, the main viewport's shutters opened. The old usage "iris" wasn't an accurate description, for all that it was a stubborn holdover from the days when circular shutters covered circular ports. These armored leaves folded back into their slots more like the closing of a fan, revealing a broad expanse of transparent glasteel. Roj had never realized before just how much light the stars produced. On all the other occasions when he had looked out naked-eye through the clearports, there had always been some sort of shipboard lighting at his back and that, no matter how dim, must always have taken the razor edge away from the crystalline beauty he saw now.

Except that not all the brilliant points of light were stars. Four of them were moving, growing larger, coming closer . . . Taking on a shape that he could recognize. Khalian warships, heading his way.

"Speed is dropping," said Minerva. "Course is holding constant. They'll overfly us in seventy seconds."

Already the Khalian ships were close enough for Roj to see the actinic flaring of reversed thrust as they dumped velocity for maneuverability. He hadn't realized before just how big Weasel warships were—or how mean-looking. That seventy seconds felt more like an eyeblink before they whipped past in a ragged formation that was far too tight, far too close, and far too fast for heavy-traffic safety, filling the viewport from frame to frame for just an instant before hurtling out again at something over half a klick per second.

"They're curious about us," said Roj, for Cully's benefit. "What happens, Colonel, if they decide this wreck's a danger to local space lanes and decide to remove the threat with a couple of plasma bolts? Or has Fleet thought of that one too . . . ?"

"Markers are more probable." The colonel's face was invisible in the darkness, but his voice was totally calm. "They'll not blow up something with such considerable salvage value."

"I wish I shared your confidence, Colonel," said Minerva. "Because I'm the one they'll be shooting at." She paused, considering a new stream of data as the now-distant Khalians reduced their speed still further and began to swing back. "More to the point, I've never heard of Khalians marking salvage before. Taking what they can carry and destroying the rest is more their style. And whatever it is they've got in mind, it's likely to happen fairly soon now."

The viewport shutters closed. "I have control, Colonel," Minerva told him sweetly, rubbing in the fact. "Except of course for the internal lighting. If you'd like to cancel manual, we're going over to silent-state battle stations . . . *Now*."

Cully might have canceled the override—or Minerva might have simply taken over, as she was quite capable of doing. Either way, the bridge lights snapped straight to the deep crimson of Condition One red alert and all the weapons systems came back to life.

"Passive tracking only, Colonel," Minerva continued in the same soothing voice. "Of course, you'd know that already. I don't want to put anything onto active status unless there's no other choice."

"We've got a lock," said Roj suddenly. "Positive guidance lock on targets one and three, data patched through and repeating on all torp homing heads. Two and four are coming on, coming on and . . . locked! We got 'em cold. If"—and he sat back from fire-control with his hands folded behind his head—"we need to fire, that is. To preserve the mission, Colonel." Cully's needless threat of a court-martial had stung more than Roj realized at the time, and it was satisfying to be able to turn the tables, even just a little. He wondered what the colonel had done to earn his promotions, because combat plainly hadn't played much of a part in it.

"The Weasels are running a close scan over the whole ship," said Minerva. "Me, the drones, the carrier. All of us. I hope, Colonel, that Fleet has done as good a job as you think, otherwise . . ." The rest of the sentence wasn't needed.

Colonel Cully hadn't moved a muscle, but as the glowing traces of targeting systems lit up the repeater screens to one side of his immobile face, Roj could see the merest gleam of moisture on his skin. So the iron man was human enough to sweat at the prospect of imminent action. Roj watched him for a moment, noting various other almost invisible signs of tension, and revised his opinion of Cully's service record at once. He was no longer the Intelligence operative sent along to make sure that mere soldiers didn't let some pangs of conscience get in the way of megadeath, but someone whose expressionless expression a much younger Sublieutenant Malin had seen before, on the face of a Marine he had watched climbing into a dropship, the same cold determination that hid the same all-too-human fear of dying. It was the

sort of expression that led to men being impossibly brave—
and impossibly brutal.

Cully was the right man to send on this mission after all,
Intelligence or not; because he above anyone else would know
what the invasion would be like if Operation FIREFROST
failed.

"The Khalia are holding station two klicks out," Minerva
reported. "They are continuing to scan. Surveillance only: no
target illumination. At least, not yet. If necessary, Colonel, I
can take out all four of them before they can react. Opinion?"

Cully thought about it for only a matter of seconds, even
though to Roj—and still more so to Minerva—it felt like an
age before he spoke. "Hold fire." The flinty relaying-of-
orders rasp was gone from his voice, at least for this. "Retain
your cover . . . but if their firing scanners come on, hit them.
On my command, and on my responsibility. Let that be so
noted."

"Done, sir," said Roj quietly, and for the first time he
really meant the honorific. "Duly noted and logged." Cully
glanced at him and nodded, a fractional inclination of the
head that was probably as much as this cold man was able to
produce. *A bit different from sitting in the dropship, Colonel.
You're starting to know how it feels on the other side of the
bulkhead, to be the one who clears the way before the drop
goes in. Not as easy as you thought, eh . . . ?*

It was going to be a question of reflexes; whether a brainship
could neutralize a first-strike situation just as the missiles and
plasma cannons of that strike were opening fire. If the question
had been theoretical, put to him over drinks in some peaceful
wardroom back on Port, Roj would have put his money on the
brainship every time. The situation was rather different out here,
where a magnified scan—had they dared to use one—would have
revealed the open torp tubes and the leveled cannons, glaring
with the IR overflow that would be spilling from both primed
sources of heat. He still had his money—and everything else as
well—riding on the brainship's speed of reaction. It wasn't as if
he had a lot of choice . . .

"They're powering up again," said Minerva. Her voice was
deadly calm. A series of active/standby lights went green on the

weapons board; even though the Khalians wouldn't be able to detect that slight change in the "derelict's" ready status, the standby backup gave Minerva that millisecond's additional edge in a quick-draw situation. Because the increase in the Weasels' power output could mean many things, including preparation to blast a traffic hazard to atoms, or . . .

All of Minerva's fire-controls went dead.

Roj had an instant of horrible shock, and then that same calm voice, threaded now with more relief than he had ever heard before, announced: "Their main drives are back on line. It looks like they're leaving . . ." For all the brain's apparent serenity, her brawn was needing to work hard to attain the same state. His fingers had clenched far too tight around the firing grips of the main plasma-cannon batteries, and as he slowly released them Roj noticed wryly just how slippery the checkered plastic had become.

Amazing, he thought, *how we've managed FTL drive, but still no cure for sweaty hands . . .*

He shifted the onboard systems from full passive into a semi-active tracking mode and put both visual projection and a graphic telemetry overlay up on the main screen. It made for a very pretty picture. The range was increasing at a very satisfying rate, three klicks, five, twelve—the separation distance jumping right up as all four Khalian vessels accelerated back to their maximum sub-light velocity. And this time they were heading out and away.

As they dwindled, becoming no more than glowing arrowheads on a long-range tactical plot in the few moments before the traces winked out altogether, Colonel Cully made a noise that could only have come from a man who had been holding his breath for an uncomfortably long time. Roj didn't turn to smile at him and didn't say anything aloud—but he looked Minerva full in the main receptor lens and gave her the ghost of a conspiratorial wink. "I think," he said obliquely, "that everything's going to be all right . . ."

It was all right, but only for as long as it took the disguised hulk to lumber into the immediate vicinity of the planet known to the Fleet as Khalia. And after that nothing was right at all.

It was well known to Fleet Intelligence that a large number of the Weasels had escaped from Bull's-Eye before the final surface assault by elements of the Marine Reaction Force, and well known too that their escape had included literally hundreds of ships. They had scattered in all directions, panicked and routed by superior forces, and had become more a threat as individual or small-group raiders than as a large military unit.

Except here, where they were gathered en masse to defend their home world.

The presence of multiple contacts crowding the passive-scan screen was a confirmation to those on RM-14376 that this was indeed their target. Certainly far more so than the Intelligence reports that had fallen so far short of accuracy where planetary defenses were concerned.

Even Colonel Cully made savage comments concerning how much else they might have gotten wrong. "Catch-22," he said grimly, swiveling slowly around in the number two command chair. "Major Murphy's Maxim. Nobody thought about orbital delivery strategic weapons over Bull's-Eye, and this lot"—indicated with a vicious jerk of his thumb at the blip-crammed screens—"got away with whole pelts. And now that somebody *has* thought about them, the Weasels we missed last time are here to stop us. At least, that's what the Weasels think . . ." A nasty smile tugged at the corner of his rat-trap mouth. "What do *you* think, Captain?"

Roj Malin glanced sidelong at the colonel and couldn't really answer at first; that he could only think how apt that "rat-trap" description had become. "I think, Colonel, that you're still not addressing enough of these questions to Minerva."

Cully shrugged, a little gesture that was more unconcern than apology. "Sorry," he said, and despite the evidence of the shrug even tried to sound as if he meant it. "In the Marines, when we have to deal with artificial intelligences, that's all they are. Artificial. RM-14376, Minerva that is, takes some getting used to."

"Never mind, Colonel," said Minerva, "when humans

were first put aboard brainships it took a while before we got used to them, too. Using a proper title helped . . ." Roj smiled inwardly; she always managed the delicate art of being patronizing without the more obvious forms of insult that, like her sarcasm, it slipped by most of the people who weren't familiar with it. "But my brawn's quite right about who to ask this time." An iris dilated with amusement way down among the elements of her main lens; as with her use of the "proper title," Cully realized what she had meant and went slightly pink about the ears.

"Then I'm asking." It was too late to compound the error; getting angry about the gentle teasing would only confirm how slow he had been to catch the joke. "What does your tactical programming have to say about this present situation . . . ?"

"This." Two of the screens blanked, then began to fill with layered schematics. "Roj and I have one advantage over any other brainship team in the Fleet: we've been in a situation like this before. When we found Bull's-Eye." Data and graphics flickered across both screens, too fast for close study. She was giving what amounted to a short lecture illustrated with sketches; the detailed briefing would follow. "Standard procedure: as we approach orbit the MARV warheads aboard each drone will be receiving constant area-correlation guidance updates right up to the point when I and they achieve breakaway. Once we're clear the preset charges and the ECM units in the troopship's hulk will detonate, not merely jamming the Weasels' scanners with standard multi-wavelength chaff, but creating upward of a thousand fragments large enough to provide long-persistence echo returns. I, of course, both visually and electronically ID as a Khalian ship, so I can make my exit more leisurely than would otherwise be possible. Satisfied, Colonel?"

"I've often wondered why I never really warmed to brainships, Minerva," said Cully. He was smiling, but it wasn't the sort of smile meant to take the sting from words. "Now I think I know. You're all schoolteachers at heart. Yes, I'm satisfied. But not very. It sounds far too pat for my liking. What about flexible response?"

Minerva might have been waiting for the question; certainly she gave no indication of concern at Cully's attitude. Rather the reverse. "I have a further advantage: despite the number of bandits in orbit, this place has nothing like the defensive intersystem of Bull's-Eye. No drones, no seeker remotes, and above all no orbital platforms. Just ships. Ships whose crews have been recently defeated and forced to flee, whose crews are tired and demoralized—and since we've knocked out their principal repair facility, ships whose systems are probably starting to fail. We've taken enough Khalian vessels apart to know how they work: modular replacement of entire units. No source for those anymore, Colonel. Nowhere to set down—because I doubt those scrappy little fields we're reading planetside are capable of handling warships."

"They're capable of rearming orbital-defense fighters," said Cully. "Unlike you I've had the advantage of seeing what noninterdicted air support can do to a drop. Among the other reasons that I'm sure you've got tucked away in one chip or another, that's why we're here—to take them out."

"I thought CASE WHITE was designated to that tasking."

"As a follow-up. Cutting-edge operations, Minerva. During the landings, not before. If you lectured less and got back to checking the main briefing, you'd know more than you seem to now."

Minerva was about to say something further, but then she faltered, a minute hesitation while she gave something her absolute attention. And when she spoke again her voice had become ice-cold and angry. "I know, Colonel. I know more than you think. I know, for instance, that there are no provisions for NBC countermeasures on that planet. None at all."

"What . . . ?"

"Unlike brawns, I'm not limited to how many functions I can control simultaneously. I've been maintaining RM-14376's onboard systems, I've been monitoring the Weasels, I've been having this pleasant little chat with you—and I've been running surveillance cameras over Khalia for one full orbit. Colonel, the place is *primitive*. Look for yourself. Both of you."

The camera images had been computer-enhanced somewhere along their route from lens to screen, and they were running by at two or three times normal speed. Minerva bled in spectrographic, thermographic, doppler-shift, and simple IR readouts as and when she felt them necessary. None of the enhanced scans had much to show: they were designed for the detection of advanced-technology power sources, and except for the spacefields and a few hot-spots that looked like reactors tacked as afterthoughts onto medieval castles, they detected nothing.

". . . Only the indigenous population that Fleet Strategic Planning is so certain will resist us tooth and nail," observed Minerva venomously. "Well, they're right enough there—because the 'indigenous population' has very little else!"

Roj had seldom heard Minerva so angry. He knew she had a stack of years' service seniority on him, and the accumulated calm acceptance that went with it. Except for now. The mission had been dirty enough when they "volunteered" for it, even when smoothed over by tactical and strategic necessity and the awareness that they were going to save millions of lives on both sides by forcing this war to a conclusion. But to learn that it meant genocide—accidentally through a lack of information, or deliberately through disinformation and a process of thought that Roj was grateful he didn't share—put a new complexion on the matter.

"How much did you know about this, Colonel Cully?" he said, wanting the man in the other chair to admit everything so that he could have a reason to cross the bridge and smash him to the floor. Roj wanted to smash everyone connected with FIREFROST, but Cully would do for starters.

Except that when the colonel got to his feet, he said the one thing that Roj didn't want to hear. "I knew as much as you," said Cully. There was no swearing on his honor as a colonel of Marines, no great demonstration of outrage; just a quiet loathing in his voice that if it was faked, gave him more right to be on the stage than on a brainship's bridge in hostile space.

Roj stood for several moments with the blood burning in his face, opening and closing his fists, feeling foolish, and stupid, and *used*. "So what do we do?" he said at last, and was surprised when the words came out without a tremor.

Cully looked at the screens and the readouts. Khalia was less than half of one AU away. "We've come this far . . ." he said carefully, but seemed unwilling to complete the thought. Roj watched him, and needed no special skill to read the colonel's face. In six days from now the men and women of the Marine Reaction Force would be in their drop positions, waiting to go, wondering as he had wondered in the past whether all the advance planning had worked or whether it was going to be only the suppression clusters on the belly of the lander that would buy them enough time to hit cover. Now he was in the position of the advance planners—and hating it. Whether they had known the truth about Khalia was immaterial. FIREFROST would work. Once the MARVs had gone in on an unprotected target—and there were thirty maneuverable re-entry vehicles to each drone—the GK-2 that they contained would blanket the planet and leave it incapable of offering resistance.

Incapable, too, of supporting any life-form higher than a vegetable. Even they, with no insects left to pollinate them, would eventually die and leave Khalia scoured clean, ready for evolution to try again from the oceans where it had all begun before. Or for the first entrepreneur with a starship and a flair for eugenics.

As a solution, it was . . . final.

And what would the Marines and the Fleet think of them after the first euphoria of victory had died away? Would they remember the lives that had been saved—or the lives that had been stolen? The end that justified the means was part of a well-turned phrase, but it failed to explain how those who employed the means slept at night, or looked other people in the face, or even met their own eyes in a mirror. Of course, they would only have been doing their duty by obeying the orders of their superior officers. But that excuse had been discredited since Nathan Hale, and by circumstances far too similar to these.

"The drones can be reprogrammed." Minerva's voice cut into the silence of their thoughts, offering neither an excuse nor a reason but a way out. Both men turned to stare straight at the main receptor lens that was as close as anyone could come to looking a brainship in the eye. Cully's face was closed, guarded, neutral; the expression of someone already too familiar with easy ways out that become harder than the original problem.

Roj . . . didn't hide anything. Relief at even the possibility of an escape from the dilemma was already lightening the somber set of his features, and before much more time had passed he would have begun to smile—had he not remembered that more than Minerva was present, and regained some sort of control over his own muscles.

"Explain." Cully, of course; possessed of a caution that came close to the pessimistic, the colonel wasn't about to let any of his carefully husbanded emotions slip away without good reason.

"Breakaway takes place as normal," said Minerva. Roj might have been hearing things born of the way he felt himself, but she sounded both excited and unconscionably pleased with herself. "After all, the charges have been placed so that they'll simulate the destruction of a battle-damaged wreck by atmospheric friction and gravitational forces. Except that instead of the drones MIRVing at once, they move out under cover of the debris and take up preselected positions in geosynch orbit over Khalia. And there they stay, with the Khalian High Command, or Planetary Council, or whatever the Weasel big bosses are called, advised of what's overhead and given the chance for"—she made a noise that corresponded to the clearing of a throat she didn't have—"an honorable cessation of hostilities."

"You're forgetting one thing." Colonel Cully's voice was as bleak as his face. "After the length of time and the number of deaths that this war has used up, what makes you think a cessation of hostilities is all that people want. Not the Marine units I've served with. Or the ones who've been watching the Omni broadcasts all these years. Try 'unconditional surrender' in your equation, then see if the Khalia will still agree to it. I suspect they'll die first." Then Cully grinned, a brief, taut skinning of lips back over teeth like a death's-head. "Of course, with seven hundred twenty canisters of binary GK-2 hanging over their heads, we can accommodate them in that choice too.''

The discussion had been interrupted by an occasional audible warning from Minerva's ECM suite as it responded to wide-band sweeps from Khalian tracking and surveillance systems. There had been nothing from target-illumination or fire-control sensors, because the Weasels had more to watch for in their own local space than the drifting wreckage of last month's battles. It was no matter now whether those battles had been won or lost, they were in the past and the future was a more immediate concern.

Until the moment when all the threat-receptors went off at once.

As the bridge lights snapped to combat-crimson and all the weapon-preheat systems kicked in of their own accord, the discussion that tried to balance the morally reprehensible against the tactically sound went out of an equally metaphorical window in the same instant, because as their IDs came up on Minerva's main screen, the sources of the new signals were all-too familiar.

There were four incoming vessels, warships all: two Delta-K corvettes and a pair of Forger-B frigates, heading in at max from out-of-system territory with their targeting sensors red-lined . . . And Minerva had long ceased to believe in coincidences.

Those four ships were the same perimeter patrol they had encountered before, returning from their sweep and finding the same chunk of combat debris they had encountered in deep space—except they were now heading for what looked suspiciously like a parking orbit over Khalia.

The Fleet and the Alliance had said many things about their Khalian opponents over the years, but ''stupid'' was not a word from which even the most ardent propagandist got much mileage. Even a child—or a cub—with the proper instruments could tell that the trajectory of this particular battle casualty was off its predicted track by a factor of several hundred million kilometers. The presence and consequent gravity well of a gas giant among the outer planets of the Khalian system would have served to slingshot any dead ship on that particular approach vector back out toward the void. Unless, of course, it was equipped with maneuvering thrusters and was still alive enough to use them—something which the Weasels were looking at right now . . .

"We're in trouble." Minerva said it in an abstracted sort of way, because most of her systems were either programming the FIREFROST drones or powering up her own defense nets, and no matter what she had boasted, it left very little over for more than the most basic voder simulation.

Cully took just one look at the screen and his brows drew together in a frown. "Explain," he said.

When the colonel was tense, thought Roj, he was a man of few words and none of them particularly imaginative. Since Minerva was busy, her brawn took it upon himself to do what was necessary for their passenger's—information, probably; peace of mind was somehow inappropriate right now. His fingers flickered across a standard keyboard with all the frantic speed of someone on deadline—and *dead* was the important element there, all right—and constructed a rough computer model of what was going on.

It wasn't just for Cully's benefit; most of what Roj sent glowing across the screen went straight into the manual-override chips on the fire-controls, because even in a brainship, now and again situations arose where the brawn had to earn his or her rations in the most basic way.

Gun-laying near enough by hand was one such way, and while the Fleet Officer's Academy had courses on it, they couldn't simulate the real thing: when the recycled air was thick with the reek of recycled smoke and the gravity grids were throwing ten-G fluctuations and when the supposed targets were glittering sequins flung all over the sky instead of a rock-steady glow on a repeater screen . . .

"They," he said, indicating the four Weasel ships, "don't like finding us here. So they're going to blast us as they probably think they should have done last time. Minerva's rigging the drones for breakaway to orbit, and I—I'm gonna try to nail them before they nail us. OK, Colonel? Clear enough?"

"Not by half," snapped Cully. He dropped back into his acceleration chair and pulled its eight-point harness into place, secured the quick-release boxes, then gestured at the firing-grips still sunk into their recesses on either side of the targeting screen in front of him. "Time you two learned that I know more about what they pay me for than you've been giving me credit for. Fire this sucker up!"

"Colonel, you're here as an observer . . ."

"Captain, you don't know why I'm here, and right now you're *way* wide of the mark. I'm giving you a direct inter-service order, mister. Hit it!"

"All yours, Colonel." Roj tabbed two controls and the gunnery control yoke popped out and down to ready position. He watched Cully grab it like a drowning man reaching for a life preserver, and guessed it was his inactivity aboard a ship at General Quarters that had been fretting the Marine. It was one thing to be aboard a troopship, all strapped in and waiting to be delivered like a lethal parcel, and quite another to be capable of doing something without being given the chance.

"Attention, attention," said Minerva in what Roj always thought of as her Red Alert voice, "mark your targets, hold your fire. Be advised that all weapons systems will remain on semi-active tracking only, until successful drone breakaway to assigned orbit has been confirmed. Mark your targets, hold your fire. Countdown of ten begins—*now*. Nine. Eight. Seven . . ."

In the few seconds that remained, Roj ran an analysis of the other Weasel ships, the ones in orbit around the home world. None of them had moved; they were still holding position and formation, unaware that anything was amiss. Either Minerva had taken the risk of activating a coincident-band com jammer to interrupt incoming signals without being too obvious about it—or the captains of the four approaching ships had scented a possible chance for glory and were keeping quiet so that they could have it all for themselves. Heading unawares into the free-fire zone of an olympus-class brain-ship, they would certainly have *something* all to themselves. Torps yes, plasma cannons yes, but glory . . . ? None at all.

". . . Two. One. Zero. *Burn!*"

A rumbling vibration passed through Minerva's hull structure as explosive bolts severed all her connections to the wrecked troop-carrier. While the charges gave a small initial backward shove, it was her own attitude-control jets that pushed the brainship clear. The FIREFROST drones followed like pilot fish in the wake of a shark, and even as the last of them slipped from the launch cradle deep within the carrier's hull, strategically located demolition charges were beginning to blow the derelict to pieces. Minerva and all twenty-four drones soon gave the appearance of just so many more pieces of the wreckage that tumbled away in an expanding cloud of debris.

"Countdown commencing to final detonation." Minerva kicked in the reaction thrusters again, another brief burn to move them farther and faster away from the disintegrating hulk. "What about the Weasels?"

"Reducing speed, some intership communication, but no general transmissions yet."

"They're confused," said Cully. "Their target started to break up before they fired a shot. But they're not so confused that they won't make sure of us this time. Look at the status displays . . ." He gestured to one particular data schematic beside the image of each enemy ship; all their combat sensor systems were fully powered and all their weapons charged. "So who takes the first strike? Us—or them?"

"What status on the drones, Minerva?" asked Roj softly, not shifting his gaze from the screen in case that might somehow prompt the Weasels into doing something dangerous.

"Guidance data is fully patched in. Go for orbital insertion?"

"Can you do it without attracting notice?"

"Once the main charges blow."

"Can we afford to wait that long?"

"We can't afford not to." There was no perspiration on Colonel Cully's brow this time, not when he controlled such firepower as he now had under his thumbs. "We wait," he said. "Too soon, they'll pick up anomalous motion from the drones and splash 'em. That would make this whole mission a waste of time. Besides"—he shifted the control yoke and tracked electronic crosshairs across each Khalian ship in turn—"they're right where we want them."

Less than a kilometer away, the troopship convulsed as its last few scuttle charges all blew simultaneously and tore its hull apart. Filaments of PDM explosive had already dismembered the old ship as neatly as a surgeon's scalpel and with such precision that when the main blast came, Minerva's tracking telemetry already knew to within a couple of meters where each of the main fragments would go. As they went, spinning erratically toward Khalia and the atmosphere that would burn most of them up, each piece of hull, each chunk of engine, had a drone to keep it company on the last long fall—at least until the drone shifted into parking orbit and left its shelter to burn up alone.

"Any reactions?"

"None. They're still coming in."

"Planetside?"

"Tracking the bits, running analyses—no, they're happy, all scanners just shut down again."

"Good. Then I think we can leave." Minerva didn't need to breathe in the conventional way, but sometimes there were noises more expressive than words. Her speakers emitted the unmistakable sound of someone taking a deep breath. "Gentlemen, secure for combat maneuvers. Battle stations, battle stations. Weapons free! Shields coming up . . . now!"

"Locking on . . ."

"Positive lock confirmed."

"Rotary one, firing! Torps away, full salvo!"

"Evasive, break right, go . . . !" The Khalia broke too, sheering away from their original line of approach as their threat receptors picked up the doppler-shift of eight torpedoes accelerating toward them at more than forty G. Three out of the four were unlucky; their helm officers picked the same evasive courses as Minerva's fire-control predictors had anticipated. They began jinking wildly in an attempt to break the homing lock, even though their crews probably knew that the attempt was next to useless. Each torp's guidance system had been individually preprogrammed before launch. No matter what an enemy might do with chaff or flares to change a radar image or an IR signature, the torp's randomized tracker would always find something, if only shape or color, to associate with its original target. There was only one really certain way to avoid a Fleet-issue Mk-12b torpedo, and that was to hit it first.

They hit five of them before the remaining three gained final confirmation of their targets and struck home. Two were a correlated pair assigned to the same delta-class corvette, and their five-kiloton warheads impacted as they had been launched, within a quarter second of each other. The Khalian corvette and every Weasel on it became an incandescent globe of plasma in far less time than that.

The last torp of the salvo hit home fair and square on the center section of one of the Forger frigates. And failed to explode. It was a fault common among the last one or two warheads in a close-grouped volley; EMPs caused both by defensive fire and by the explosions of other warheads often scrambled even these hardened electronics. They didn't mean the frigate shrugged the impact off. It had been struck amidships by a missile that weighed some thirty-four hundred kilos, and this one had achieved its terminal velocity of slightly more than forty-seven klicks per second when it punched into the Forger's side.

With the generation of that much friction, pyrophoric ignition did the rest. The Forger's demise wasn't quite so ostentatious as being struck by a combat-yield thermonuclear warhead, but it flared up as brightly and as finally as any match-head ever struck.

The last Delta had fallen prey to the same disease as the last torpedo, its electronics fried by an EMP slashing out of an epicenter four hundred meters away. Its crew had fallen victim to something much simpler: the gamma radiation from that same explosion, at an intensity far higher than their ship was shielded against. Had its hull been thick enough to protect the Weasels inside—say thirty centimeters depth of lead for every square centimeter of surface area—their atmosphere-capable vessel would have been too heavy to ever leave the ground.

And that left one.

The last Forger-B came scything through the massive cloud of irradiated chaff that was all Minerva had left of two of its consorts, and all its guns were firing in a frenzy of destruction. Its own torpedoes were expended, or forgotten, or ignored as not being intimate enough. That was something Roj and Minerva had encountered before, a Khalian captain becoming so angry that what he wanted most in all the worlds was to rend his enemies with teeth and claws, and was now forced to resort to its closest equivalent. They had nailed several Weasel ships because of that—and had come damnably close to being nailed themselves.

"Mine," Roj heard Colonel Cully whisper almost to himself, and despite his better judgment held off the final pressure that would have launched another salvo of torpedoes.

"Roj?" he heard Minerva ask. There was apprehension in her voice.

"He wants them, he can have them. But stand by on override in case he—"

The warning didn't need finishing. Cully had been tracking the Forger since the engagement began, apparently paying no heed to any of the fire-control inputs without which most humans wouldn't have gone near a brainship's weapons. Either that, or he had processed the data almost as fast as Minerva herself. When his thumbs finally crushed down on the twin triggers of the main plasma cannon they seemed to lock there in a firing frenzy almost as intense as the Weasels' own, laying down a pattern of energy bolts along their approach that looked almost thick enough to walk on.

But then, even though they were the Bad Guys, the Weasels were doing that too.

It just wasn't fair. . . .

Especially when just in the instant that the Forger impaled itself on the point of Cully's cone of fire and tore itself apart in a great blossom of molten metal and little squealing burning Weasels, there was a most unholy bang somewhere aft and Minerva's entire structure shuddered.

"We're hit . . . !

"I'm hurting . . . !" For all her metallic body, all of her

sleek size and power, in that instant Minerva was the little crippled girl she had been before the brainship program took away her useless body and gave her one that never suffered pain. Until now . . .

"Oh, God, we're going in . . ." said someone softly as Khalia filled the forward screens. The whole planet reeled sideways, steadied for an instant—then fell right out of the sky onto their upturned faces.

And all the lights went out.

". . . get up, Captain. I said, you're still alive, so get up."

Despite the noises of encouragement from a voice that was as much like Colonel Cully's as it was like anything else, Roj Malin was reluctant at first to open his eyes. It had been so still, so dark and quiet, so peaceful . . .

The ship was still around him. There was air to breathe, heat to keep the ultimate chill of deep space at bay, and only the artificial gravity felt strange. It took him several confused moments to realize that it was real, and no longer the simulated one-G of Earth standard.

"We got down in one piece," he heard Minerva say. "Just. I had to pull almost twelve G at one stage so that we didn't look like something coming in to land. I countered with the artificials as best I could, until they blew."

It hurt to move, and now Roj knew why. If his seat harness had been cutting into him at twelve times normal gravity, it would have been doing a passable imitation of a cheesewire. He didn't bother to look, but there would be puffy red gouges running in nice geometric patterns all over him to mark where the restraint straps had been. At least they hadn't chopped anything off. He had seen that, once. . . .

"Minerva," said Cully in the voice of a man with things on his mind, "we landed safely—but can we get off again?"

"I'll let you know." The diagnostics board was a constellation of LEDs as Minerva checked her own health, and she didn't sound as if she wanted to discuss the matter with strangers.

"What about outside?" Roj's attempt to get out of his acceleration chair was more a series of connected winces than the usual smooth movement, but at least he was able to do it unaided. Cully didn't offer to help anyway. He was more interested in the readouts from a bank of instruments on one of the other bulkheads.

"Outside is a little hot," he said enigmatically.

"Temperature? Enemy ground forces?"

"Rads. A residual of three hundred plus, dropping fast. The shielding can handle it. Looks like we brought what was left of the Forger down with us—so I suppose you were right after all." Cully smiled the nasty smile that Roj had never come to terms with. "About the enemy ground forces. Ground—and grilled."

"Wonderful. Jokes. Just what I needed to make me feel better."

"Don't knock it, Captain. At least you're still alive to groan."

"Yeah, I've noticed." Roj groaned some more and flinched as his flightsuit chafed raw skin, then forgot all about it as Minerva's voder came back on line with a crackle like the diffident clearing of throats.

"Diagnostics complete, gentlemen," she said. "Do you want the good news, the bad news . . . or the worse news?"

"Are matters so serious that you have to resort to clichés?" Cully wasn't smiling anymore, although whether that was to give weight to his remark or because of genuine concern, his still features didn't say.

"Clichés always begin as the simplified obvious. It's their simplicity that leads to overuse." Minerva sounded as stone-faced as the colonel looked. "Now do you want to hear about this or do you not?"

"Minerva," said Roj wearily, "get it out of the way so that we can start doing something about it, will you . . . ?"

"Right." The main screen flickered for a moment, then with seeming reluctance formed the schematics of an olympus-class brainship disguised as a Khalian Fencer B-4 frigate. The vessel's outline was disfigured by leprous-looking blotches of yellow, indicating those areas where Minerva had sustained systems damage during the brief, savage dogfight three hundred klicks beyond the atmosphere. As she spoke a small blue triangle moved around the display to point out what Roj privately considered "areas of especial interest."

"Hull integrity was breached by particulate damage here, here, and here. The fragments in these areas here and here were irradiated, so the compartments here and here are hot—that means you can forget about going back to your cabin for clean socks, Colonel. We can manage without them, and so I'm sure can you. However . . ." The pointer changed from blue to red, never a good sign. "I lost most of the modulars here and here. My com system, gentlemen, and most of my primary navigational units are now a thing of the past."

"That was the good news?" said Cully.

"No, actually that was the bad. The good is that despite the damage I think I can still lift clear of Khalia before the CASE WHITE mud-movers arrive and turn us into a radioactive blot on a glass landscape."

"You think?" Roj knew Minerva well enough by now to pick up on her cues, and this one was fairly definite.

"Uh, yeah. I did mention worse news. Primary navigation—like for instance, taking off. The only way we'll get off-planet is by some creative cross-modular insertion. I'm not carrying any line-replaceable spares, but the FIREFROST systems ought to—"

"Oh no you don't!" Cully was on his feet, face dark with anger and the sudden suspicion that he had been maneuvered slowly and subtly into this position from the very beginning.

"You've suddenly become very passionate, Colonel. Now sit down again *and let me finish.*"

"Best do it, Colonel." Sitting quietly in front of the com board, Roj didn't need a brain other than his own to know that there would be no coded transmissions leaving RM-14376 for anywhere right now. Neither the orbiting drones, nor the approaching Fleet, nor even from the bridge to the vessel's rearmost compartments. Right now, shouting was the only long-distance means of communication that they had available. The problem would be in getting this particular colonel of Marines to realize the problem. Roj sympathized a little; without FIREFROST the assault would have to go ahead regardless of on-planet resistance or off-planet support, and

Cully had been at the sharp end of such operations too many times to regard the prospect calmly.

Against that was the fact that if they could lift off and rendezvous with the vanguard of the CASE WHITE units, they could at least warn them of the situation. Maybe the GK-2 bombs could be activated by someone else, somewhere else. Maybe; it had been made fairly clear before they left the orbital facility over Bull's-Eye that the control codes for the MARV drones were as unique as Cryptography could make them, in case of accidents.

". . . and even if there *was* some way to deliver the warheads," Minerva was saying calmly, "we've got as little NBC protection as the Weasels."

"What? What's wrong with staying right here?"

"Colonel, the access hatches for those modules are all mounted on my outer casing. They're meant to be opened by a ground crew while I'm in atmosphere drydock." She was being just so patient with him, when Roj knew from the undertones of her voice that she would have preferred to grab Cully by the hair and shake some sort of sense into him.

"The radiation outside is going to cut things close enough as is. At present rate of decay it'll be relatively safe in fifteen hours thirty-seven minutes. Allow an hour for modular substitution, hour and forty-five minutes for prep and preflight from cold . . . The invasion battlegroup will enter orbit in eighteen hours and predrop bombardment will commence in eighteen hours plus twenty five minutes. By my math, we'll have three minutes to get the hell out of here."

"Spacesuits," said Cully with the air of one putting forward an irrefutable argument.

"All the pressure suits I carry were in one of the hot compartments. What was it you mentioned before: catch-22? Well, meet catch-23. We wait."

They waited; and then they waited some more; and only when Minerva judged that it was safe did they venture outside. Colonel Cully had been right in the literal sense as well as in his interpretation of the radiation readings beyond Minerva's climate-controlled environment. Sweat was streaming down both his and Roj's faces before they were half done with the module swap. It was small wonder the Weasels had an expansionist nature, if this place was where they had originated.

"Connections complete, standard check!" Roj yelled in the general direction of the remote pickup they had run out from the bridge, and stepped back from the access hatch as Minerva ran power into this latest unit. There had been five blowups already, when circuitry designed for the microwatts of a missile guidance system revealed it only when the gigawattage of a starship's flight instruments ran through and fried its chips. There was still a splinter bedded somewhere in Roj's shoulder from the last time but one, and he was well past taking any further chances.

Even if they were already running late.

There was a constant desire to keep looking at his chrono, and at the far-too-rapid countdown of its timer. Cully, protected by rank or by a sheer lack of concern, wasn't so particular. The colonel glanced at his wrist on an average of once every minute, following it each time with a nervous glance skyward.

Roj was more concerned about the Khalia. It was impossible to believe that their landing here had gone completely unnoticed, wilderness though it might be. At the very least, they were a friendly ship, a fencer-class shot down in combat on the very fringes of the home world itself, and surely that rated a rescue. He wondered if rescue tugs on Khalia were armed, and if not, whether Minerva could smoke any intruder before it got a message off about who was and wasn't to be rescued. . . .

The spray of heavy machine-gun fire went clanging in silvery splashes across the brainship's hull just as he closed the last-but-one inspection hatch, and he felt a half-spent ricochet slap against his shoulder in an attempt to keep the silver of ceramic company. Even though the distorted slug did not leave more than another bruise among the criss-cross laid there by his straps, it would be a spectacular affair—assuming he lived long enough for all its colors to develop. That was something that seemed less than likely, because the next burst of fire chewed up the ground between where he had dived for cover and the entrance/exit port leading to Minerva's dark, cool, and above all armored interior. As if to prove it hadn't been a fluke, the next two bursts chopped into exactly the same area, as if promising what awaited the first man to make a run.

And he was unarmed, on top of everything else. Sidearms weren't quite as necessary on a brainship as they might be on an MRF dropship, but there were a couple of autorifles in a secure cabinet at the back of the bridge. Right now, they were as far away as Port.

Correction, one of them was still in the cabinet. From the sound of it Colonel Cully had the other, because the weapon's chattering in short, controlled bursts was coming from so close that it had to be the colonel firing. He hoped. He was right.

"Notice something, Captain?" shouted Cully above the crackle of gunfire. "There's only one of them!"

"Only one Weasel?" The statement seemed to need some sort of reply, and that was the only thing that came to Roj's mind. It was probably wrong anyway, but he was more concerned with keeping his head out of the path of an un-ricocheted slug than he was with thinking up the right an-swers to this most practical exam in firefight analysis.

"No, man! Only one gun! Get into the ship and—" The rest of it was lost in a shattering bellow from overhead as Minerva's A and X turrets traversed toward the distant ridge that was the only place where the Weasels could be hiding and opened the line of fire. It wasn't the precise placement of shot required by deep-space combat, but saturation gun-nery of the old school over a range of one klick, and it trans-formed the rock and soil and vegetation of that ridge into a smoldering primordial sludge.

"Ready to go!" In the clanging silence after the plasma cannons shut down, Minerva's PA sounded insignificant. Only the words were important. Already heat and vapor were be-ginning to flow from the vectored-thrust nozzles of her lift jets. Roj scrambled to his feet, closed the final hatch with a slap of one hand, and all but dived through the entry-port. Despite being encumbered by the awkward bulk of the big autorifle, Cully was right on his heels.

He stumbled in the doorway and the weapon went clattering across the floor of the airlock. Roj scooped it up, scorching his fingers on the hot barrel-shrouds, and turned to punch the big, red, friendly door-secure button. Then he saw the reason why Cully had dropped the gun. . . .

The colonel was staring down at the front of his tunic with a slightly astonished expression on his face. There was no pain, no anger, just a faint surprise. And in the middle of the tunic, in the middle of his chest, was a long thin metal spike.

"That's why—kept our heads down," he said, quite calmly, biting the words off short to conserve what air was left to him. "Only one gun. Plenty spears. If close enough. Minerva was right. Primitive." Cully grinned, and shrugged, and coughed a spray of blood all over the wall. "Effective too," he said, and died.

"Get the door closed, Roj!" snapped Minerva, her voice coming harshly from one of the wall repeaters. The vibration of its speaker sent little trickles of Colonel Cully running from the grille. Roj grimaced, and hit the button centuries too late. As the massive slab of metal hissed down its runners, he saw, in the far distance, a blink of white light maybe half a kilometer from the ground. The expanding fireball that was either a nuclear or an FAE came an instant later, but the door slid shut and secure long before blast or sound could reach him.

The Fleet, and CASE WHITE, was here at last.

Forty seconds later Minerva was clawing for altitude and orbit and the scores of friendly ships that were starting to fill the sky over Khalia. Roj tried to think of excuses all the way to orbit, then remembered the look on Cully's dying face and gave the whole thing up as a waste of time. Because FIRE-FROST or not, the invasion was under way. . . .

INTERLUDE

37.78974CR1.5
The Military as a subculture

Every officer must be cognizant of the fact that by its
sheer size and nature the Fleet, or any large military
organization, constitutes its own culture. Often a culture
with patterns of behavior and acceptance far removed
from the society it protects. This was recognized by the
prespace democraterians who, at the expense of effectiveness, insisted upon basing their military structure on
levies that were never acculturated by a military society.
This led to such forces as the French Levee in Masse
and the American National Guard attempting to use men
in situations requiring behavior patterns of which they
were incapable. The unfortunate result of this misplaced
policy, including the loss of two of the moons of Jupiter,
the primary gas giant in the home system, is historically
apparent. Given a culture that cannot accept its own actions, each individual will soon come to view itself as a
separate culture, or revolutionary. Unfortunately there are
few limits placed on behavior by this self-identity as is
evidenced also on Hress when one Marine . . .

37.7945CR3.6
  Few situations are more likely to create horror than

any action involving a large number of civilians. A comparable situation can only be found when two opposed cultures clash. Inevitably neither survives intact, and often one is completely extinguished. Values that either side hold as basic are reexamined while the personnel involved are under extreme duress. Extremes of behavior are the rule, not the exception. These can range from psychotic violence to "going native." The result is often surprising, and just as often renders even the most elite unit incapable of further combat until reindoctrination.

FULL CIRCLE
by Jody Lynn Nye

THE SPACE-TO-AIR CRAFT circled high, and then began a dive at a sharp angle through atmosphere, positioning itself for maximum accuracy. Marine Sergeant Alvin Shillitoe, called Tarzan by his mates, peered into the video pickup slaved from the eye at the nose of the craft. There were no portholes in the capsule in which he and his company were contained.

"On target, sir. Prepare for jettison." The pilot's electronically transmitted voice tingled shrilly in Shillitoe's ear. The big Marine nodded brusquely, ignoring the lurching jolt that followed the announcement. Some of their equipment was so blackdusting old. Well, they weren't wasting any of the new stuff on his men. The mission was slated as an easy one—a walkover.

"Brace for separation," he ordered. He put on his helmet and locked in the air-recirculation unit. The capsule was supposed to maintain atmosphere all the way down, but it never hurt to make sure that everyone made it there without going brain-dead from oxygen deprivation. Many of his Marines followed suit as Alvin began repeating key points from their ISA briefing.

"We're not going to have any real trouble securing the landing strip. Just get in, show our smiling faces, and take possession of the strip and any buildings that overlook it. It's on the edge of the Weasel city where the brass are planning a secondary assault later in the schedule. No major military bases visible from orbit, so they say we have a chance of being ignored." Alvin paused, glanced at the three new bloods added less than a week before, and his voice hardened. "Don't count on it. They probably have plenty of weapons and high explosives. So do we, but these are civilians.

"We don't want to use them if we don't have to. Give them the order to lay down arms and leave, and you two sound like you mean it."

"Like they warn ours," a voice grumbled. Shillitoe pretended he hadn't heard anything.

This last instruction was to Pirelli and Dr. Mack Dalle, who had studied Khalian customs and language. The tall, thin researcher looked out of place among the muscular, focused Marines, but he was more of a trooper than he looked. And more of one than he would have been comfortable admitting to himself. Pirelli was real smart, but he took too many chances. You had to give him a job and make him stick to it.

"All we've gotta do is hold that strip for two hours max., which'll give the big carriers long enough to find our beacon, confirm the all-clear, and start landing troops. If we're assaulted, we neutralize enemy units. After that, our job is finished, unless we want to join in the assault on the city so you can play more patty-cake with the Khalia."

A few of the Apes growled their consent. They'd taken casualties on Bull's-Eye and were anxious to get some revenge.

"They're the same Weasels we've been fighting, chief." One of the heavy weapons specialists who hadn't bothered to seal up yet, Vic Zanatobi, piped up supportively. "Nothin' new down there, just a lot of those hot-blooded fur grebles." Zanatobi smoothed back his shock of blue hair and clapped the suit helmet onto his head. It was adorned next to the faceplate with the sideways smile of a brilliant yellow banana:

the company badge. Yellow was for Admiral "Dynamite" Duane, but the design was their own: Tarzan's Apes.

"Technically speaking, we're hairy mammals too, you know," Mack offered cheerfully, putting on his own helmet and locking it down.

"Yeah. Look out who you insulting." Corporal Utun grunted from a few seats farther down, unsheathing her sword a few inches and slamming the hilt back into the scabbard. She showed her teeth in a friendly grimace before sealing her headgear. Her crony Jordan patted the muzzle of the plasma cannon secured at his feet and checked his safety straps. Wearing pressure suits, they had little mobility in atmosphere and full gravity. A collision could send a loose item ricocheting around the cabin, smashing and denting equipment, not to mention the damage to personnel.

"Detaching." The pilot's voice was audible to everyone now through their helmet com units. There was a huge cracking noise on either side of the capsule, and a wild lurch. Shillitoe's head snapped back sharply. The landing boosters were firing. Good. They must have released close to Khalia's surface.

The capsule hit with a thud and a hiss as it burned along the ground, sending jarring vibrations through their spines. As soon as the hatch blew open, the Marines sprang through, covering each other until they were all out, forming into a loose circle with backs against the hot metal sides of the landing craft.

"Air's good, chief," Dockerty confirmed what they had been promised. "Nitrogen, O-two, lots of long-chain carbon trace molecules. Probably stinks, but it's okay to breathe." The chemical analysis scrolled up the screen on the upper right inside Tarzan's helmet. On his left, blips representing each Ape were dispersing according to plan.

"Keep sealed for now."

The capsule had seared an area across the far end of a primitive landing strip about two hundred meters long, which was flanked by stone buildings two or three stories high. Two of the structures had huge double doors that covered the entire side facing the strip.

"Hangars," Foxburg stated the obvious.

Without warning, a hot red line etched itself in the earth at their feet.

"Laser!"

"Up there!" The company rolled out of sight of the tallest building on the strip. Its many windows and the set of stairs in the front suggested that it was the administration building, built by those unknown humans Marines had first encountered on Bull's-Eye. It was plain compared to the gaudy wooden shedlike structures beyond the airfield. Weasels didn't go for windows much, especially not big ones. Three more red flashes showed in the casement on the uppermost floor, and three streaks bubbled in the metal side of the capsule. By then, every Marine was out of sight or behind it.

"They know we're here. Shed the suits. We're going to need to move fast. Utun, cover Jordan. Jordan, take out those two hangars. Shout a lot so they vacate before you blow the buildings, but if they don't get out, that's their tough luck. Spread out. Pirelli, Doc, tell 'em to vacate that big place. I don't want 'em firing down on us the whole time. Do it!" The Marines in concrete gray uniforms and the medic in white sprang into position.

Pirelli and Utun wriggled out of the enveloping suits worn over their ground-attack gear and threw themselves to the ground at opposite edges of the capsule, returning fire toward the sniper. The silent laser shots left red-hot, hissing stripes on the casement as the unseen gunner leaped for cover, screaming.

"We only winged 'em. Dammit, they're so fast." Pirelli grunted.

"Attention, you in the tall building!" Mack shouted in Khalian. The language was not easy for humans to pronounce, especially at high volume. The hissing and growling took most of the lining out of one's throat. "Vacate the structure at once, or we will destroy it."

Jeers and defiant howls rang across the empty airstrip. Utun laid down covering fire for Jordan as he snaked across the open with the heavy plasma cannon on his back. When he was clear, she ran across to him, etching a pattern of hot lines on the building's face with her laser rifle. Jordan took aim on the hangar next to the administration building and fired.

The charge hit directly in the center of the hangar doors. All of the Apes gave it a three-count and covered their heads with their arms. Mack dropped his gun and stuck his fingers in his ears just as the building leaped into the air with a volcanic roar and disintegrated. The blast knocked the medic backward onto his rear.

In the window of the administration center, the sniper took advantage of the Apes' covering pose to shoot at them again. The shot drilled a tiny hole through Viedre's alloy-tipped boot. He screamed and hit the dirt. This time when the sniper exposed himself, Ellis and Dockerty both scored on him. The Weasel lurched and fell, gun and all, out the window.

Small, furry forms appeared in the doorway, dodging irregularly to avoid becoming targets themselves, and scurried down the ramp. None of them were carrying weapons. By their personal ornamentation, the Marines judged them to be Priests. Shillitoe ordered the gunners to ignore them.

"They're going to get help," Pirelli warned the sergeant.

"Let 'em. Reports said there were no troops within a hundred klicks." The Khalia, moving at speed, vanished into the shrubbery.

Mack flipped over onto his belly and made his way over to Viedre on elbows and knees. He flattened himself to the ground behind the wounded Marine and drew his diagnosti-kit around.

"It's already cauterized," he assured the wounded Ape, "but I'll numb it. See me later so I can examine that foot when we have time. And don't kick anything."

"Krim, why did I have to be wounded first?" Viedre puffed, holding his leg and grimacing. The heavy equipment pack he wore made it hard to sit up. "I'll never hear the end of it."

"Why am I down here instead of back on the *Elizabeth Blackwell* doing research?" Mack groused companionably. He took a quick reading to make sure Viedre wasn't going to go into shock, but his suit's trauma drugs hadn't even kicked in. The hole was clean, and it would stop hurting on its own in a few hours.

"Man, isn't this a nice little vacation from your boring old job?"

"If it is a job anymore. I'm spending so little time there, it's dwindling to a hobby."

The sergeant's bark interrupted them. "Rest time's over. I want all this area including the admin building and the strip secure. Jordan!"

"Sarge?"

"Blast that other hangar. Are you waiting for Hawk Talon to come out of it? Move it!"

From inside the capsule, the Marines offloaded the flat, round beacon, a unit with its own powerful but short-life power source. Foxburg took charge of the paint sprayer and ran a huge, irregular oval around the area the Apes intended to hold. Before the preparations were complete, Utun let out a screaming war cry.

"Sarge!" The big, golden-skinned woman was on her belly in the dust, firing her laser rifle at hundreds of Khalians, large and small, who appeared suddenly, swarming over the rubble from the destroyed hangar. These were obviously not soldiers. Many of them were old and moved more stiffly than the other Khalians they had ever fought, and many were very small, only half as tall as the adults.

A few of them had laser rifles, from which they returned the Marines' fire, but most had spears and polearms, unmistakably homemade from the local bamboo, and farming implements. Utun kept firing until she was engulfed by the wave of Khalians.

"Halt!" Tarzan's echoing bellow made them pause briefly, but the mob continued to advance on the Marines, flowing around Utun, who was no longer moving. Jordan shouldered his way through them and stood over the body of his friend, knocking away spears and claws with the empty plasma cannon.

"Doc, she's hit!" Jordan yelled. "Come here quick!"

"She'll last!" Shillitoe thundered. "Defend yourself. Doc,

get under cover." Then he yelled over the unit intercoms, "Drive the locals out of the perimeter."

Mack seized his medical supplies and fled for the far side of the administration building. He had spotted an open-faced enclosure attached to the main structure beside the ramp. It was probably the airstrip's garbage dump, or worse yet, the outdoor toilet, but it was out of sight.

"Drive them back! Fire at their feet," Tarzan boomed, his command suit amplifying his voice as he moved back toward the mob of Khalians. His company closed in around him, forming a semicircle that hemmed in the Khalia and forced them, on pain of scorched fur and claws, back past the painted circle. They were a ragged assortment, teeth and claws flashing in multicolored fur, snarling as they went, without even the minimal order or discipline that had been present in their soldiers.

As the last one was forced over the line, Pirelli announced to them in their own language, "Do not pass this circle again." To underscore his order, he squeezed off short bursts from his laser rifle to etch the line deeper into the packed dirt. "Or it's death to you."

His speech was ignored. The mob broke left and right around the line of Marines and flooded into the enclosure. Screaming and waving spears and digging mattocks, a knot of them made for the beacon. Five Marines dashed after them, intending to head them off before they could damage the unit. The Khalia's short little legs didn't carry them very fast, but they could turn and maneuver at the speed of thought.

Dockerty shot one after another until his rifle was beaten out of his hands by a big Khalian with a polearm. Another Khalian jabbed him with its spear before he swept his sword out of the scabbard and slashed at it. His pack and long flak vest served him as shields, protecting his back and chest. Those still left vulnerable his arms and legs. He stabbed and parried the light bamboo poles until he was side by side with Ellis.

"You face north, I'll face south," Ellis panted, turning so

that their left arms were between them. "Where did all these long rats come from?"

"It's the whole goddamn village. I swear the babies are back there with their rattles."

There was a whistling noise. A dart hit Ellis in the side of the face and clung to the flesh by its point until the Marine pawed it away with the wrist of his sword arm. Blood poured out of the gash. "Yeow, shit!"

"Is it poisoned?" Dockerty demanded.

"Don't think so. Doesn't feel like it. Just hurts." Ellis worked the side of his jaw carefully and winced. "Black holes take them, they've got throwing sticks or something." Another dart whistled between them, but missed, falling at their feet. Dockerty ground it into the dirt with his boot and backhanded a Khalian who was trying to batter him with a digging stick. The Weasel snarled and sprang for his neck to bite him. Ellis raised the rifle clasped against his left side and burned a hole between the Khalian's eyes. It fell against the back of Dockerty's legs.

"Fire for effect! Back! Drive them back!" Shillitoe bellowed.

Viedre and Marks pursued a trio of Khalians armed with bulky-looking laser pistols up the ramps of the administration building. Their heavy packs made it impossible to keep up with the Weasels. The Marines followed them all the way to the top floor of the building, where the Khalia were leaning out of the windows, firing their lasers down at the rest of the company. Marks shot one and shoved the second one away from the window with his elbow, rolling it against the wall. When it stumbled to the floor, Marks tried to stomp its throat with his boot heel, but the Weasel curled away from his blow and fled on all fours. Marks chased it down the ramp.

Viedre whacked the third across the lower back with the stock of his rifle. The Khalian dropped its weapon, which fell from the window. There was a cry of triumph below. Some other Weasel must have grabbed it.

The ceiling in this room was almost six feet high, obviously built for humans. Viedre straightened up as the Khalian he had disarmed jumped for him, claws and teeth bared. He tried to train the gun on it, but it whisked out of his sights before he could thumb the trigger stud. It darted under the gun and grabbed him around the chest, tearing at his uniform and reaching for his throat with its teeth.

Its claws scored through his uniform and arms but caught in the fabric of the flak vest. Blood poured out of the lacerations. Viedre tried to shake the Weasel loose, but it hung on, digging its back legs into the flesh of his thighs and bearing him over backward to the stone floor. Blows to its head and back with the stock didn't seem to hurt the Khalian, so Viedre threw the rifle aside. With his teeth gritted, he forced his hands up and under the Khalian's jaw, pushing the teeth away from his neck. The Weasel seemed to be as tough and limber as a snake, and it was angry. It kept hissing something at him in its own language. Viedre changed his grip to throw the Khalian off, and it snapped at his wrists.

Ignoring the pain in his legs, Viedre gathered his strength, and with a wrench turned himself over with the Khalian still clinging to his chest, and flung himself on the ground. The Khalian wheezed as the air was knocked out of it, and let go its grip. Panting. Viedre seized it by the neck and belly fur and slammed it against the wall. Weasels weighed little for their size. A human could defeat one easily in a contest of strength. The Khalian squealed and raked at him with a back foot. Viedre slammed it against the other wall and back again until it stopped moving. Blood welled out of its mouth as Viedre threw its body to the floor.

Marks appeared in the doorway. His uniform hat was gone, and his red hair hung around his sweaty face. "You okay?"

"I'll live."

"Krim, but you're a mess."

"Forget it. Help me downstairs." Viedre picked up his rifle and limped out.

At the bottom of the ramp, they burned the steel door closed behind them so no more Weasels could use it as a vantage point, and then joined Tarzan and most of the other Apes in driving a herd of Khalians over the perimeter.

"Hey, help me here!"

Sokada found himself standing alone in the middle of a

solid crowd of Weasels. Yelling for backup, he sprayed laser bolts around him. That killed about ten of them, but the rest saw what was happening to the others, and ducked under his field of fire whenever he faced their way. Two of his fellows had been torn to pieces by the mob after they were shot by snipers out of the administration-building window. Tammer had been shot in the hand and then holed through the back before he fell. He was still screaming when they tore him apart. Colwyde had taken two shots square in the face, and had a line burned across his chest. He had been dead before the mob reached him.

Sokada realized that no one could hear his shouts over the war cries of the Khalia. The gun was pulled out of his hands, and a set of teeth attached themselves to his fingers, chewing into the flesh. Gasping with pain, Sokada drew his sword with his free hand and cut off the head of the Weasel biting him. With the laser fire no longer keeping the mob at a distance, the Marine was surrounded by furry bodies stabbing at him with spears. They understood his disadvantage without his laser rifle against their natural armament of teeth, claws, and thick, hairy hide.

Mechanically, he slashed, parried, and turned, around and around, until the Weasels' faces blended together in a toothy, furry mass. As long as his arms were moving, he was able to avoid taking much more damage there, but his right leg hurt from a deep stab wound in the thigh where a parry had failed to turn a thrust from a halberd blade, and his bruised left knee felt as if it was going to give out.

A badly aimed slash with a polearm missed taking his ear off, but the flat of the blade hit him solidly in the side of the head. Sokada roared with pain and redoubled the speed of his attack. He was walking backward, slipping and stumbling over the bodies of wounded or dead Khalians, as he tried to get near enough to the stone wall to put his back to it.

He risked wiping the sweat off his face with a bleeding hand. Another Weasel jumped for him, and he spitted the creature on the dripping sword blade. The others took advantage of his blade's entanglement to rush in and claw at him.

Sokada lifted a foot and thrust the body off the sword and into their faces.

They no longer had any individuality. When they moved, he attacked them; when they stopped moving, he ignored them.

At last the granite wall was against his back. Sokada kicked out and stabbed, trying to stay upright. To his relief, the throng seemed to be thinning out, moving off to his left toward the ruined hangar. Tarzan and half the company were moving the crowd away from him.

He called out as they passed. "Sarge! Colwyde and Tammer . . ."

"I saw 'em. Watch out!"

A white and brown Khalian had seen Sokada glance away from the fighting, and launched itself at him. It grabbed his wounded hand and began to chew it off at the wrist. Sokada's eyes filled with tears, and he ground his teeth in pain and fury.

"Damn you, you stupid little rodent-toothed monster!" He battered the Weasel over the skull with the hilt of his sword until its legs went limp. He kept pounding until he felt the bone give, and the bloody jaws parted to release his hand. The tendons were showing through the ripped flesh.

"You miserable piece of vermin. I'll take your skin back as a souvenir. I'll use it to wipe my ass!"

Dropping his sword, he drew his dagger. He grabbed the Weasel corpse by the muzzle and flipped it over. Starting with a cut across the throat, Sokada started to skin the dead Khalian.

A very small Khalian squirmed under the fighting line of Marines and ran toward him. Dashing its spear to the ground in front of Sokada, it threw itself on the body between it and screamed defiance. It made a grab for the knife, which Sokada whisked out of reach, and dropped down protectively across the body.

"Krim take it, what's it saying?" the Marine demanded, trying to get its prize back.

"You killed its mother," Mack shouted from the corner of the building. "It doesn't want you to cut her skin off."

"This is its mother?" Sokada asked, drawing back. "I . . . Shit, I'm sorry." He let go of the body and backed away, but not before the child clawed a furrow down his leg with a lightning slash of its claws. Stunned, Sokada didn't seem to notice. He limped quickly away, out of Mack's line of sight, around the corner of the outbuilding. In a moment, Mack could hear him throwing up.

The child alternately howled and whimpered over the torn body, whispering endearments that Mack could just barely understand. He, too, was sick about the vicious turn that their mission had taken. Both sides seemed to have forgotten that their enemies were living beings, with families and emotions. Mack studied the child, wishing there was something he could do to comfort it.

He noticed then that there was blood seeping through the black fur on its shoulder and pooling on the ground. The child paid no attention to its wounds as it moaned and cradled its mother's body. Its grief was too deep. Mack's instincts as a healer refused to let him ignore an injury, even if it was one of the enemy. He stopped and berated himself. This child wasn't the enemy. The Marines were the invaders here. None of these civilians had ever seen a human world. Even as he reached for bandages Mack realized why the Khalia had been so vicious to human civilians, if this was how their own reacted.

Mack moved out of the shelter, an antiseptic-anesthetic pad already unwrapped. Keeping his voice low and soothing, he addressed the child in its own language.

"Easy, little soft-fur. Be calm. You're a brave warrior, yes, you are. You're wounded. This will make it stop hurting, and then you can rest. I mean you no harm."

It paid no attention to him as he crouched over and walked slowly toward it. But as soon as he was within arm's length, the child tried to shred Mack's face, but missed. The injury made its reactions slow. It let out a cry of pain. Mack easily avoided the flashing claw, grabbed the wrist, and clapped the pad onto the open wound.

Like the closing of a switch, the child's expression changed abruptly from an openmouthed snarl to a blank wariness.

Mack held up a synth-skin plaster. "This will cover the wound and make your shoulder feel better until it heals."

"I will bleed and die, like a warrior, and they will sing of my death," the young Khalian snapped proudly.

Mack smiled at his bravado. "You should think of growing up, so you can die in a more worthy battle. There are so few of us you don't have a kill of your own."

"I can kill you."

Amused, Mack sniffed and curled his lower lip, the Khalian equivalent of a shrug. The youngster recoiled, eyeing him. Evidently Mack had done the gesture correctly. "For how much honor? I'm unarmed. I am only a healer."

The child squinted and bristled his whiskers suspiciously. He was still not letting Mack get too close. A quick glance around showed that all the armed Fleet personnel were still engaged in battle with many of his fellow villagers. Mack knew what the Khalian was thinking: there wasn't any way to accomplish a heroic death without getting in the way of a senior warrior. He'd be more likely to earn a bite on the ear than a kill.

"If you're a healer, do you swear on your honor as a (nontranslatable insult) not to poison me?"

"I do," Mack promised. Carefully putting his knee down on the child's discarded spear so it couldn't be snatched away and used on him, Mack cleaned and sealed the wound. There were other scratches, none serious. Mack swabbed them out and left them alone. Khalians set great store by their battle scars. By the look on his young patient's face, shock was beginning to set in now. Mack led him back to his sheltered position and sat him against the wall with a rations bar and a container of water.

The doctor hurried back to see that all Khalians still on their feet had been driven back behind the bounds of the circle. Tarzan and the others were merely keeping them outside.

"Don't shoot at 'em unless they stick a toe over the line," he shouted in Alliance Basic, his voice carrying easily to all positions. "Our orders are only to hold this landing strip, not depopulate the planet. Sound off. I want to hear your acknowledgments.''

   ''Jordan, aye.''
   ''Utun, aye.''
   ''Dockerty, aye.''
   ''Viedre, aye.''
   ''Marks, aye.''

The voices came from around the circle, shouted from behind the building and from its upper floors, and echoed weakly by Sokada, still behind the outbuilding. Only twenty-two. Mack added his ''aye'' when his turn came, and looked for the missing three. Two were dead, lying not far from where he had seen the young Khalian. There was no hope that they might be alive. He treated Utun and four others for minor wounds. Utun sat perimeter watch with the plasma-cannon tripod braced against her chest, snarling back at the Khalians she was guarding. It was then that Mack saw the missing Ape and hurried over to him. The other Apes saw him, but were too busy holding back the mob to react.

Pirelli, bleeding from a dozen slashes and bites, was on his back just on the other side of the wall in the destroyed hangar next to the administration building. Mack checked his tracer several times to make sure it was showing life, not a blue light for death. It was hard to believe that the man could have sustained so much trauma and yet live. The new medical packs seemed to be a real improvement. He would need substantial reconstructive surgery when they were lifted off-planet.

Shillitoe loomed hugely over a cluster of growling Khalians who stood just outside the perimeter between the building and the ruin. The circle behind him was dotted with the bodies of Khalians. In the center, Dockerty stood guard over the beacon unit, now flashing its steady rhythm to the skies. The villagers watched it with growing alarm. Mack suspected they thought it was a bomb.

Suddenly, two adult Khalians dashed over the line toward the beacon. Accurately, dispassionately, Dockerty gunned them both down. There were gasps and growls from the others. A couple more started forward, urged by three elders

wearing the office of bard, but they glanced at the gun sights
trained on them and remained where they were.

"You stay on your side, and no one will get hurt," Shillitoe
announced, fanning the muzzle of his rifle at the crowd. The
villagers backed away, but surged forward to the line again.
"Yeah, crowd it all you want. I'm not turnin' my back on
you."

Mack translated his order into Khalian and repeated it several times so the whole circle could hear him. He paused near
the ruins where he heard a faint groaning.

"Hello?" he called. The noise stopped. Mack switched to
Khalian. "Answer?"

"Here," came a low murmur. Mack followed the voice
into the rubble. Behind a heap of broken rock and mortar lay
an aged Khalian female. When she saw Mack coming toward
her, she growled fiercely.

"Kill me," she dared him.

"I don't kill."

"Coward."

He smiled. "I'm a healer. Let me help you."

"What kind of (nontranslatable insult) are you?" It was
the same term the child had used.

"One who tries to prevent unnecessary death," Mack said,
assessing her injuries. "A wise warrior learns to fight another
day."

"What are you doing?" demanded Sanborn, the Marine
patrolling that arc of the circle.

"I'm doing triage on this old female," Mack explained
patiently. "She's been holed through the belly, and her right
forelimb is crushed. I think the bone is broken."

"If she's hurt, put her out of her misery. She's only a Khalian."

"Hold your water," grunted Sokada, limping from around
the side of the administration building. "Sergeant!" he
shouted. "Request permission to render assistance to injured
local!"

"What?" demanded Shillitoe from across the compound.
"Yeah, sure," he answered, not sure he had heard correctly.

Sokada himself was heavily bandaged and his one arm was nearly useless.

"How's the light here for you, Doc?" Sokada asked.

Mack, pleased at Sokada's show of humanity, glanced at the rough ground, and then up at the sun. "I think it would be easier for me if I could examine her in the full sunlight. How about up there, near the end of the runway?"

Sokada slung his rifle over his shoulder. "Sure, Doc. C'mon, Sanborn, give me a hand."

"Awww, what the hell." The new blood eyed the mob as he edged toward them.

With great care, the three humans lifted the old female and carried her to a flat, open sunny space between the two destroyed hangars. She struggled and cried out, causing another stir at the perimeter. Ellis and two of the others had to fire a few bursts in front of the villagers before they subsided.

"I am a sacrifice for my people. Kill me and let the children alone," the old female demanded as Mack bent over her.

"We're not going to kill anyone else," he assured her, dabbing antiseptic on her arm before injecting a painkiller. The stomach wound had damaged no vital organs. Certainly her lungs were in good shape. His medical scanner showed only entrance and exit wounds through the belly wall, the muscles, and the layers of skin. "See? No one is shooting." She was fortunate he had one of the few med scanners ever programmed for Khalian anatomy.

"You are kinder than the others were. They said you would kill us all."

"Not at all. By the way, what does (nontranslatable insult) mean?" Mack tried to match her pronunciation.

"Ones with as little honor as hair. But you must have more hair than what shows. I will not call you that again."

"Uh." Mack wasn't ready to explain human hair growth patterns to her. "Let me know if this hurts." Mack felt down the forelimb until he found the break. It was a clean snap, needing only to be realigned and splinted. He twisted, and the ends of the bone were once more in line. Using a ventilated plastic bandage that stiffened quickly when exposed to air, he splinted her limb.

"A warrior never complains of pain." The old female struggled to sit up as soon as Mack moved his hands. She had some sort of medallion around her neck.

There was a gasp from the host of Khalians at the circle's edge. Many moved from where they had been herded to the point closest to the old female. A younger Khalian started to move toward her, but saw a Marine staring at him and changed his mind. Mack gestured to Sokada.

"Can you get Pirelli over here? Careful. He's in bad shape."

The two Marines took their wounded mate by his arms and legs and lifted him. With an anguished cry of pain that nearly made them drop him, Pirelli regained consciousness and started to struggle in their grasp.

"Hey, Doc, he's delirious! We can't hold on to him."

Mack gave his Khalian patient a final glance and ran to help. He wrapped his arms around Pirelli's legs, but that only made the injured Marine more frantic. Mack decided the big man must be having a reaction to the new drugs in his suit's medi-pack. He changed his grip, and got a knee in the chin.

A squeal from the perimeter attracted attention from the other Marines. Four Weasels were making their way quietly into the circle, over the protests of the others, who were trying to keep them back over the line. All four wore the trappings of bards.

"It's death! It's death!" the other Khalians cried.

Tarzan spun at the commotion and pointed his rifle. "Positions!" he barked.

"No, wait," Mack shouted over the command frequency, turning with his arms out to stop the company from opening fire. The other two men lowered Pirelli to the ground and readied their own weapons. "Wait. I think they're helping." Mack tried to assure them.

"Yeah?" the sergeant replied, cautiously lifting his eye from the rifle sight but not lowering the weapon.

The four Khalians spread a thick cloth on the ground and then twitched their ears approvingly as Mack dragged the still struggling Pirelli onto it. Then they took their places beside the humans at the sides of the cloth. One of them gave a sharp nod to Mack to show that they were ready. "On the count of three," the doctor told the Marines. "One, two, *three*!"

Though the villagers didn't understand the words, they understood the inflection, and helped to hold the now well-wrapped Pirelli still while the stronger humans carried him to the cleared space. Without speaking, they let go as soon as the Marine was lowered to the ground, and obediently started back toward the perimeter.

"Well, I'll be a son of a supernova," Tarzan opined. "Men, get the other wounded where Doc can take a look at 'em."

"What other wounded?" Zanatobi asked. "We've got two dead."

"Those others," Tarzan said, pointing to the weakly twitching forms of wounded Khalians strewn about the landing strip. "Come on. Our orders are to secure this position. They don't specify how. Mack here shows us how to do it without further casualties, and you want to argue. Mack, get your helpers to come back."

"Yes, sir!" Mack was surprised at the enthusiasm in his voice. Tarzan was smiling as well.

"Krim damn it, I think that's the first order I ever gave you you didn't argue," the veteran commented.

"Yes, sir!" Mack returned, doing his best imitation of a salute.

Then everyone got busy healing some wounds.

INTERLUDE

Admiral Dav Su Allison, retired
Rules of Command
41.45428D2.2
Field Diplomacy

As the purpose of any action by the Fleet is determined by political and economic necessity, there may be
occasions when field personnel must deal with diplomatic matters far beyond their normal purview. In order
to best prepare for such circumstances, it is necessary
that every officer and, ideally, all personnel be thoroughly indoctrinated on the full range of immediate and
long-range goals. If this cannot be done, it is indicative
that there has been a severe breakdown at the Flag level
of command. As propaganda rarely reflects the true purposes of any military conflict accurately, careful briefing
is mandatory.

There is no accounting for the opportunities that may
have been lost by field officers being unwilling or unable
to react to diplomatic initiatives. By their very nature,
such situations are transitory and fragile. There are numerous records of occasions when such an action was
taken, both successfully and with varying degrees of disaster. An example of the former is Claremont's Peace,
which led the way for the eventual integration of the

Fleish Ergonic into the Alliance. Captain Claremont far
exceeded his authority, but emerged with a beneficial
result. (Ed. note: Fleet records are incomplete on the
subsequent commands held by this officer. He is believed
to have been placed in command of a long-range explo-
ration mission that was subsequently lost.) An example
of where a similar action has had a less fortunate result
would be the negotiation by Marine Sergeant Snyder with
the Slein League. While his efforts did result in the end
of hostilities in the first Pelic War, it also virtually guar-
anteed the occurrence of the far more destructive Second
Pelic War.

Just as a diplomat would be inept at combat, field personnel should acknowledge their own limitations, regardless of the temptation. A line officer should recognize
the need for a diplomatic specialist, just as he or she
would call for trained medical or engineering personnel
in a different set of circumstances.

The guidelines that must be obeyed whenever a field
officer finds himself in a diplomatic posture are:

1. The officer should take only those actions needed
to stabilize the situation.

2. In no circumstances . . .

THE END
by David Drake

THE RED SHIFT Lounge was the sort of bar where people
left their uniforms back in their billet, so the sergeant who
entered wearing dress whites and a chest full of medal rib-
bons attracted the instant attention of the bartender and the
half-dozen customers.

The unit patch on the sergeant's left shoulder was a black
shrunken head on a white field, encircled by the words 121st
MARINE REACTION COMPANY. The patch peeped out
beneath a stole of Weasel tails, trophies of ten or a dozen
Khalians.

The Red Shift was part of the huge complex of Artificial
Staging Area-Zebra, where if you weren't military or a military dependent, you were worse. Everybody in the lounge
this evening, including the bartender, was military: the two
men in a booth were clearly officers; the two men and the
woman drinking beer at a table were just as clearly enlisted;
and the stocky fellow at the far end of the bar could have
been anything except a civilian.

But no uniforms meant no insignia, no questions about who
had the right to go find a mattress with who . . . No salutes.

And none of the problems that occurred when somebody

figured a couple hot landings gave him the *right* not to salute some rear-echelon officer.

But down-time etiquette didn't matter when the guy in uniform was a sergeant from the Headhunters, the unit that had ended the war between the Alliance of Planets and the Khalia.

The War between Civilization and Weasels.

"Whiskey," ordered the sergeant in a raspy, angry voice.

"I thought," said one of the officers in diffident but nonetheless clearly audible tones, "that the One twenty-first shipped out today on the *Dalriada* at eighteen hundred hours."

The clock behind the bartender showed 1837 in tasteful blue numerals that blended with the dado lighting.

"For debriefing on Earth," the officer continued.

"And the parades, of course," his companion added.

The sergeant leaned his back against the bar. Something metallic in his sleeve rang when his left arm touched the dense, walnut-grained plastic. "I couldn't stomach that," he said. "Wanna make something of it?"

"Another beer," said the stocky man at the other end of the bar. His voice was mushy. The bartender ignored him.

"No, I don't," said the officer. "I don't suppose I would even if I were on duty."

"Bartender," called his companion. "I'll pay for that whiskey. As a matter of fact, Sergeant, would you like to—"

He paused. The first officer was already sliding out of the booth, carrying his drink. "Would you mind if we joined you?" his companion said, getting up and heading for the bar before he completed the question.

"Naw, I'm glad for the company," the sergeant said. "I just couldn't take—I mean, *peace* with the Weasels? We had 'em where we wanted 'em, by the balls. We shoulda kept going till this"—he tugged at his Weasel-tail stole—"was the only kinda Weasel there was!"

"I'm proud to meet a member of the Headhunters," said the first officer. "My name's Howes"—he stuck out his hand—"and my friend here is, ah, Mr. Lewis."

Beyond any question, the two men were commanders or even captains when they were in uniform.

"Sergeant Oaklin Bradley," the Headhunter said, shaking hands with both officers. "Sorry if I got a little short . . . but 'cha know, it tears the guts outa a real fighting man to think that we're going to quit while there's still Weasels alive."

The bartender put the whiskey on the bar. Bradley's back was to him. The bartender continued to hold the glass for fear the Headhunter would bump it over.

"You were there at the surrender, I suppose?" Howes said as he picked up the whiskey and gave it to Bradley.

The woman, an overweight "blonde" in a tank top, got up from the table and made her way to the bar. She was dead drunk—but familiar enough with the condition to be able to function that way.

"Aw, Babs," said one of her companions.

Earlier, the trio at the table had been having a discussion in loud, drunken whispers. Just as Sergeant Bradley entered the lounge, Babs had mumblingly agreed to go down on both enlisted men in an equipment storage room near the Red Shift.

If her companions were unhappy about losing the entertainment they'd planned for the evening, it didn't prevent them from joining her and the two officers in the semicircle around the uniformed hero at the bar.

"Oh, yeah," Bradley said. "I was there, all right." He'd waited to speak until chair legs had stopped scraping and everyone was close enough to hear easily. "We landed right in the middle of the Weasel Presidential Palace or whatever. . . ."

"High Council Chambers," Lewis murmured.

"Yes, yes, I'd heard that," Howes said. His eyes were greedy as they rested on Bradley's fringe of Weasel tails. "The Khalia worship strength, so just reaching their capital put the Alliance on top of their dominance pyramid."

The man at the end of the bar stared into his empty mug, turning it slowly and carefully as if to make sense of his distorted reflection in the bottom.

"We killed so many of 'em you could float a battleship in

the blood," Bradley said, licking his lips. "Never felt so good about anything in my life. We blew our way into the very fucking center of the place, caught all the Weasel brass with their pants down . . . and Cap'n Kowacs, he said we had to let 'em surrender instead a burning 'em all the way we shoulda done."

Bradley tossed down his liquor in a quick, angry motion, then slapped the empty glass on the bar. Babs shifted closer so that one of her heavy breasts lay against the Headhunter's biceps.

"Well, it did end the war," Lewis said, examining his fingernails and looking vaguely embarrassed for disagreeing with the hero.

"*That* part of the war!" Howes retorted sharply. "There's still whoever it was behind the Khalia to begin with."

The bartender refilled the whiskey glass.

The Headhunter at the bar of the Red Shift Lounge remembered. . . .

In the belly of Dropship K435, Captain Miklos Kowacs squinted to focus on the image of their target. His holographic display stayed rock-steady as they dived toward the huge Khalian complex, but Kowacs's own eyes and brain vibrated like dessert gelatin.

Speed through an atmosphere meant turbulence, and the Lord knew that to survive, the Headhunters were going to need speed as well as electronics that spoofed the Identification: Friend or Foe signal from the Weasel fortress.

Every second Marine in the three line platoons carried a man-portable rocket launcher. "Man-portable" because men were carrying them, not because they were light or handy. Most of the Marines who didn't have launchers lugged three packs of reloads.

The rockets were to disable the missile launchers of the Khalian base. Even when that job was done, the Headhunters wouldn't have to go underground after the Weasels: three of the Marines were strapped under thirty-kilo tanks of DPD gas—

That was designed to sink through the tunnels of a Khalian burrow and kill every living thing that breathed it.

There'd been plenty of room aboard the Attack Transport *Dalriada*, the K435's mothership, but the Headhunters were overequipped to fit comfortably onto the dropship itself. Marines squatted shoulder to shoulder, bumping one another and cursing bitterly. . . .

Knowing, among other things, that the weight and bulk of the rockets that the mission required meant that they'd had to leave behind the body armor that they'd otherwise have been wearing during an assault like this.

Of course personal armor wouldn't matter a damn if the ship bit the big one while they were all aboard her.

The units aboard the *Dalriada*'s other seven dropships had normal missions: land on the fringe of a defended area and attack. The 121st was different. Last time out, the Headhunters had captured a Khalian courier vessel; now the whole company was shoehorned into a secret weapon that pretended to *be* a Weasel ship, telling the target not to fire on them as they raced down to cut Khalian throats.

There were various ways the local Weasels could configure their IFF. Faint lines across Kowacs's hologram display recorded the burning tracks of the first two drones sent ahead of K435. At the third try, the fortress hadn't fired, so Operations was betting that K435 could get in untouched if it sent the same IFF response as that last drone.

Operations bet a single hundred-Marine chip. The Headhunters were betting their lives.

". . . seconds to touchdown!" the flight deck warned. A break in transmission erased the figure, but if they were *seconds* close, K435 was well within the defended envelope.

"Wait for it!" bellowed Sergeant Bradley over the unit frequency as he saw inexperienced troopers rise to jump out before the dropship landed.

No missile explosion, no hammering flares from autoloading plasma weapons. They were all going to live—

Until the Weasel ground personnel got done with them. That was fine. Weasels were what the Headhunters had come to meet.

Too many new Marines on this drop. There'd been too fucking many casualties in the Bull's-Eye operation. . . .

Kowacs felt a minuscule lift in K435's bow as the shock of the vessel's approach was reflected from the ground. An instant later, the braking motors fired at full thrust and hammered the rows of squatting Headhunters down against the deck plating.

"Now!" Kowacs, Bradley, and all four platoon leaders shouted as explosive bolts blew away the dropship's hatches and the 121st Marine Reaction Company, the Headhunters, lurched into action.

The world was bright and hot and smelled like brown flames.

An orbital-defense missile roared up from its launcher as the Marines shook themselves out onto the flat roof of the fortress. The sound of the three-tonne missile going supersonic just above the launch tube was earsplitting.

A Headhunter fired her hand-held rocket launcher while she was still aboard K435. Backblast made that a dangerous trick—but this wasn't a desk job, and starting to shoot instantly was a pretty good response to the shock of landing and the missile launch.

The Weasel missile tube was built into the fabric of the fortress. The small Marine round guided for the center of the opening, then fired a self-forging fragment straight down the tube's throat. Even if the armor-piercer didn't penetrate the launcher cap while the next anti-orbital round was being loaded, it was almost certain to jam the cap in place and prevent the Weasels from using that tube again.

The Weasel fortress was a jumble of huge flat boxes, with point-defense plasma weapons inset at each corner and heavy missile batteries buried deep in their cores. K435 was supposed to have landed on the highest of the twenty to twenty-five cast-concrete prisms, but that hadn't worked out: a box to the west overlooked the one on which the Headhunters were deploying, and the Weasel plasma guns could depress at any instant to sweep the whole company to a glowing memory.

"Delta, check two hundred twenty degrees," Kowacs ordered his Weapons Platoon. His helmet's artificial intelligence put him at the top of the pyramid of lieutenants assigning sectors and sergeants highlighting specific targets for the Marines of their squad. "Clear the high—"

There was a deafening crash and a blast of static—a plasma discharge radiated all across the radio-frequency spectrum.

Corporal Sienkiewicz stood beside Kowacs because her strength and ruthlessness made her the best bodyguard he could find in a company of strong, ruthless Marines. She'd just fired her hand-carried plasma weapon, a heavy tube that looked delicate against her husky two-meter frame.

A Khalian gun position vanished; then the whole top edge of the concrete prism stuttered with dazzling plasma bursts and long tendrils of quicklime burned from the concrete and spewed away in white-hot tendrils. Delta had its own belt-fed plasma weapons set up on tripods, and they didn't need Kowacs's orders to tell them it was everybody's ass if they didn't nail the close-in defenses before some Weasel brought the guns under manual control.

The noise of plasma weapons, rockets, and rocket warheads made it hard for Kowacs to think, much less hear any of the message traffic on his earphones. Although Kowacs's helmet damped the worst of the racket, shockwaves slapped the skin of his face and hands like huge hot raindrops.

Squad leaders with echo-location gear were using the noise to map all the surfaces of the Khalian fortress. When holographic images on a sergeant's helmet visor indicated a missile tube in his squad's sector, he relayed the target to a Marine with a rocket launcher.

The Headhunters' top-attack rockets ripped and snapped all across the concrete jumble. Occasionally a blast of smoky yellow flame indicated that one of the big Khalian missiles had blown up within its launcher.

But the Khalia weren't shooting anymore.

Kowacs turned around so that his unaided eyes could confirm what his visor display already insisted. Through the skeletal ribs of K435 and across the fortress, as well as on his side of the landing vessel, nobody was firing except Kowacs's own Marines.

Missiles didn't rise to engage the ships in orbit. Plasma weapons didn't chew themselves new firing slits so that they could bear on the Marine landing force. . . .

Unbefuckinglievable.

There was a momentary lull in the gunfire as the rest of the Headhunters realized the same thing. Then Sergeant Bradley screamed, "Door opening!" on the primary unit push, and three rockets streaked simultaneously toward the northwest corner of the block on which the Marines had landed.

The leaves of the hidden steel trapdoor rang like bells as they flew apart under the impact of the self-forging fragments. There were swatches of fur in the blast debris also.

"Double it!" Kowacs ordered, but there were already three more rockets in the air and three more sharp explosions over the sally-port, chopping Weasels into cat meat before their counterattack had time to get under way.

Kowacs was more agile than most of the Headhunters because he was burdened only with his personal weapons. He began running toward the shattered trapdoor, shouting, "Gas carriers to me!"

You'd've thought the rocket blasts would've kept the Weasels down for at least a few minutes. More furry, yellow-fanged heads popped out of the sally-port even before Kowacs got out the last syllable of his order.

He shot as he ran, spraying the area with a dozen ricochets for every bullet that counted—but ammo was cheap, and at least a dozen other Headhunters were firing along with their captain. The vivid white fireball of a plasma burst hid the target momentarily; Sie had saved back one charge for an emergency like this.

The Weasels had been waving something.

More Weasels rose out of the half-molten pit where the trapdoor had been. They vanished in a maelstrom of bullets and grenade fragments.

Kowacs paused twenty meters from the sally-port to reload. A Marine with one of the green-painted gas cylinders caught up with him. Sienkiewicz was giving the fellow a hand with his load.

More Weasels leaped from the fortress. Kowacs aimed but didn't fire. Other Marines ripped the fresh targets into gobbets of bloody flesh.

The Weasels were waving white flags.

"Cease fire!" Kowacs shouted. Still more Weasels were coming up. "Cease fire!"

There were ten or a dozen unarmed Khalians in the next group, all of them waving white flags. Some were females.

A Headhunter fired his assault rifle. One of the tripod-mounted plasma weapons vaporized the Weasels with three bolts.

More Weasels came up from the crater.

"*Cease fire!*" Kowacs screamed as he ran forward, facing his Marines as he put his body between them and the Khalians.

Facing most of his Marines, because Sie was on one side of him and Sergeant Bradley was on the other. Both noncoms were cursing their captain, but not so bitterly as Kowacs cursed himself and the command responsibility that made him do *this* when he should've been shooting Weasels.

Nobody shot. Nobody spoke. Kowacs's panting breath roared behind the constriction of his visor.

Kowacs slowly turned to face the Weasels again. His lungs were burning. He flipped his visor out of the way, though that left him without the heads-up display if he needed it.

There were twelve Khalians. They stood on the lip of the crater, waving their small square flags. Each Weasel had its nose pointed high in the air, baring the white fur of its throat. Their muzzles were wrinkling, but Kowacs didn't know whether that was a facial expression or just a reaction to the stench of blast residues and death.

Miklos Kowacs had killed hundreds of Weasels during his Marine career. He'd never before spent this long looking at a living one.

"Helmet," he said, "translate Khalian."

He splayed the fingers of his left hand, the hand that didn't hold a fully loaded automatic rifle, in the direction of the Weasels. "You!" he said. "Which of you's the leader?" as the speaker on top of his helmet barked the question in Weaseltalk.

None of the Khalians wore clothing or ornamentation. The one on the left end of the line lowered his nose so that he could see ahead of himself, stepped forward, and chattered something that the translation program in Kowacs's helmet rendered as, "Are you Fleet Marines? You *are* Fleet Marines."

"Answer me!" Kowacs shouted. "Are you in charge?" The concrete seemed to ripple. It was solid, but Nick Kowacs wasn't solid just now. . . .

"We wish to surrender to Fleet Marines," the Weasel said. He was about a meter forty tall, mid-breastbone level to Kowacs. "Are you Fleet Marines?"

"Goddamn," Bradley whispered, his scarred left hand wringing the foregrip of the shotgun he pointed.

"You bet," said Nick Kowacs. His brain was echoing with screams and other memories and screams. "We're the Headhunters, we're the best." *Weasels never surrendered.* "You want to surrender this whole fortress?"

"That too," said the Weasel. "You are fighters whom we respect. Come below with us to receive our surrender, Fleet Marine."

Sienkiewicz laughed.

"Bullshit," Kowacs said flatly. "You tell your people to come on out, one at a time, and we'll see about surrender."

"Please," barked the Weasel. "You must come into the Council Chamber to take our surrender."

"Bullshit!" Kowacs repeated.

He risked a glance over his shoulder. The three Marines with gas cylinders, kneeling under the weight of their loads, were in the front rank of waiting troops. "Look, get your people up here, or—"

The Khalia had no equipment, but they had been born with tusks and sharp, retractile claws. "Then I have failed," the speaker of the group said. He raised a forepaw and tore his own throat out.

"—almighty!" Bradley blurted as Kowacs choked off his own inarticulate grunt. The Weasel thrashed on the seared concrete, gushing arterial blood from four deep slashes. The furry corpse was still twitching when a second Khalian stepped forward.

"Come into the Council Chamber with us, Fleet Marine," the new envoy said. "Only from there can the surrender be broadcast to all."

"No!" shouted Sergeant Bradley. The Weasel raised his paw; sunlight winked on the clawtips.

"Yes!" shouted Captain Miklos Kowacs, feeling the ground shiver like the dying Weasel before him.

"Ah, sir?" said one of the Marines carrying a gas cylinder. "*All* of us?"

Lieutenant Mandricard, the senior platoon leader, had faced his platoon around to cover the Headhunters' rear while the rest of the Marines were shooting Weasel pop-ups. He glanced over his shoulder at the company commander.

Kowacs pointed a finger at Mandricard and said over the general push, "Gamma Six, you're in charge here until I get back, right? If that's not in"—*how long?*—"six zero minutes, finish the job."

He nodded toward the gas cylinders. And smiled like a cobra.

"Sir," said Bradley, "we can't do this."

Kowacs looked at him. "I gotta do it, Top," he said.

"Hold one," said Corporal Sienkiewicz. She'd unharnessed one of the gas carriers and was now—

Godalmighty! She was molding a wad of contact-fused blasting putty onto the tank of gas. If she dropped the heavy cylinder, the charge would rupture it and flood the whole area with DPD!

"Right," Sienkiewicz said as she examined her handiwork. "Now we're ready to go down."

Bradley swore coldly, checked his shotgun, and said, "Yeah, let's get this dumb-ass shit over with."

Kowacs hadn't told Sie and the sergeant to accompany him; but he knew they wouldn't accept an order to stay behind. "G—" he said to the Khalian envoy. His voice broke. "Go on, then."

The eleven surviving Weasels scrambled into the blasted entrance. Kowacs strode after them.

"I'll lead," said Sienkiewicz.

"Like hell you will," Kowacs snapped as his rigid arm blocked his bodyguard's attempt to push past.

The entrance was a stinking pit. A crowd of Weasels, all of them carrying flags, filled the floor below. The metal staircase had been destroyed by the first volley of rockets; since then, the Khalia had been scrambling up wooden poles to reach the roof and their deaths.

Shattered poles, corpses, and charred white scraps of cloth covered the concrete floor on which living Weasels pushed and chittered in a cacophony that the translation program couldn't handle.

"Back!" barked the Khalian envoy, raising both his clawed forepaws in symbolic threat. "To the Council Chamber!"

The Khalian mob surged down the hallway like a shockwave traveling through a viscous fluid. There were lights some distance away, but the Headhunters' blasts had destroyed the nearest fixtures.

Kowacs looked down, grimaced, and dropped. His boots skidded on the slimy floor.

"Watch—" he said to his companions, but Sie was already swinging herself down. Her right hand gripped the edge of the roof while her left arm cradled her lethal burden like a baby.

Bradley must've thought the same thing, because he said, "Hope the little bastid don't burp," as he followed into the Khalian fortress.

"Come this way!" ordered the envoy as though he and not the Headhunters were armed. The Weasels' demonstrated willingness to die made them very hard to control.

Pretty much the same was true of Marines in the Reaction companies too, of course.

The ceiling was so low that Kowacs, stocky rather than tall, brushed his helmet until he hunched over. He expected to hear Sie cursing, but the big woman didn't say a word. She was probably concentrating so that she didn't drop the bomb in her arms and end all this before—

Before it was supposed to end. Not necessarily different from the way it was going to end anyway.

The hallway curved. For a moment, Kowacs's helmet picked up the crisp commands of Gamma Six as Mandricard put the Headhunters in as much of a posture of defense as the featureless roof permitted. Reception faded to static, then nothing at all.

They came to a bank of wire-fronted elevators and a crowd of waiting Khalians. "Come with me," the envoy said as he stepped into the nearest cage.

The cage was small and low; three humans in battlegear and a Khalian filled it uncomfortably. As the elevator started to descend, Kowacs saw a horde of Weasels pushing into the remaining cages.

Bradley began to shake. The muzzle of his gun wobbled through tight arcs. "It stinks . . ." he mumbled. "It *stinks*."

He was right, of course. The air circulating in the Khalian burrow smelled of Khalians, and that was a stench worse than death to a man like Bradley, who'd seen what the Weasels left of his little daughter on Tanjug. . . .

Or to a man like Nick Kowacs, whose family had been on Gravely when the Weasels landed there.

Kowacs shivered. "Top!" he said harshly. "Snap out of it. You're not going claustrophobic on me now."

Bradley took off his helmet and squeezed his bald, scarred scalp with his left hand. His eyes were shut. "It's not the fuckin' tunnels," he said. "Not the tunnels. All these Weasels . . . I just, I wanna—"

Bradley's fingertips left broad white dimples on his skin when he took his hand away. The Weasel envoy watched the sergeant with bright black eyes.

No one spoke again until the cage stopped and the Khalian repeated, "Come with me," as his paw clashed the door open.

Kowacs couldn't guess how deep in the earth they were now. There was a sea of fur and tusks and chittering Weasel voices outside the elevator. Many of this crowd wore ornaments of brass and leather, but Kowacs didn't see any weapons.

He stepped out behind the envoy, watching the passageway clear before them and wondering if the Khalia would close in again behind the three humans.

It didn't matter. They were *in* this, he and Top and Sie, as far as they could get already. At least the tunnel ceiling was high enough for humans, even the corporal with her burden of death.

The envoy led through an arched doorway. The chamber within was huge even by human standards.

The chamber was full of Khalians.

The smell and sound and visual impact stopped Kowacs in his tracks. One of his men bumped him from behind.

Kowacs closed his eyes and rubbed them hard with the back of his left wrist. That made it worse. When he didn't see the room filled with Weasels, his mind quivered over the memory of his mother, her gnawed corpse thick with the musk of the furry monsters that had—

"No!" Kowacs screamed. The distant walls gave back the echo, cushioned by the soft susurrus of breathing mammals. There was no other sound.

He opened his eyes.

A group of Khalians was coming forward from the crowd. There were twenty or more of them. They wore jewelry and robes patterned with soft, natural colors.

They were very old. Some hobbled, and even those Weasels who were able to walk erect had grizzled fur and noticeably worn tusks.

Weasels don't wear clothing. . . .

There was a great sigh from the assembled company. The aged Khalians gripped their robes and tore them apart in ragged, ritual motions. Some of them were mewling; their facial fur was wet with tears. They fell to the floor and began writhing forward, their throats and bellies bared to the Marines.

The Weasel in the center of the groveling line gave a series of broken, high-pitched barks. The voice of Kowacs's helmet translated, "Khalia surrenders to you, warriors of the Fleet Marines. We are your subjects, your slaves, to use as you wish."

"Come to the Council Chamber," the Weasel envoy had

*said. The High Council of Khalia. They weren't surrendering
this fortress—*

"Khalia surrenders—"

They were surrendering the whole Khalian race!

"—to you, warriors of the—"

Bradley's shotgun crashed. Its airfoil charge was designed
to spread widely, even at point-blank range. The load sawed
through the chest of the Khalian speaker like so many miniature razors. The Weasel's tusked jaws continued to open and
close, but nothing came out except drops of bloody spittle.

The aged Khalian nearest the dead one began to chant,
"We are your slaves, warriors of the Fleet Marines. Use us
as you will. We—"

Sergeant Bradley's face was that of a grinning skull. He'd
dropped his helmet in the elevator cage. There was no reason
left behind his glazing eyes. "You'll die," he said in a sing-
song voice, "you'll all—"

He fired again. His charge splashed the skull of the corpse.

"—die, every fucking—"

Kowacs gripped the shotgun barrel with his left hand. The
metal burned him. He couldn't lift the muzzle against Bradley's hysterical grip.

"Put it down, Top!" he ordered.

The moaning of the crowd was louder. Waves of Khalian
musk blended sickeningly with powder smoke.

"—are your subjects, your—"

Bradley fired into the dead Weasel's groin.

"—Weasel in the fucking uni—"

"Down!" Kowacs screamed and touched the muzzle of his
assault rifle to Bradley's temple where a wisp of hair grew in
the midst of pink scar tissue. Kowacs's vision tunneled down
to nothing but the hairs and the black metal and the flash that
would—

There was a hollow *thunk*.

Bradley released the shotgun as he fell forward unconscious. Sienkiewicz looked at her captain with empty eyes.
There was a splotch of blood on the green metal of the gas
cylinder and a matching pressure cut on the back of Bradley's

skull, but the sergeant would be all right as soon as he came around. . . .

"On behalf of the Alliance of Planets," Kowacs said in a quavering voice, "I accept your surrender."

He covered his eyes with his broad left hand. He shouldn't have done that, because that made him remember his mother and he began to vomit.

"Hey, Sergeant Bradley," said one of the enlisted men in the Red Shift Lounge, "let *me* get 'cha the next drink."

The man in whites toyed with his stole of Khalian tails. "We shoulda kept killin' 'em till everybody had a Weasel-skin blanket!" he said. "We shoulda—"

Somebody came into the bar; somebody so big that even Sergeant Bradley looked up.

The newcomer, a woman in coveralls, squinted into the dim lounge. She glanced at the group around Bradley, then ignored them. When she saw the stocky man at the far end of the bar, she strode forward.

The sudden smile made her almost attractive.

Bradley's hand closed on his fresh drink. "If there's still one Weasel left in the universe," he said, "that's too many."

"Sar'nt?" murmured the drunken blonde. "Whyn't you'n me, we go somewhur?"

"Hey, cap'n," said the big woman to the man at the far end of the bar. "Good t' see you."

"Go 'way, Sie," he replied, staring into his mug. "You'll lose your rank if you miss lift."

"Fuck my rank," she said. Everyone in the lounge was looking at them. "Besides," she added, "Commander Gold-stein says the *Dalriada*'s engines're broke down till we get you aboard. Sir."

She laid the man's right arm over her shoulders, gripped him around the back with her left hand, and lifted him in a packstrap carry. He was even bigger than he'd looked hunched over the bar, a blocky anvil of a man with no-colored eyes.

"You're always gettin' me outa places I shouldn't a got into, Sie," the man said.

His legs moved as the woman maneuvered him toward the

door, but she supported almost all of his weight. "Worse places 'n this, sir," she replied.

"They weren't worse than now, Sie," he said. "Trust me."

As the pair of them started to shuffle past the group near the door, the woman's eyes focused on the uniformed man. She stopped. The man she held braced himself with a lop-sided grin and said, "I'm okay now, Sie."

"Who the hell are you?" the big woman demanded of the man wearing the Headhunter uniform.

"What's it to you?" he snarled back.

"This is Sergeant Bradley of the 121st Marine Reaction Company," said one of the enlisted men, drunkenly pomp-ous.

"Like hell he is," the big woman said. Her arms were free now. "Top's searching bars down the strip the other direc-tion, lookin' for Cap'n Kowacs, here."

Kowacs continued to grin. His face was as terrible as a hedge of bayonets.

The group around "Sergeant Bradley" backed away as though he had suddenly grown an extra head.

The imposter in uniform tried to run. Sienkiewicz grabbed him by the throat from behind. "Thought you'd be a big hero, did ya? Some clerk from Personnel, gonna be a hero now it's safe t' be a hero?"

The imposter twisted around. A quick-release catch *snicked*, shooting the knife from his left sleeve into his palm.

Sienkiewicz closed her right hand over the imposter's grip on his knife hilt. She twisted. Bones broke.

The knife came away from the hand of her keening victim. She slammed the point down into the bar top, driving it deep into the dense plastic before she twisted again and snapped the blade.

"Big hero . . ." she whispered. Her expression was that of nothing human. She gripped the Weasel-tail stole and said, "How much did these cost 'cha, hero?" as she tore the tro-phies away and flung them behind her.

The bartender's finger was poised over the red emergency button that would summon the Shore Police. He didn't push it.

Sienkiewicz's grip on the imposter's throat was turning the man's face purple. Nobody moved to stop her. Her right hand stripped off the uniform sleeve with its Headhunter insignia and tossed it after the stole.

Then, still using the power of only one arm, she hurled the imposter into a back booth also. Bone and plastic cracked at the heavy impact.

"I'm okay, Sie," Kowacs repeated, but he let his corporal put her arm back around him again.

As the two Headhunters left the Red Shift Lounge, one of the enlisted men muttered, "You lying scum," and drove his heel into the ribs of the fallen man.

Kowacs found that if he concentrated, he could walk almost normally. There was a lot of traffic this close to the docking hub, but other pedestrians made way good-naturedly for the pair of big Marines.

"Sie," Kowacs said, "I used to daydream, you know? Me an old man, my beard down t' my belt, y'know? And this little girl, she comes up t' me and she says, 'Great-grandaddy, what did you do in the Weasel War?' "

"Careful of the bollard here, sir," Sienkiewicz murmured. "There'll be a shuttle in a couple minutes."

"And I'd say to her," Kowacs continued, his voice rising, " 'Well, sweetheart—I survived.' "

He started to sob. Sienkiewicz held him tightly. The people already standing at the shuttle point edged away.

"But I never thought I *would* survive, Sie!" Kowacs blubbered. "I never thought I would!"

"Easy, sir. We'll get you bunked down in a minute."

Kowacs looked up, his red eyes meeting Sienkiewicz's concern. "And you know the funny thing, Sie," he said. "I don't think I did survive."

"Easy. . . ."

"Without Weasels t' kill, I don't think there's any Nick Kowacs alive."

INTERLUDE

Admiral Dav Su Allison, retired
Rules of Command
46.8475A1.1

. . . the League years a firm policy of exploitation was established. Even in the early empire nonhuman races' treatment was related more to their similarity to humanity and their physical attractiveness to mankind than for their real value. During the golden era of the High Empire, all races achieved a functional equality. During the millennium that followed the flight of the last Emperor, the treatment of aliens varied greatly depending on local conditions.

The Fleet, today, attempts to use alien personnel in a manner for which their unique natures best suit them. In some cases this means simply not accepting such races as the Janna as recruits, even though their presence would likely improve the quality of life for shipboard personnel. In other cases the employment of nonhuman militia widens the envelope of where even bio-modified personnel can function effectively. Purely practical consideration mandate the use of the members of certain nonhuman races in specific circumstances. No being other than the Kurles of Hamilton's World could survive in the sensory-depriving conditions required of distant monitoring stations. Nor could any but the short-lived Paglea operate under extremes of radiation.

Still, the vast majority of the personnel of the Fleet is human. This is the result less of xenism than the recognition of the logistical necessity. For any navy to efficiently provide all of the needs of its personnel, a multiplicity of requirements must be avoided. The environmental support needed for a truly multiracial force would be staggering. Its requirements would, of themselves, preclude any level of combat effectiveness. In view of this, just as parts are standardized, so also must be the bulk of Fleet personnel. Taking into account mankind's fecund nature and proclivity for violence, man has logically held the responsibility for manning the Fleet since its inception as a defense force for the Original Thirteen.

Beyond sheer necessity, mankind has proven itself quite adept at combat. Few species share or understand our admiration for destruction. Without exception, those that do are counted as mankind's staunchest allies or bitterest enemies.

RESISTANCE

by Christopher Stasheff

"It lies!"

The messenger quivered with indignation, drawing himself up on his hind legs—in indignation, yes, but also to bring his own eyes level with Steetsin's, where he reclined on the couch from which so many of his ancestors had delivered judgment.

Around them, the Great Chamber of Wedge Hold stirred to the mutter of Steetsin's warriors. Above their heads hung the tattered banners captured in hundreds of years of fighting. The walls boasted their trophies, too—ancient weapons from celebrated battles.

There were a few more recent—sidearms and slugthrowers once carried by officers and men of the Fleet.

"Chief of the Wedge Sept," the messenger insisted, "this missive was penned by the Clan Chieftain's own hand!"

"It cannot have been!" Steetsin snarled. "Never would a Khalian chieftain stoop to such cowardice!"

"How can it be cowardice, if the Clan Chieftain does it?" the messenger demanded.

The Syndicate envoy leaned close to Steetsin's back and murmured, "How can the Clan Chieftain have done it, if it is cowardly?"

The answer was clear, and Steetsin did not shy from it. "If it was the Clan Chieftain in truth who wrote it, he must have taken the Terrans' pay!"

The messenger spat an oath in sheer shock, before he managed to control his outrage. His voice quivered with rage as he said, "It is not cowardice, but the honorable respect due an adversary who has proved himself worthy."

He did not explain; he did not need to. The Fleet had driven the Khalia back on all fronts, had captured Target in spite of the Khalia's furious defense, and now had invaded the home world itself! They might be hateful, but they were mighty—and being mighty, they were worthy of allegiance.

And being the victors, Khalian honor demanded that the Khalia accept whatever task the Fleet assigned them, so long as it was in battle.

Yet they had slain Steetsin's mate and cubs on Target and, what was worse, had slain them unknowing, when the city in which they denned had exploded in flame. That, Steetsin could not forgive—nor could he truly think of the men of the Fleet as allies. "Therefore does the Chief of Clan Ruhas say that we must be done with war-for-hire, and ally with the Alliance Fleet, who had proved themselves worthy—and be done also with the Syndicate, who have sought to buy our honor, and have lied!"

"Be still!" Steetsin flowed off his couch, claws out, lips writhing back in a snarl. "I will hear no evil against the councillor who has advised me so long and so well! Kartwright is no liar, but a tried and valiant warrior, who has watched with me in the cold of the night and has stood by my side through many battles. Speak not against him, or his kind!"

Cartwright smiled and inclined his head in gracious acknowledgment of Steetsin's praise.

The messenger's lips writhed back in a harsh laugh. "What! Are we to hear no wrong of your Syndicate shadow, who would have honor for coin, and say the Chief of Clan Ruhas lies?"

"If he speaks truly, let him come here to the Hold of the Wedge and speak it to my face! Let him stand against the upbraiding of a vassal who has ever been honorable and true!

Until he does, the Khalia of the Wedge Sept will harry any human of the Fleet who comes near!''

"Then up and out!" the messenger sneered. "For an army of the Fleet even now rolls through your valley, coming to your gate with tokens of friendship—and its gunboat circles overhead!"

Steetsin stood rigid. Then he hissed, "If they come, they bring destruction, not gifts—and we shall know you for the traitor you are!"

Running steps, and a soldier burst into the Great Chamber. "Lord Steetsin! The Blind Eyes show an army within the Wedge, and a scout overhead!"

Steetsin spared the messenger a look of hatred.

"Go up to your battlements," the messenger urged. "Look down and see that they are truly humans of the Fleet—and count any weapons you may see, that are more than side-arms!"

"I go," Steetsin hissed, "and if I see cannon, you shall die!"

Cartwright was only two paces behind Steetsin, in spite of the steep incline of the tower steps. The Chief noted the fact with grim satisfaction as he came out onto the battlements—as he had said, Kartwright was a warrior. He leaped to the crenels and reared up, forelimbs resting on the stone—stone that had been laid down by his father (dead in battle ten years ago), with money given them by the Syndicate—money, and the use of gigantic shambling machines that had cut and lifted the stones. He looked down, as his father had before him, and his grandfather, and all his forefathers, over the Wedge—the two rivers, dimly seen off to each side, that flowed toward each other, meeting in a point as they flowed into the Great River. Beyond its waters lay the domain of Clan Chirling—allies now, but for hundreds of years, enemies. Hundreds of years, until the Syndicate had come and shown them won-drous weapons, that could be theirs if only they would fight the Fleet. He felt a stab of shame, quickly buried—there was no surprise that the Khalia had hearkened to the Syndicate's promises, for who would not at the sight of weapons that could reach to the horizon, and ships that could carry an army to the stars? They must have been wonders indeed to Steet-sin's grandfather, and he could not be amazed that all the Khalia had put aside hostilities to pounce on the contemptible humans of the Fleet . . .

And here came the contemptible ones, marching ten abreast in a long flowing carpet, down the valley and up toward his gates.

He stared again at hairless skin and unclawed hands. How could such creatures know of fighting? It should have been so easy . . .

But it had not been, and the Chirlings were his friends now, had been the shield on his back at Target, and the enemy was now his ally . . .

The memory rose up of his mate and cubs, a memory sheathed in flame, as he imagined it must have been when the bomb struck, and the hatred raged up again. What honor could they have, who cared not if they slew families and cubs? How could the Chiefs of the Clans have made peace, and allied with the Fleet? Better to have died one and all, each and every Khalian! He had to admit to a certain sneaking admiration for the enemy, for their tenacity and their fighting skills—but the hatred was still there, over all.

"It is true, Kartwright," he hissed. "I see no rocket launchers, no cannon. They come in peace—as much as an army can do."

"And how much is that?" Cartwright breathed at his shoulder. "What will happen if you admit them within your gates, Steetsin?"

Steetsin stood rigid, and the lifelong animosity of one raised to regard the humans of the Fleet as his enemies rose to the fore, and with it the hatred in flames. "Gunner!" he snapped to the soldier nearby. "Bring down that gunboat!"

The soldier was too well trained to hesitate or argue. He turned to his cannon. Its barrel rose, swiveling, and a huge gout of flame burst from the muzzle. Its thunder shook the turret as the energy bolt split air aside, and the gunboat lit with a brief dazzle.

"A force-shield!" Steetsin spat. "Treachery!"

But the gunboat had been too close for the shield to absorb all the energy—an edge was twisted, scorched. Not enough to cause any great damage, no, but enough so that the gunboat spat back at him, a lightning bolt that seared the air near Steetsin and blasted two crenels off the turret. By the time they started to fall, Steetsin was already down under the stone. "What friends are they who fire!"

"Ones who insult you." Cartwright was down beside him. "So little energy, so small a shot . . ."

"They shall learn the anger of the Wedge Sept!" Steetsin howled, leaping to his feet. "All warriors! Arm and form for a sally! As your grandfather did, against Khalian thieves!"

"No-o-o-o-o!" The cry split the air, freezing all the warriors in surprise. The messenger leaped into motion, a brown blur streaking toward the gate. Too late, Steetsin realized his error—he should have had the warrior bound hand and foot and cast into the dungeon. But he had not, and the Khalian rose up next to the gate, forelegs reaching out to the great bar.

"Kill him!" Steetsin screamed, but none of his warriors moved against the Clan Chief's messenger. "Burn him!" And Steetsin himself leveled his sidearm, but too late, too late, for even as the gun leaped in his hand, the messenger had wrested the bar from its staples. He leaped in pain as Steetsin's bullet took him; he fell crumpled in the dust, dead—but the huge gate swung inward, and the army of the Fleet filled the portal.

"Fight!" Steetsin howled. "Slay as you retreat!" For he knew the Hold was lost.

Finally, his warriors came alive. These were no loyal Khalians they faced, but the age-old enemy, tales of whose cruelty and cowardice had filled their ears almost from birth; these were the monsters who had somehow overwhelmed them. Not a warrior among them but had lost a wife or a comrade on Target; not a warrior among them but bore his own store of hate for the Fleet. Guns racketed all around the courtyard. Humans of the Fleet fell, gouting blood, but others took cover behind the gate or ran for the flimsy protection of carts and dead bodies. Guns barked in Fleet hands—puny sidearms and rifles, but so many of them, so many! And Steetsin's men began to fall . . .

"To the postern!" he screeched as he fled down the tower stairs. "To the tunnel!" as he raced for the great portal in the side of the Great Chamber. "Down and away!" as his men began to file down to the escape passage.

Steetsin himself ran to join the rear guard, to heat his barrel to melting with bullets for the humans of the Fleet, knowing that Kartwright was nearby, would follow, would shadow him, even though Steetsin could see him not . . .

When the last of the men had stumbled through, Steetsin ran the pads of his paws lightly over the tunnel wall, found the third brick from the top, lifted it, and pressed the button underneath. A hundred yards away, on the other side of the river, a muffled explosion sounded. Steetsin turned away, the knowledge bitter within him that one wall of his ancestral Great Chamber was now choked with a jumbled mass of stonework—but no enemy would follow through the blocked mouth of the tunnel. "Raid leaders!" he called. "Tally your men!"

His lieutenants counted quickly and reported in. Only two thirds of Steetsin's warriors had come out of the keep. His neck fur bristled at the thought. "So many comrades slain! Yet we shall avenge them." He looked about him, gimlet-eyed. "Where is Kartwright?"

There he came, turning away from a warrior with a wounded arm—bandaged now, and healing, thanks to Kartwright's Syndicate medicine. "Do you seek me, Steetsin?"

For some reason, the man's atrocious accent suddenly grated on Steetsin's nerves—now, after all these years! He told himself again that the human mouth was not made for Khalian shrills and whistles, and schooled himself to patience. "What say you, Kartwright? How shall we desecrate this messenger's memory, he who opened our gate to the humans of the Fleet? For surely, he deserves to be forever abhorred!"

But a wordless protest sounded from a hundred throats, and Steetsin turned, shocked. "How can you speak well of him!" he shrilled at his men. "He, who betrayed us!"

Now, now they were silent. They stood, eyeing one another uneasily.

"What—would you defend him, but not have the boldness to tell why?" Steetsin demanded. "Raznor, speak! You, who are my second in command! How can you defend the vile action of this traitor!''

Raznor glanced at his captains, then turned back to Steetsin. ''I do not, Chieftain—but he placed his faith in the Clan Chief, and was loyal to him.''

Steetsin stared.

''He must have known he would die,'' Raznor explained, ''but even so, he stuck fast to his word of loyalty. Such courage must be admired; wrongheaded or not, his memory should not be desecrated.''

Steetsin's eyes narrowed, but he said nothing. Truly, there was nothing to say.

But Raznor was not done. ''Who are we, to forswear loyalty to the Chief of our Clan? Tell, Steetsin—what cause have we to think he betrayed us? For surely, it is not for us to say what is best or worst for all Clan Ruhas!''

Steetsin swelled with the horror, the enormity of it. ''How could you have forgotten, forsaken the memories of your glorious comrades?'' he shrilled. ''What! Do you not remember their suffering? Do you not remember the fall of Target?''

Then he took up the tale, began once again to recount the atrocities of the Fleet, to remind them of the falling fires, the twisted limbs, the charred wreckage and the wasted lives, of the eternal oblivion of male cubs who would not now have their chance to prove their courage, to gain their honor, of females who would not win through to ever-life through the honor of their sons.

When he was done, not a one of his warriors but trembled with hatred and rage, held barely in check; not a one who would not have lashed out at any human of the Fleet who came near—and, indeed, several eyed Kartwright with cold hostility. But the man had courage; his smile scarcely faltered as he edged fractionally behind Steetsin. ''They are ready, Chieftain. Turn them where you will.''

Steetsin knew where. He scanned the line of his warriors slowly, eyes burning. ''From this time forth, the human of the Fleet will bemoan his fate! He will wish he had never come to the Wedge! In every way that we can, we will harry him! We will slay his stragglers, we will rend his supply trains! There shall be no trade, no crops—until at last, he abandons our Hold!''

''All honor to the Chief of Clan Ruhas.'' The Marine captain bowed, as though he meant what he had said.

Ernsate believed that he did—that all the Fleet officers did. They may have hated the Khalia as old enemies do, but they respected them as valiant warriors. In those who had begun to see how the Khalia's nobility had been twisted and abused by the Syndicate, that respect had turned to honor.

Therefore, Ernsate inclined his head in imitation of the human's greeting. ''The Chief of the Clan gives honor to his noble ally. I hope you are well, Captain English.''

''I am well. I trust the noble Chief is also?''

''In good health.'' Ernsate tried to contain his impatience; the ritual was necessary. Still he was rather abrupt in saying, ''It is the welfare of my Clan that concerns me, their welfare in body and in honor.''

''Surely there can be only the slightest of stains on the honor of Clan Ruhas!''

So. Word of the Wedge had come at last to English. ''Only a slight stain, that my warriors seek to banish. The time has not come when I would have to go myself to the Wedge.''

''Great honor would indeed come to a chief who would so care for his warriors!''

Yes, it was that necessary, then. ''I have heard that the Chief of the Wedge Sept has feet made of mist.''

''It is true that none can find the tracks that show where he or his sept have been. Yet it is true also that he is a valiant warrior, that his claws are sharp and his grip harsh.''

Steetsin's ambushes had done great damage, then. Ernsate rose up in decision. ''I must go in person. So valiant a chieftain deserves the honor of personal care from the Chief of his Clan.''

''All praise to Ernsate,'' the captain murmured, ''honor to the Chief of Clan Ruhas!''

''They come, Lord Steetsin!''

Steetsin nodded, eyes on the plume of dust that rose from the roadway below. They were perched on a slope, hidden

among trees and scrub. Off to his left, a group of ants came
around a curve. *Ants*, he thought, and noted the metaphor's
aptness with wry appreciation. So were the Fleet, at least in
moral stature. They knew nothing of honor, of nobility. "Be
ready, Kartwright."

"I shall follow you as I always have, Steetsin."

The Chieftain nodded, satisfied. "The shield on my shoulder, yes. Be alert—they come!"

The slow-moving column wound along the road opposite
them. When its rear was just past the Wedge Sept's hidden
flank, Steetsin squealed in sudden rage and leaped from cover,
bounding down the slope toward the soldiers of the Fleet,
knowing that his warriors would follow, would fall upon the
column all along its length, and that Kartwright would follow
them, alert to protect any stragglers.

There they were, the smooth-skinned, flat-faced fools!
Steetsin raised his sidearm to give the first shot, sword gleaming in his other hand . . .

Khalians rose up in the midst of the Fleet soldiers.

Khalians rose up, and Steetsin stopped.

Khalians rose up in such a fashion as to be so thoroughly
intermingled with the humans that Steetsin could not be sure
he would not hit one of his own kind. He stilled, trembling
with frustration, and all his warriors froze, as he did.

But through the stalled throng, Kartwright churned and el-
bowed, coming up behind Steetsin to hiss in his ear, "These
Khalians are traitors!"

The words freed Steetsin; as always, he felt a gush of gratitude toward his Syndicate ally, even as he screamed, "Traitors!" and fell on the Khalians before him, sword raised to
slash, sidearm leveling . . .

Another Khalian rose up, head and neck above the others,
taller, with russet highlights in his fur.

Steetsin froze again, staring, appalled. "Chieftain of my
Clan!"

"Even so," Ernsate returned. "Put up your arms, Steetsin.
The men of the Fleet are worthy warriors. We have both
buried our dead; they are our allies now."

Steetsin stood trembling, paralyzed by conflicting emotions, loyalty warring against hatred . . .

"No real Clan Chief would command such dishonorable action," Kartwright snapped.

"Be still, worm!" Ernsate commanded. As the humans of the Fleet stepped forward, hands reaching for Cartwright, the Clan Chief lifted his gaze to the warriors of the Wedge Sept and cried, "Lay down your weapons! Declare your peace with these worthy warriors! *They* shall now be your arms and shield!"

"He has betrayed you!" Cartwright fairly screamed. "Your own Chieftain has betrayed you!"

The words kicked Steetsin into action. He hurled himself at Ernsate, sword lashing, sidearm coming up, shrieking, "Traitor! Seller of honor! Die!"

Khalians howled and leaped to block him, but they were too late—Steetsin was already on the Clan Leader, sword slashing . . .

And cracking against Ernsate's steel armguard, as his other hand sprouted claws, ripping open Steetsin's chest, and the first hand closed around his neck, probing, slashing . . .

Then the sky reeled about him, faces streaked, the earth slammed up into Steetsin's back, and red haze overlaid all, the haze of his own blood pumping from his throat, dimming the faces, the sky, dimming all into darkness.

Ernsate stood, chest heaving, filled with the elation of battle and triumph but already beginning to feel the sadness, the grief that must have its vent in screaming, sooner or later, at the death of a valiant vassal and a gallant clansman.

He looked up, eyes narrowing. "Have you the corrupter, then?"

"We have," said the Marine officer, and two of his men yanked Cartwright before Ernsate, hurling him down at the Khalian's foot . . .

Hurling him down, but he came up screaming, a slender blade in his hand, hidden somewhere within his clothing, and Ernsate slashed at him—but already, the man was crumpling from a kick in the kidneys, driven by a Fleet man.

They stood, chests heaving, glaring at the Syndic who writhed before them in agony.

"This was the true enemy," Ernsate told the Marine captain. "Not a traitor to your kind, no, for he is not one of yours—but a traitor to me and mine, for he abused Steetsin's trust."

The captain nodded, his face flint. "You take him, then. He is yours."

The men of the Fleet cried out in involuntary protest, but as quickly silenced, glaring at the shuddering Syndic, hatred of enemy overcoming loyalty to kind.

"It is justice!" the captain snapped. "What will you do with him, Lord Ernsate?"

"We will suck his knowledge from him," Ernsate stated. "Then he will die, for his crime against my Clan." He beckoned to his own men, crying, "Come, take up the body of Lord Steetsin—for surely, he has died bravely and with honor! Let him be interred in the Hold of the Wedge with his ancestors, and let his funeral be sung with all pomp and ceremony, his weapons ranked beside him—for, though misguided, he strove with all his might for Khalia, and the glory of his Clan!"

All the Khalians rumbled agreement, and Steetsin's warriors took up the body, turning their faces toward the Hold.

"And what of this scum?" demanded Raznor, with a hiss.

Ernsate's face hardened. "He shall be buried below Lord Steetsin, naked and bereft of weapons, that he may serve Steetsin's ghost for a footstool, and be his servant in the Everlife."

The ranks of human soldiers stirred with disquiet, but the captain called out, "It is just! Let him who has betrayed the spirit now serve that spirit! And let this deed be sung!"

"Let it be sung," Ernsate echoed, "for today died a valiant warrior, and tomorrow shall die his evil shield. Warriors, bear him solemnly! All clansmen, chant his glory!"

Thus the column moved away toward the dark mass of the Hold, stark against the sky, and the keening lament rose to mark its way.